PROLES

Proles

A NOVEL

BARRY BERGMAN

SERVING
HOUSE
BOOKS

FOR LIZA

Natasha has just come up to the window from the courtyard and opened it wider so that the air may enter more freely into my room. I can see the bright green strip of grass beneath the wall, and the clear blue sky above the wall, and sunlight everywhere. Life is beautiful. Let the future generations cleanse it of all evil, oppression, and violence, and enjoy it to the full.

—Lev Davidovich Bronstein (Leon Trotsky), February 1940

Well, the new Nixon is older, to begin with. Perhaps he has acquired, I should hope, some more wisdom.

—Richard M. Nixon, April 1968

1.

Some sharp-tongued *critique de cinéma*, the belle of Manhattan cultural circles, famously lost it at the movies.

Simon Bussbaum, some smart-mouthed *pisher* from Queens, quietly found it there.

Actually he stumbled across it in Celluloid and Social Change, a one-credit elective and the only class Simon, with no use for a degree, bothered attending. Revelation came in the form of a Super-8 print displayed on a torn, tripod-mounted retractable screen in a makeshift classroom in the bowels of the college library. The portable projector hummed and clicked and made you worry the sprockets would catch and the film stock melt, the story replaced by a two-dimensional lava lamp. It made *Simon* worry, that is, no one else having the slightest interest in a scratchy, black and white exercise in earnest, Mexican-accented neorealism. The rest of the student audience, eyes dilated and heads on their flip-up desks, would have happily pledged their firstborn sons for the sweet relief of an impromptu, psychedelic meltdown.

City of Emeralds. Sy himself thought it an artless movie, bereft of believable dialogue and wanting in plot and production values. The big-deal critic had dismissed it as propaganda, noting, in a preamble to her withering judgment, the blacklisting of its writer, director, *and* producer. ("That makes four strikes," she'd observed, "if we count the protracted, shambolic walkout these fellow travelers from Tinseltown have stooped to use as fodder for what is, in sum and substance, a Soviet-style morality play.") The rumpled lecturer, less cleverly than he imagined, pronounced it "black and white and Red all over."

Just the same, the film struck Simon as curiously unfettered by ideology, more Woody Guthrie than Daily Worker. A heartfelt plea for fair play for the common man, a faded bumper sticker made vibrant, in spite of itself, by the artlessness of the telling. Sincerity—as Natalie Wood said to Sal Mineo in a movie by Nicholas Ray—that was the main thing.

Natalie spoke the truth. This, though. This *was* the truth.

City of Emeralds, aka *Ciudad de Esmeraldas,* recounted the tale of dirt-poor Chicano copper miners—backed by their resolute, dirt-poor wives—demanding dignity and equal pay in a place called, what else, Emerald City. Based on a bitter strike that stretched from 1950 to '51, the film had barely survived a campaign of hysterical, Strangelovian obstruction led by the likes of Joe McCarthy, Howard Hughes, and Ronald Reagan. Its leading lady was deported, vehicles belonging to cast and crew shot at by gun-toting patriots. Technicians refused to work on it. Theaters refused to show it once it was finally made.

A few card-carrying thespians aside, *Emeralds'* cast consisted of miners, miners' wives, and, in supporting roles, the townsfolk of Mineral City, New Mexico, site of the actual strike. Starring as José Castillo, the hardhats' intrepid leader, was Naldo Galvan, his real-world counterpart. Galvan's screen presence put you in mind of Bogart, if Bogie had swapped his felt fedora for one of those straw farmworker-style cowboy hats—rugged features, hint of an overbite, bemused tough-guy expression—and was reading his lines from cue cards. Galvan's performance, charitably, was stiff. Being a working-class hero had to be hard. For Naldo Galvan, clearly, playing one was harder.

Still, only the haughtiest of *haut monde* connoisseurs, poison quill poised in a Village arthouse, would have the temerity to pan his acting chops via thousands of well-chosen words in the nation's foremost journal of art, culture, and taste. The man had *lived* the part. Certifiably battle-tested, *el McCoy real.* Compare and contrast: Humphrey DeForest Bogart, born to wealth, never worked an assembly line or pushed even a single pencil. A proud Democrat, Bogart had turned tail after taking a bit of flak for defending, briefly, the Hollywood Ten. He was a star by then, 1948, the year *Key Largo* came out. And here he was, afraid of a cross word from Walter Winchell. So how tough was Bogie, really, when the cameras stopped rolling?

The lecturer, a balding corduroy man with a sad ponytail, was a lapsed lit prof who now viewed the written word as a tool of the ruling elite. He knew every unknown filmmaker from Chelsea to Alphabet City and peppered his talks with gratuitous, ingratiating allusions to pot. Sy could picture him scribbling notes in his study while Lou Reed droned about heroin.

Yet he, too, seemed sincere.

For Simon Bussbaum—whose travels had taken him as far west as Palisades Park, on the Jersey side of the GW Bridge, and, once, with no need even to flash his fake ID, south to the nation's capital, where he watched the Yippies fail to levitate the Pentagon—the film was his burning bush, the home version of Chuck Heston on the sacred mountain. Sy's dingy classroom epiphany lacked the grandeur of Cecil DeMille's big-budget spectacle. It lacked any grandeur at all, like the outer boroughs from which he'd sprung. But grandeur wasn't the point. He, Simon Bussbaum, had been touched by a higher power, a power both higher and more powerful than the wooden, unnameable God of Israel, voiced by Charlton Himself, in *The Ten Commandments*.

And Simon's bush—two reels of translucent plastic which, wait for it, *did not burn*—was neither a lame special effect nor a figment of mind-altering chemicals. If his classmates were mostly wasted, Simon Bussbaum was soberer than a cloistered monk, under the influence of nothing other than strange, disquieting, utterly substance-free spirits.

Until he emerged from the library, in fact, surfacing squint-eyed into the bright, bucolic grounds of the campus, he'd hardly thought about weed or alcohol all day.

* * *

He hitched home in the morning. Once inside the apartment he tossed his backpack on his bed and made for his brother's room, finding its door half-open. Unlike his own pristine room—cleaned as always to a fare-thee-well, in his absence, by his mother—his brother's was in disarray and gave off the funk of a locker room, minus the sweetly sickening scent of Right Guard aerosol spray and bargain-basement cologne. Smack in the middle was the source of the funk, sprawled face down on his bed, nose in a book, surrounded by other books. Swimming in books. His right hand floating above his head, clutching a lemon-yellow highlighter, uncapped and ready to go. Reading a book, for Jake, was an act of aggression, like going to war. Highlighters were his weapon of choice.

Jake was studying to be Trotsky. He had started to look like Trotsky.

Simon knocked on the jamb to get his attention. Jake paid him no mind. "Three words," Simon declared, trying to sound triumphant. "*City of Emeralds.*"

His brother glanced up and went back to his reading, unimpressed. His default posture. Simon stood in the doorway and raised his three inadequate words with a blizzard of verbiage, hoping to convey to Jake—who, as usual, was right now deep in the weeds of Marxist theory—the momentousness of what still felt, a full twenty-four hours later, like illumination, a vision of the cosmos Simon hadn't known he'd been waiting for.

Illumination, though, defied reason. Maybe, like the lecturer said, the yearnings of the heart ran too deep to be conjured with language alone.

Or maybe he just lacked the right words.

Jake half-listened, rolling onto his back, avoiding eye contact. He signaled his boredom by using his T-shirt to polish his pie-shaped lenses, a style of eyewear the masses associated less with Lenin's man Trotsky than Lennon of Liverpool, whose screeching wife broke up the Beatles. He checked them against the light from the window, then maneuvered the specs back into his Jewfro.

"Sy," he said. "Don't be a *putz.*"

City of Emeralds, explained Jake—removing his glasses again, a B-movie doctor about to tell a patient he has weeks to live—was built on lies. Narratively, ideologically, historically. Also, Sy supposed—Munchkins chattering in his head—morally, ethically, spiritually, physically, positively, absolutely, undeniably, and reliably. But Jake's point wasn't that *Emeralds* was Red propaganda. His point was that it was the *wrong sort* of Red propaganda.

"So it's, what, not Trotskyite enough? Not revolutionary enough? How many workers even saw *La Chinoise*?"

"Trotsky*ist*," said Jake. "We say Trotsky*ist*."

"Trotsky*ist*, then. Ist ist ist. Trotsky*ist*."

This seemed to satisfy Jake, who went on with his lesson. "Godard's a Maoist. A French intellectual. Even the Maoists don't want him. But

Emeralds is worse. It's a pipe dream, a happy ending. It tells the working man everything will be fine, that loosening the capitalist yoke is enough. But it won't be. I mean, maybe for folks in Beverly Hills. But people working assembly lines, killing themselves in steel mills? Slightly less fucked is still fucked. They get the message they don't need a revolution, they just need to tweak the system. And the system wins.

"But you wouldn't know that, spending your life in a corporate propaganda factory."

"I'm not spending my life there," Sy replied. "I'm just not losing it in Vietnam."

How Jake had managed to dodge the draft was a mystery. Also, most likely, illegal.

Sy was sorry he'd brought it up. Jake was a bummer.

But Jake was just getting started.

Had the lecturer mentioned how those heroic workers—José Castillo, real name Naldo Galvan, and all the others playing themselves in the movie—had fared after the closing credits? How their brotherhood of choice, the International Union of Mine, Mill, and Smelter Workers—there at the birth of the CIO in 1935, only to be purged like lepers during the Red Scare—would be swallowed up by the United Steelworkers of America? How that class-collaborationist union, hemorrhaging dues-paying members in the mills of Chicago and Cleveland and Pittsburgh, spent the '60s muscling its way into zinc and copper in the arid air of the Sun Belt?

How *Emeralds'* noble warriors, back in the real world—in Mineral City, New Mexico, a name that sounded as made up as Emerald City— were betrayed, abandoned, and left for dead by the cowards and sellouts in Big Labor, Inc.?

"He told you all that, right?"

Simon shrugged noncommittally. Jake possessed a deep reservoir of information, much of it suspect. He was a unity of opposites, a Marxist allergic to labor, a materialist who lived in his head. A negation, perhaps, of the negation, a concept Simon had never grasped but which Jake had fully embraced.

He'd convinced their parents he was looking for work, and would get his own place once he found something suitable. But nothing, for Jake, would be suitable. He wanted to be Trotsky.

Amid a lengthening list of confusions, Jake's latest passion was pride in his proletarian roots. Which, to the extent these might have existed, had skipped big chunks of the family tree. Their grandfathers were merchants, supposedly, one in jewelry and the other in rags. Their father wore a necktie to work. There might have been a prole or two hiding among their ancestors, who lived and died in Russia and Eastern Europe, best guess, long before there was Hitler or World War II, or even a World War I. But nobody ever talked about their ancestors.

Jake, it turned out, had passed through Tucson—Tucson, *Arizona*, just next door to New Mexico--the last time he went missing, Crashed with an ambiguous cadre of local lefties. They weren't Trotskyists. Trotskyists weren't ambiguous. It was modern-day Stalinists who declined to announce themselves, who dressed in the wholesome clothing of popular movements. But Jake doubted they were Stalinists. They were too young to be Stalinists.

Then again, who wasn't? Lepers had better PR than Stalin. Khrushchev himself had disavowed Stalin a generation ago. These desert lefties never mentioned Russia or China either, not a word about communism, socialism, any isms at all. They seemed like a club. They were devoted to keeping the fires burning for Galvan, now a dissident in the USWA, nonferrous division. Jake had forgotten all but one of their names. All he knew was they worked for ThreeCo, which stood for CoCoCo, which stood for the Cobra Copper Company.

Sy wanted to hug him, almost. Jake knew people who knew Naldo Galvan? Alive and well and living in Mineral City?

He crossed the threshold to grab a pencil stub and wrote the lefty's name on a page he tore from a spiral notebook. Hitched back to school the next day. He found a decent-sized roach in the pocket of his only suit, wrapped in a yarmulke from some distant cousin's bar mitzvah. He sat cross-legged on a pillow in front of the TV, wearing the skullcap, watching cartoons and staring at the name he'd scribbled with what he saw now was an eyebrow pencil. He tried to imagine Trotsky's eyebrows. The name was smudged but legible.

Howard Shackleford. Thick dark letters. Sy could see his reflection on the TV screen, so that from a certain angle Porky Pig stuttered the end of every 'toon in a yarmulka. He sat through Daffy Duck, Bugs Bunny. Tweety and Sylvester. After a while he realized he hadn't eaten all day. He got up and poured some cereal into a bowl. The milk had gone bad so he ate the cereal dry. Washed it down with a beer.

He turned off the set, read the back of the cereal box. Toyed with a crossword puzzle in an old New York Times. But he wasn't able to focus.

Mineral City. Naldo Galvan.

From his Trotskyist brother, of all people, he'd got the key to the treasure.

Assuming, of course, Jake wasn't yet completely deluded. And Sy wouldn't be fleeing to Canada.

* * *

The war was winding down, but the draft went on, the fates of America's less fortunate sons hinging now on the roll of a Pyrex tumbler. Come December he drew triple threes in the lottery, ensuring he would never be locked in mortal combat with Ho Chi Minh's or anyone else's army. Word of his pardon came via a tavern TV. The magic digit had just escaped the announcer's throat when he leaped from his barstool, grabbing people randomly by the shoulders, grinning and cackling like Jimmy Stewart back from the dead. He hugged the kid on the next stool, whose number hadn't come up yet, and whose wonderful life, for all Sy knew, might be the last one snuffed in a Vietnamese rice field.

He had escaped the death machine.

But so would the kid. Barely a month later Nixon would sign the Paris Peace Accords and ditch his draft for a volunteer army—the better to stifle protests—and not one of that year's contestants was inducted. But nobody knew that then. Anyway, he was gone. Off to the Southwest to join *la lucha* and consort, time permitting, with the local *señoritas*. The desert loomed, a liminal borderland between plunderer and Indian, man and Gila monster, not-yet and long-ago. He could taste the copper dust, feel the nauseating gutwrench of wild peyote. He could taste the future.

He slept the sleep of the dead, only better. He was alive. Next morning he had the operator put him through to the outfit Jake had told him about, ThreeCo, which stood for CoCoCo, which stood for the

Cobra Copper Company. The woman who answered the phone said they weren't hiring. But she wished to be helpful, and offered to mail Simon an application to keep on file. She called him Hon. Her father and husband both worked underground at ThreeCo, she said, and someday her son would, too. She'd started her office job a month after she got her high school diploma. She would have told him anything he asked her about. She was a long way from New York.

January came and went. The application arrived on Valentine's Day. It included a questionnaire. Q: "Why do you want to work for the Cobra Copper Company?" A: "I have a passion for copper." Q: "Have you ever been arrested, or convicted of any crime, misdemeanors included? If so, explain in the space provided below." A: "___________________." Q: "Are you able to lift a 50-pound bag over your head?" A: "~~Depends~~ Definitely."

He had been arrested, once. He'd been trying to hitch a ride out of a wide spot on Highway 17, where a long-haired older man in an orange Bug had dropped him on his way to Poughkeepsie. The three of them heading back to school after Christmas break. A light snow was falling. Cars slowed down to give them the middle finger. But it was too cold to stand around getting the finger. They took a break in an army-navy store, where one of the group, an acquaintance called Gordy, purchased a large American flag he meant to hang upside down in his room, most likely, or use as a curtain. No sooner were they back at the highway than a deputy pulled up. Ordered them to open their bags. This was illegal even in Nixon's America. But they didn't have any pot, and a person could disappear down the memory hole in some of these podunk towns. Cooperation felt like the play.

Then the cop saw the flag. What were you gonna do with that, he demanded, his tone newly belligerent, the *were* suggestive of imminent confiscation. Burn it, muttered Gordy, what else? Simon hated Gordy, at that moment, more than he hated the cop. The cop hated Gordy. And not just Gordy, but Gordy's flag-burning comrades. They'd crossed the line from stoners to insurrectionists. The cop was a vet, by the looks of him, still on Team Tricky Dick, had his fill of commies halfway round the world. Wasn't having them here.

Get in the car, he said, and watch your hair. A funny cop. At the station he parked his prisoners on a bench with a view of some empty jail cells. Said he was phoning the justice of the peace, though it might have been his wife or the guy at the Texaco. It was a quick call. The JP couldn't hear their case till tomorrow, he reported, which meant they'd have to spend the night in the hoosegow. It also meant he'd have to feed and water them and cancel any after-dark plans he might have had for himself.

"Jeez," he muttered. Or possibly "Jews." Though Jeez was a Jew, so six of one. Either way it was dawning on the cop that he'd wrung all the fun he could wring from this little caper. Abuse of power had its limits.

He'd cut them a break, the officer said finally. Let them pay a fine and be on their way. They had, all told, sixty-two dollars and change. The cop pocketed fifty and kept the flag. Then he drove them back to the highway, right to the spot where he'd picked them up. Warned them to keep their noses clean. Simon knew what he meant. Gordy was Italian, in fact, a lapsed Catholic. In the land of the WASP, though, probably close enough.

The cop flashed the peace sign and pulled away. The snow had stopped, and the three got a ride from a middle-aged man in a Lincoln. He had salt-and-pepper sideburns and a baby blue polyester suit, and he'd lost a son in the war. He took them most of the way back to school, stopping once at McDonald's to buy them burgers. They found that hilarious, doing a McDonald's drive-through in a Lincoln. But they felt bad about his son, and comported themselves respectfully, answering his questions about how they liked school and what their majors were and how did their football team look this year, which none of them had ever once contemplated. Simon said it looked promising. They lied when he asked about pot, because you never could tell about people. But he didn't smell like a narc. Probably just thinking about his kid.

Sy wasn't sure getting pinched for hitchhiking qualified as an arrest. In any case he doubted the cop kept records of that kind of thing. Gordy, had he been a cop, would have kept records. But Gordy wasn't as smart as the cop.

Sy mailed back the application. Told everyone he was leaving.

His father's response, when he broke the news, was to sneer audibly and shake his head at having spawned what he called a matched pair of subversive elements. His mother said he was throwing his life away. Tears were not shed.

Jake looked up from his reading, mumbled something about leaving himself. So leave already, said their father.

And then, nothing.

Simon hitched back to school. It was midterms week—all he had, as far as he knew, was an essay test on "Hollywood and the blacklist"— when he heard from ThreeCo. A different woman, older-sounding than the first, asked to speak with a Mr. Bussbaum. Sy told her she could. There was a pause. "I'm him," he explained. "Simon." She said she was glad to meet him. Everything was in order, the only hiccup being his living thousands of miles away.

He assured her this wasn't a problem.

They scheduled a meeting for two weeks out. Sy took his suit and his heavier clothes to the Salvation Army, along with a dozen cartons of books and records. Found a couple of duffel bags with working zippers. He wouldn't need much. He'd been renting a converted laundry room off-campus, month to month, with the help of a student loan and the odd dishwashing gig. You were supposed to give thirty days notice. But he'd had to pay a month's rent in advance. So they'd come out even.

There was nothing else tying him down. Louise, an aspiring Laura Nyro he'd long expected to dump him, had finally dumped him. And it turned out Uncle Sam didn't need his services in the Postal Service any more than he needed them in the army.

He got some maps from the auto club and a bus schedule at the Port Authority. Made a deposit sight unseen—using some leftover loan money, which the bank would be wanting back once they heard that he'd flown the coop—on a place he found in a Tucson paper they had at the 42nd Street library.

He met a couple of high school friends in Jackson Heights for beers and eight-ball, an old favorite haunt under the el, and promised to stay in touch. A girl he knew had a birthday party at a bar in Jamaica, where he got to say some goodbyes. She'd heard about Louise and said maybe she'd come visit sometime in Arizona. They both knew she wouldn't. He hung around till he figured his family was sleeping.

He set an early alarm. Showered and stuffed the bags with clothes and miscellaneous belongings. He left a note for his parents, another one for his brother. Then he took the E to the Port Authority. The train was crowded and ripe, the terminal more so. The city was swarming with rats, half of them human. Project babies petted the rodents. New York, New York, a hell of a town. The people rode in a hole in the ground. The Port Authority was the crossroads, the place they sold their souls for a piece of the action.

Parting was short and sweet, the antithesis of sorrow.

* * *

It was a three-day trip, the landscape rising and falling and changing colors beyond the grime-streaked windows. Accents mutated as the bus lurched from depot to depot. Simon bought some Robitussin in the Midwest somewhere and slept when he could. Once he dreamed he was in a moving tomb. Woke in a rolling hearse with a chemical toilet.

His mind was a muddle when the bus reached Tucson. There were no cabs at the station. He phoned a company with an ad in the yellow pages. He washed his face in the men's room, bought a cold coffee from a vending machine, then went outside to wait for his ride. It was after dark, spooky hot, not the familiar relief of a New York summer night but vaguely mystical. The moon gleamed in the starless sky, a dime on a blanket of Yankee blue. He waited at the edge of the parking lot, the night so deep and silent he lost his bearings and had to turn to face the depot again.

He was almost sorry when the car arrived. He rode with his head so far out the rolled-down window the driver had to shout to ask him to keep it inside the vehicle. Simon rolled down the other window. Endless sky gave way to the light from street lamps, single-story houses, fitful oncoming traffic. But the car smelled like the desert.

His new home was a second-floor shotgun flat. As promised, the landlord had left the key in an envelope inside the mailbox. The bedroom was in the back, beyond a small living room and a kitchen just off the entrance. He showered and scarfed a day-old sandwich. Slept and slept.

He woke in a pool of sweat. The place had no central cooling, nothing but distant cousins of air conditioners in two of the windows. He plugged them into the outlets, showered again, walked till he found some breakfast. Then he walked some more. At eleven fifty-eight a blinking bank sign flashed ninety-six degrees. An hour later a different bank flashed ninety-nine.

The heat was as advertised. A dry heat. And another upside: flesh everywhere. College girls, waitresses, nurse's aides, clerk typists. Spectacular sun-kissed things in their peasant blouses and colorful Mexican skirts, tanned young arms and shoulders and breasts, smiling radiant faces upturned to the mountains, the heavens, eager and open and welcoming.

He cruised the abandoned campus, ambled up Fourth, which the cabbie had told him teemed with street people in winter. Then downtown. There was a hardware store called Ronstadt's with a tractor in the window. The Chicago Store, whose window featured electric guitars and drums. He went inside and listened to long-haired cowboy pickers singing Dylan and James Taylor tunes or just noodling in air-conditioned comfort. A mandolin player did a wistful version of "Ripple," a Grateful Dead tune awash in water imagery. Pigpen was newly dead, grateful or not, but no one played any Pigpen tunes.

Once he'd cooled off a bit he grabbed a Coke at a nearby café, then found a phone booth. The phone book was still there, skinny but unmolested, dangling on its chain. H. Shackleford picked up on the second ring. There's no Howard here, he said. H stood for Harold. Jake, big surprise, had misremembered it. Sy said why he was calling. H. Shackleford definitely remembered Jake.

Harold disliked phones. They agreed to muster in two days at the Happy Enchilada, a taquería in South Tucson. Sy assumed this meant the southern part of town, but it was more like South Dakota, an inexplicably separate entity. He waited forever for a bus, which let him off at a corner across from the Enchilada. Like everything else with doors and windows, the bus was bone-chillingly cold.

Harold was seated at a table with a couple of friends when he pushed through the door. All facing in his direction, like the Last Supper. Sy shook hands with Harold, then with his two apostles. The apostles also worked at the ThreeCo smelter.

"Everyone calls it Freako," Harold told him.

"Everyone but the bosses," said Dwight, a dull-looking post-adolescent with freckles and tousled, sandy-colored hair. Harold and Lencho, stocky and Aztec-looking, nodded agreement.

"And that's *all* the bosses," said Lencho. "Bosses are bosses. Freako, Steelworkers. They're just alike."

"Fungible," Harold said. "Get it? Because they're like fungi, see. You can't tell them apart, and they'll kill you if you're not careful."

He was mid-twenties, bright and self-consciously nonchalant, an alien mimicking human characteristics. Short and frail-looking, neatly combed hair and a voice in an upper register. Made more sense in a classroom than a copper mine.

Sy found the joke labored and unfunny. But he wanted to show he got it. "Mushroom humor," he said.

Harold plowed ahead. "The point is, the local's in the company's pocket. That's something we're trying to fix."

Sy said Jake told him they might know Naldo Galvan.

"Jake," said Lencho. His tone, like the breed of his left-wing tendencies, was ambiguous. "He's some kind of a Maoist, I guess."

"Trotskyist, more like."

"Socialist Workers?"

Sy shook him off. "Not much of a joiner."

Nods and knowing looks.

"Anyway, sure," Harold said. "Naldo Galvan. Still in Mineral City. You've probably heard the story. Steelworkers raided Mine Mill, installed their puppets as officers of the local. Naldo's nobody's puppet. So now it's a two-front struggle. Same as here."

Harold was sizing him up, deciding how much to reveal.

"*City of Emeralds* was inspirational. Naldo Galvan especially."

"Got that right," Harold said. "So let's get you hired."

"That was the plan."

"Don't sweat it." This was Dwight. "If you were good enough for the army, you're good enough for Freako."

"Or even if you weren't." That was Lencho.

"They mean surface," Harold said. "Mill, smelter, refinery. Underground's a higher bar."

"Underground, gotta be good enough for the *navy*," said Lencho.

They gave him a primer. Cobra Copper was a subsidiary of Mongoose Mining and Metallurgy—known as Mother Mongoose, or MoMMy—perched on a mother lode fertile enough, Simon gathered, to outlast not just the four of them but also, assuming he survived, generations of Bussbaums to come. The complex occupied thousands of acres and included, besides the smelter, the mill, and the electrolytic refinery, the world's most prolific underground copper mine, a bunker of tunnels a mile wide and nearly as deep.

The smelter, all things considered, was the way to go.

The probationary period was the wrinkle. Six months, per the union contract. The upshot being Freako could terminate new employees with prejudice, no questions asked. The union wouldn't lift a finger. The union never lifted a finger.

"So you'll have to lay low for a while," Lencho again.

Sy promised he would. They shook hands again, as if some urgent matter had been settled. And then he left, H. Shackleford, aka Harold, never having offered to buy him lunch, or even a cup of coffee.

* * *

You could die waiting for buses in Tucson. Walking too. And he had no idea, still, how he'd get to his interview. He needed a car.

Or a truck. Twice now he'd spotted a sky blue '49 Chevy, gun rack at the back of the cab, in a Safeway parking lot. Handmade for-sale sign in the passenger window. He peeked inside and noticed, in the side-view mirror, a man in a straw cowboy hat watching him. This was per usual on the subways. Oglers galore. You shot them a look, or moved to another part of the train, or stepped off and back on to a different car. A Safeway lot in broad daylight posed no danger at all.

The man waited till Sy acknowledged him. "*¿Quieres comprarlo?*" He had a sun-weathered look, as if he'd been picking grapes since before trucks were invented.

Simon had done some Spanish in high school. "*¿Dinero?*"

The man smiled crookedly. "*Sí. Claro que sí.*"

Sy was about to say, "*¿Cuanto?*" But the man was a step ahead. "Three hundred. Brakes good. Tires good. Engine rebuilt, ninety thousand. Granny gear. Three hundred. Cash on the barrelhead, *¿me entiendes?*"

The man's name was Frank. He proffered the keys and they climbed in. The odometer read 93,600. Frank pointed at the floor, directing him to step on the starter button. The engine turned right over. Frank pulled the for-sale sign off the window and held it in his lap. Sy headed west on Speedway beyond the Interstate until he reached a clutch of squat buildings he took for a prison but which turned out to be a community college. Mountains loomed on his right, and sandy dirt dotted with stumpy green trees on either side stretched into the distance. When he came to a cross street, he signaled left, but there was no traffic. "Granny gear," he now understood, meant the transmission. First was lower than low. Better to start in second.

The truck had an old-school windshield, two smallish rectangles side by side. But the height of the cab made for a formidable view, lending the ride a sense of rickety stateliness, like a carriage drawn by a broken-down horse. Frank switched on the radio—people discussing Watergate in Spanish—and switched it off again when he'd proved it worked. The brakes didn't need to be pumped. Back at Safeway Sy told him he had only a little cash in his pocket, and hadn't yet opened a local bank account. But he'd be starting at ThreeCo soon, What about an out-of-town-check for three-twenty-five?

Frank pondered this for a moment. "Three-fifty," he said. "*¿Vives aquí?* You live in Tucson? Put your address," indicating the checkbook Sy had produced. He copied some information from Sy's New York license and handed over the pink slip.

The form, Sy noticed later, declared a title transfer for a hundred and fifty dollars, cutting Frank's reportable income by more than half. Frank had arranged to have the document pre-notarized.

Or maybe he'd stolen the seal. Sy hoped he had. That was a better story.

* * *

His interview was noon the next day. He grabbed coffee and eggs and toast at a downtown diner and headed north on Acorn Boulevard, over the dusty Calambre riverbed, then on to Acorn Junction, where the road veered east toward Acorn proper and dead-ended finally in Cobra City, a wholly owned subsidiary of the Cobra Copper Company.

The radio was all preachers and mariachis. The preachers had high-lonesome voices that rattled the truck's speakers, most noticeably when beseeching the Lord. The mariachis came through okay till they gave way to the Bible thumpers. Simon felt on the cusp of an out-of-body experience. Only the body was somebody else's. Somebody else's body, somebody else's skin, somebody else's life. Somebody else's truck. The truck wanted a dog. A big slobbery one, slobbering out the open window. Slobbering was underrated. The heat was punishing. The breeze burned his skin, or whoever's skin he was in.

The smokestacks came into view when he turned east. On straightaways they loomed in the distance like floating dynamite sticks. But straightaways were rare. Mostly the drive resembled a sideways Cyclone ride, a roller coaster of roadkill and dead man's curves. The steering wheel had more play than he remembered. He imagined driving this route after dark, or before daybreak, even as he feared letting his mind wander from the task of staying alive. The road was unforgiving, the plunge steep and rugged as the end of a noir chase scene. At last he spotted a sign for CoCoCo Road and drove a mile down the chewed-up blacktop till he came to a high gated fence. Behind the fence was a trailer that served as the company office. He sponged his armpits as best he could with a wad of Kleenex. After a minute or so a man in a khaki security uniform unlocked the gate and waved him in.

The interview was perfunctory, conducted by a different man in a short-sleeve shirt and bolo tie who wanted to see if Sy had most of his fingers and at least a smattering of English. The question about being arrested, which Sy had declined to answer, never came up. When he'd proved his fitness for service the man asked for a local address and phone number. Sy would need to replace his New York license with one issued in Arizona. He also needed a phone. The man thanked him for coming in and promised to call him once they'd made a decision and Sy had a phone.

He recalled what the apostles had said about Freako's standards. He was as good as hired.

The trip back was less trying, the dynamite looming now in his rear-view mirror.

Back in town he stopped at the phone company and placed an order. The installation guy showed up two days later. As soon as he left Sy dialed Freako and spoke with the woman who'd sent him the application when he called from New York.

"Thanks, Hon," she said. "Good luck."

* * *

He bided his time at Chuy's Bunny Ear Café, watching the Watergate hearings on a black-and-white Zenith portable perched by the register. Horizontal bars fluttered skyward, past the ghosts and snow, in an endless loop. There were two of everything.

The place was just off the UofA campus. Home, when school was in session, of the raging Wildcats. Chuy, best guess, a previous owner, the counterman being a gringo's gringo. But a Mexican-style café wanted a Mexican-style name. Sy took "bunny ear" for a type of cactus, deducing this from the storefront window, the *pièce de résistance* of which was a crude sketch of a prickly, hospital-green rabbit-faced succulent munching on a carrot he planned to wash down, evidently, with a cup of joe. Squiggly lines, indicating steam, rose from the cup. Chuy's was geared to college kids, coffee and soft drinks, packaged pastries, *pan dulce*, what passed in this part of the world for bagels. The counterman talked back at the TV. Aside from the TV itself—Sy didn't yet have one of his own—this was the Bunny Ear's main attraction.

He was sitting at the counter, taking in the proceedings, when the counterman had a Eureka moment.

"Claghorn!" he shouted, pleased to have solved some private mystery. Jabbed his finger at the screen in a knowing way, like a drunk at a high school reunion. "Claghorn, who that is. Ol' Senator Claghorn."

Simon had never heard of a Senator Claghorn.

"Senator *Beauregard* Claghorn?"

He shook his head.

"From the Fred Allen radio show?"

The man seemed confused. "You mean *Fog*horn *Leg*horn?" Sy caressed his empty cream-colored mug, which was indestructible and comforting in its heft. "Because absolutely."

There was a humming of appliances, freezers and refrigerators and air conditioning units. Onscreen a man with owlish glasses and a child's haircut sat at the witness table, reading from a prepared statement in a flat voice, never looking up from the page.

"Cartoon rooster? 'Camptown Races,' always whacking that dog with a two-by-four?"

The counterman eyed him over the marbled bar. His head pitched forward like a man whose neck had been snapped by a noose, then sprang back to life, eyes brimming with newfound purpose. As if he'd been hypnotized and awakened, suddenly, by a trigger of some kind, a commonplace word, say, imbued with a special power by the hypnotist. Deep furrows formed beneath the brim of his Cleveland Indians cap. "Son, Ah said, son," he said finally, thumbs hooked in imaginary suspenders. "Ah believe you got in mind a whole 'nutha rooostah—Roostah *Cog*burn, that is."

Probably never missed a reunion.

"Tha's a joke, son," still with the thumbs.

"Okay."

"Before your time," the counterman sniffed. Himself again. The drawl dispatched, he spoke now in a fruited-plain accent that matched his cap, its blue felt dome set off by Chief Wahoo's crimson face and horsey pearly whites. "The Duke, though—heck, my own kids won't go see *True Grit*, and they're old enough to know better. They like that Dustin Hoffman, Jack whatsisname, Nicholas. Nicholson." He shook his head in a way that suggested disgust or sadness or bemusement. "All his wives been Mexicans, Wayne. Three so far. That's a fact."

This was not a fact. Simon Bussbaum knew a few things about Marion Morrison, stage name John Wayne. He wore a rug. He'd made his 1968 pro-war propaganda piece *The Green Berets* with LBJ's blessing and the Pentagon's full cooperation. He'd dodged military service in favor of Hollywood, even after Pearl Harbor. In younger days he'd been not just a cheerleader for Nixon's House Un-American Activities Committee—HUAC, authors of the Hollywood blacklist—but a Bircher in good standing. Wife *número dos* had been Mexican, but the others hailed from Panama and Peru. These were the facts.

Still, all this jabber about fictitious deep-South senators and Hollywood cowboys had made him uneasy, stirred some latent paranoia of being branded a tourist or, worse, a carpetbagger. Plus he wanted to watch the hearing.

"Y'know, with a name like Bunny Ear, you'd think you'd get better reception."

The counterman studied the picture. Fiddled doubtfully with the antenna, each fiddle causing the ghosts to lurch in formation from one side to the other, cutting right-left-right like slalom skiers in the Limbo winter Olympics. After every few cuts he took a half-step back to gauge his progress. When he tired of this he coaxed a Pall Mall from a pack in his shirt pocket and struck a kitchen match against some unseen part of his person, possibly the zipper of his fly. Then he pulled up a director's chair on his side of the counter and returned to the hearing, which was oriented a degree or two nearer to upright but was in every other respect one thousand percent unchanged.

All America was watching. There was nothing much else to watch, all regular programming preempted, all eyes belonging to housewives, shut-ins, the institutionalized, the incarcerated, the unemployed, the night laborers, and anyone else in viewing range of a cathode ray tube at this particular moment trained, like it or not, on Sam Ervin, meaty paw clutching a candy-striped gavel. A lovable redneck he was, Senator Sam, all jowls and eyebrows and wry country-lawyer twinkliness. His star witness, the penitent bagman John Dean, had about him the weaselly air of a hall monitor, the Mister Peabody specs a relic perhaps from grammar school, selected initially by his mum as a hedge against blows to the face from brutish classmates and retained in later years as a sort of fetish. Seated behind him were more lawyers and an unnaturally poised woman wearing a high-necked dress, presumably his wife, her platinum hair stretched tight in a debutante's bun. In her left ear, the one to the camera, shone a big globe earring. It sparkled beside its double like the larger and hotter-burning of twin suns.

"What did he know," the counterman said, "and when did he know it. That, like the man said, is the question."

"Not much of a question."

"String him up, you're saying, then give him a fair trial."

"Works for me. It's what the Duke would do."

"Not for Nixon. McGovern maybe." He laughed and extended a bony right hand. "Name's Spencer. Call me Spence."

Spence. A good muscular handle, hardy and unpretentious as meatloaf.

"Bussbaum," he said. "Call me Sy."

"Welcome to Tucson, Sy. New York, right? *I'm walkin' heah!* Lawng Island, am I right?"

"Ratso Rico. Rico Rico Rico. Saw that in New York, matter of fact."

"So, Long Island?"

"Queens. Close."

They watched for a while in silence, Dean's monotone mingling with the appliances.

There was a lull in the action. He was ready to go. "So, Cleveland. Alan Freed, Cuyahoga River. Gaylord Perry. About all I know."

"You're one up on me. Never set foot."

Sy indicated his baseball cap. "Just a Tribe fan?"

"When in Rome," Spence said. "Tucson, my fish-out-of-water *amigo*, is the officially sanctioned, authentic winter home of the Cleveland Indians. Like the sign says. Big road sign, practically a landmark. It's on postcards. How'd you manage to miss that?"

He dug in his pocket for change. "Not much chance to explore yet."

He slapped some coins on the counter. The ferocity of the climate came as a shock. It was the same shock he experienced every time he emerged into the open air, as surprising as it was predictable. He took a moment to gather himself beside the bunny-faced cactus, the steaming cup of joe.

The heat splashing his face, burning his eyes, rising in waves from the sparkliest, most immaculate sidewalk he'd ever seen.

* * *

The call came in a week or so. He'd been assigned to the smelter, beginning with Wednesday's C shift. This being Freako time, Wednesday's C shift began Thursday at midnight. For reasons of prestige, he supposed, the letter *A* was reserved for day shift, so you worked all eight hours of any day's graveyard shift, designated the last shift of the day, the first third of the next. Nobody seemed to find this odd. You got used to it.

He was detailed to anodes. The job paid four ninety-two per hour, more than he'd ever made in his life. He'd need boots with metatarsal guards. A combination lock. Coveralls were suggested. ThreeCo would furnish the rest.

He called Shackleford. All he'd say on the phone was that it was easy money. Good place for Simon to get his sea legs, quote unquote, while he was still on probation. He'd learn soon enough what an anode was.

What it was was a slab of copper. There were twenty-two slabs in each of three concrete carousels, squarish sheets of smoldering metal glowing like jack o'lanterns in the dark of the smelter. The wheel, thick as a stack of Manhattan phone books, ground slowly, creakily, as if powered by hamsters. The air ranged from stifling to suffocating. You were grateful for any hint of a breeze, any faint whiff of oxygen. Thirty-some yards away, carved out of a corrugated wall at the end of the building, an open garage-style door framed the night, the darkness corrupted by glimmers of sky and unnatural amber light. The orbiting slabs drifting by, in the foreground, like buttered toast on a lazy Susan.

A finished anode weighed eight hundred pounds. Sy's station was Anode Wheel Number Two. This was about all he knew, the sum of the mumbled orientation he'd got at the top of the shift from his new boss, the anode foreman, a fireplug with a face that looked to be gouged out of rawhide. The face made him think of a chew toy for a very large dog. The dog made him think of a fireplug.

"You figure out how to operate this piece o' 'quipment," the boss had told him, presenting him with his regulation fourteen-pound sledge, "you'll be all right."

In fact he thought he might heave. His gut had been in a knot since the moment he saw the smokestacks again. Disturbing by day, at night they mutated into shimmering, spectral pillars of smoke, unearthly enough to make you question your own fleshly being. They stood vigil over the complex like gun towers in hell. He labored to breathe as he trudged from the lot to the locker room, his various symptoms emulsifying into a blended, generalized dread on entering the smelter proper. Freako after dark had the ambience of highway construction projects glimpsed from speeding cars in the dead of night, drive-bys of jackhammers and blowtorches and spotlights, compounded tenfold by deep immersion and intimations of disaster.

The smelter itself was a cavernous, ramshackle Big Top featuring spark-spewing furnaces, splashing cauldrons dangled from cranes like murderous marionettes, rapids of liquid fire tumbling down in harrowing dayglo ribbons. Danger was everywhere, lurking beneath the dull roar and the rotten-eggs stench. Everything black and orange, darkness and firelight, a waking nightmare Halloween. He lingered awhile by the entrance, willing himself to turn back but paralyzed by the terror of a possible misstep and the gravity of what seemed some dense and desolate planet. The gravity enhanced by the heft of his spaceman costume, shiny and cumbrous and already steeped in a pungent marinade of sweat.

These were the basics of his ensemble:

— A fire-resistant orange jumpsuit, which, when he first saw his reflection in Steinfeld's fitting room, had conjured memories of Pete Townshend abusing his Fender at the Fillmore East;

— A virgin aluminum hardhat, bright as the gibbous moon, bobbing and bouncing about his ears;

— An army-green respirator, yellow filter casings like the eyes of a mutant housefly, to be hung from his neck and deployed during ground-level cloudbursts of sulfur dioxide;

— Shiny, silvery Tin Man gloves that reached practically to his elbows;

— Steel-toed Redwings, metatarsal guards attached, worn this inaugural night with Dr. Scholl's walking socks of a thickness he'd supposed, incorrectly, would spare the backs of his heels from blisters;

— Buddy Holly-style safety glasses, replete with Coke-bottle lenses and built-in blinders. These were sturdy enough to pound nails and slid regularly to the tip of his nose, which was no more useful for breathing than for load-bearing, clogged with a tarlike substance that could pass, in certain discredited belief systems, for the Snot of the Gods.

Also, for good measure, you weren't allowed to roll up your sleeves.

The best you could say for the job was you were mostly stationary, and so less likely to get crosswise with something lethal. The work put Simon in mind of breaking rocks, minus the shackles and gun-wielding guards and chain gang songs, poems of constant sorrow shaped by the clang of the prisoners' hammers. Drudgery past belief. The glimmering wheel moved at a crawl, a pace more conducive to sleep than music. As the metal cooled in its casts, a hydraulic cylinder rose from beneath whichever slab was inching toward him, tilting, when it worked, at a forty-five degree angle from its upper corners. The objective being to make sure the slab broke free of its mold by whaling on any slab that clung to the concrete, repeating as often as needed to get it unclung.

It was a job fit for a chimp. It had to be done by humans, Sy supposed, because there weren't enough chimps hungry, submissive, or suicidal enough to take it on. He kept drifting off. He'd be roused periodically by an explosion, like a cannon off in the distance, or the metallic squeal of heavy equipment, or the pounding of one of his fellow hammerers. Or, once, by the yelp of his foreman's voice.

"Bussbomb," the high-pitched bark of a small yipping dog. "*Bussbomb.* You wake the fuck up now, boy."

He did. Woke right the fuck up. Grabbed his sledgehammer, dropped its head on the nearest slab. Rinse and repeat. The third blow was the charm. The anode popped loose, inclined slowly, slowly returned to rest. The fireplug watched, rocking on his heels like an Irish cop. They stood there, side by side, wheel groaning, anode after anode rising and falling again, without human encouragement, in its concrete cast. Then the foreman waddled off to bark at some other poor sonofabitch.

Sy glanced anxiously at his watch, its hands luminous in the shadow cast by the upturned bell of his silver glove. It said twenty past three.

* * *

Next he knew it was daylight. Five thirty one. Did the math. Eight minus five-thirty-one. Just shy of two and a half hours. A hundred forty nine minutes, nine thousand seconds give or take. An eternity, calibrated.

And yet, miraculously, shift change. He'd drifted off again when he felt a tap on the shoulder. Stocky Chicano, American flag decal on his hardhat. Simon's relief. The man greeted him, or sent him off, with a little salute. When Sy looked back he was sipping a cup of coffee and reading the paper, boots resting on the rim of the anode wheel. A man in his element, serene, unbothered by the prospect of imminent death from a downpour of wayward magma. A man who, were it not for the presence of plastic-hat bosses on day shift, might have shown up for work in pajamas.

Sy shuffled off, past the anode wheels and the converters, three hulking furnaces and two less so, on toward the locker room. Around him advanced a ragtag army, as single-minded as rent-a-horses on their way back to the stable. Not people he cared to shower with. At any rate not this morning.

He stepped out of his coveralls in the lot and detoured to the company town before setting off for the mountain road back to Tucson. The coffee was freshly brewed and too hot to drink. He tore a small square out of the lid and holstered the cup in a cheap plastic holder that hung awkwardly from the dash, a gift accessory from Frank, on the far side of the stick. He was petrified. He'd just cheated death in the smelter and here it was again, this time in the form of a pinball somersault down the side of a mountain. With no one behind him he stayed in second gear and rode the brake. Focused on keeping his eyes on the yellow line and his hands on the wheel.

In time his terror subsided. The more he relaxed the more he feared falling asleep. He reached across the cab for his coffee, which had gone lukewarm. He was able now to work the radio dial, changing stations according to mood and safety demands, a gauntlet of barkers and crooners, shards of high-pitched homilies alternating with bits of brass flourishes and strummed guitars and trilled whoops and hollers. This was his mountain soundtrack, a fitful rhythm of sermon and serenade, bluster and melancholy. Eventually static snuffed out the preachers and McCartney and Wings flitted in, piteous fallen Beatle, heralding Sy's return to lower altitudes with some fatuous hummable dance-hall shtick. His adrenals began to settle and fatigue set in.

He had a premonition. It would be this milk run stretch, after all, that ended in doom. With this in mind he spent the rest of the trip scouring the dial for hard rock bands, hoping power chords at top volume would keep him alert enough to reach his apartment. His hope was rewarded. He threw open the door and collapsed onto his mattress.

Sleep proved elusive.

The bedroom was a humidor. The mercury on his souvenir Statue of Liberty thermometer hovered around ninety. The swamp coolers—those faux air conditioners in two of the windows—were useless. Tucson was the opposite of a swamp. Sy smelled like copper, his skin dusted with a thousand toxic substances. He wanted a shower. But his mattress was on the floor, and the physics of locomotion from this position were too much. In his weariness he'd neglected to close the blinds, he saw now, and resigned to live with this as well. He studied the bare bulb in the ceiling fixture, a beached whale in the desert, naked and sore and sweating.

There was beer in the fridge, as unattainable as the world beyond—mountains, desert, sunsets in Technicolor, *señorítas* in various shades of bronze. What he'd seen of Arizona, pre-Freako, had made him feel like a troubadour, his heart silently crooning mariachi tunes to passing strangers. Life *during* Freako was another thing altogether. As for life after Freako? This seemed, at the moment, entirely hypothetical.

He'd just dozed off when a crack of thunder rocked him awake. Rain pounded the window, spidery bolts of lightning sliced the eerily purple sky. Still drowsy, he lay in bed awhile, enjoying the rush of cool and suffused in something like awe at the immensity of the spectacle. Before he could get to his feet this brief, unexpected night was turning again to day. The clouds vanished and soon the sun was back and with it the heat and the sounds of the everyday world and his broken and restless sleep.

In a dream he stepped out of the Chicago Store and there, in Ronstadt's window, stood Linda herself. She was the Linda of Stone Poneys days, bangs and lips and hula hoop earrings and liquid almond-shaped eyes and the voice of a Siren, drawing him closer and closer, all the more when she sang about different drums and how she had to be leaving. Turquoise-tipped fingers fondling the microphone in a provocative manner. In the dream he was not, like Ulysses, lashed to a mast. He broke the window with three blows of his regulation fourteen-pound sledgehammer. She was gone, though, by the time he'd made his way up from the sidewalk. Just him and the tractor.

He picked himself up off the mattress, finally, wanting a shower more than he'd ever wanted anything in his life, more even than Linda of Stone Poneys days.

* * *

After his second night he scored some dexies from his relief, a man known as Dr. Hernández. Kept a pharmacy in his lunch box. Broad smile with lots of gold. Hernández displayed a vial of pills between his thumb and fingers and gave it a little shake. It was one of those plastic prescription vials, urine-yellow, childproof twist-off cap. He stopped rattling it so Simon could read the label. The original doctor's name was blacked out with a Magic Marker, along with the patient's.

Sy had left his wallet in the locker room. But his credit was good. Golden smile from the doc. "I know where to find you, bro."

Big assumption on his part. Sy's status with Freako was day to day, minute to minute. He fantasized about escape. Magic, mule, hostages. Laundry bin, like in Hollywood jailbreaks. He had to remind himself he could leave whenever he liked. He was, after all, a white man, more or less, in America. With college credits. There had to be other jobs in Arizona. If not there were other states.

Still, to fold after two shifts? What of Naldo Galvan? What of *la lucha*, the people of Mineral City?

He would soldier on. Speed would help. The nickel bag was a sort of luxury option, something to take the edge off. His plan was to vary the dose each night till he found the sweet spot, just enough to power him through the night without keeping him up all day. Hernández inspired him. He was older than Sy, though probably not as old as he looked—not so much aged, Sy suspected, as weathered. An old Freako hand, at any rate. And if Hernández could survive Freako for years, plus a tour or two in Nam—inferring this from his flag decal—Sy could survive a week. And if he could survive a week he could survive two weeks, a month, a year. And after that? Anything was possible.

Was this Quang Tri, after all? Was he surrounded by swamps and jungles, by Vietcong intent on sending his imperialist ass home in a box? He was not. He was surrounded by Circle Ks, gleaming red-arrow logos like three-fingered hands reaching awkwardly for the sky. His truck was parked near the stacks, springs and signposts of this mountain-ringed valley of ashes. If all else failed he could drive to California, find a commune, learn a trade, A world of possibilities, waiting. For him, that is. For Hernández, not so much. Hernández was screwed. And he stood, as much as possible under the circumstances, with Hernández.

When the going gets tough, Nixon said, the tough get going. Simon got drugs.

The dexies were the shape of a shield, almost a heart, the halves like left and right ventricles. One ventricle did the trick. He still dozed off at the anode wheel, but shallowly, catnaps light enough to hear the approach of the foreman or the operator of whichever wheel was idle. You were supposed to wait for someone to spell you before taking your lunch break—thirty minutes, per the union contract, travel and hand-washing included. This was entirely self-policed.

He passed the night smoking cigarettes, one after the other, the glowing tips like fireflies in the dark. Once home he'd light a joint and douse his neck with rubbing alcohol, a technique he'd used during the odd New York heat wave.

Time was upside-down. His alarm clock rang each evening as the moon peeked over the mountains. Then he'd shower and hit the Copper Penny, an ersatz IHOP seconds from the Interstate where you poured your own bottomless cup of coffee from a mustard-colored urn they left at your table. On his way out the waitress would fill his family-size stainless-steel thermos. Then he'd stop at a Circle K for smokes and a breakfast burrito he might get to by four or five in the morning.

By then he was filthy. Dust was everywhere. Copper dust, rock dust, garden variety dust. Before you could eat you had to hike to a concrete latrine, primitive and foul as an unlocked gas station restroom, over by the converters. Laundry-style basins, doorless stalls, vandal-proof mirrors of polished steel. The latrine announced itself via a cast-iron door with the word *"Hombres"* spray-painted in guardrail yellow, bracketed by fire-engine red exclamation marks pointing alternately north and south, an embellishment perhaps by a second artist.

Both the word and the punctuation seemed superfluous. *Mujeres* in Freako's employ were limited to clerical duties and confined to remote locations, far from the *hombres'* room. But the splash of color did add a kind of grace note to a dismal setting, as wistfully uplifting as subway graffiti. Inside, above the door, someone had painted a red arrow and the legend "Mexico 115 *millas.*" This referred to Nogales, which lay two hours to the south, an hour's drive from Tucson.

After washing up he walked back through the anode floor and beyond the corrugated wall of the smelter. He'd discovered a quiet spot on the loading dock, overlooking a holding area for forklifts and front end loaders and other heavy equipment. The air at that hour was the most bearable he'd experienced in Arizona. The burrito was cold and flavorless. If there was a microwave somewhere, no one had brought it to his attention.

No one, really, had spoken to him at all. The anode department wasn't conducive to conversation. Human-generated sound was absorbed by the oceanic background thrum of industrial hardware. You worked alone, anode wheels being large and spaced well apart. This was fine by Simon. He was less than conducive himself.

After four midnight shifts he was sleep-deprived, sluggish, and, within the limits of his emotional register, morose and hostile. Generally out of sorts. Often, as he waited to dislodge a copper slab, he floated above himself, observing himself, a space-suited alien armed with a rubber hammer. Lost in space, insensible save for the dull ache in his back and shoulders.

Entering night five he popped his usual ventricle of Dexedrine and then, still dragging after an hour or so, swallowed the other. This worked fine for the short term. But it left him speedy when he wanted to sleep. Instead of knocking him out, his morning smoke further muddled his mind, while the dexies made the rest of him restless and fidgety. He'd sleep later. Too tired and indifferent to shower, he headed back out, sleepwalking unsteadily toward the campus.

The undergrads had gone home or retreated to cooler climes, Aspen, Minneapolis-St. Paul, Flagstaff. His clothes smelled and he hadn't shaved for days, yielding not so much a beard as a vague aspect of haggardness. Dishevelment suited him. His insides were askew, his circadian rhythms blown to bits and reinterpreted as free jazz, syncopated in impossibly complicated ways. Truth in advertising. He was wilting from the outside in. Small children eyed him suspiciously, and the feeling was mutual. Who did they think they were?

Why were they even here? That is, why were their *parents* here? Simon had come on a mission, and even so he'd rather have been in Mineral City. He wondered if New Mexico was cooler. This was a different order of heat from the smelter, with its underworld trappings, the lava flows and the acrid odor of sulfur and the benighted state of its inhabitants, as dead as they were alive. Being outdoors at noontime you felt as if you'd ventured too close to the sun.

Which, in the astronomical scheme of things, you had.

By his seventh C shift, in fact, Sy was adjusting to zombie life. He discerned a perverse wisdom in having graveyard drag on for two full weeks, with no days off to scramble your cycles. Plus you got four days off when you were finally done. This was your reward for keeping the smokestacks blowing for fourteen consecutive nights.

Halfway there. Week two would be better. His terror of molten lava had eased, and he'd mastered the ins and outs of bashing a slow-moving wheel with a rubber hammer. He'd rediscovered a will to live, practically, and the hope that he'd get the chance. For now he just wanted some rest.

It was with this singular ambition that he was tromping back to the locker room, nodding to the few men with whom he had a nodding acquaintance, when the sparkplug pulled him aside. He wore a smug half-grin that implied he not only had a secret, but that the secret pertained to Sy. He held a half-sheet of yellow paper, pinching it by a corner with his thumb and forefinger, as if dangling letters of transit from Casablanca.

The shift was over, though. And the Allies had won. Sy just wanted to clock out.

"Got your new orders, Bussbomb. Movin' up in the world, looks like."

Couldn't be good. Sy braced for the punchline.

"Been promoted. Onward and upward."

The sparkplug gave him the form. Reclassified as a converter puncher, effective swing shift Saturday.

Sy stared at the letterhead. Freako's logo was a cobra wrapped around the pole of an American flag. The snake was curled into the shape of the letter S, forming a dollar sign that was equal parts venomous and patriotic. The logo seemed inspired, if a bit on the nose. It took him a moment to make the connection to the cobra in the company's name. Exhaustion was eating his brain.

Go ahead and shoot, Rick told Ilsa, you'll be doing me a favor.

"Promoted," he said. "Huh."

He scanned the form, searching for an escape clause.

"Promoted. Twenty-two-cent bump, last I checked. That's *per hour,* son. Don't take it so hard."

But he did take it hard. He had no clue how to punch a converter. He'd seen it from a distance, punchcar operators scudding to and fro along a narrow track as they rammed steel bars into metal-flapped eyelets the size of tennis balls. The flaps ran the length of the furnaces. As the bars penetrated the flaps the holes hissed and spit sparks back in return, and once or twice he'd caught a glimpse of a puncher straddling the track, hammering on the front of the car with another rod. It looked more physically taxing than wielding a bona fide hammer, and given the sparks and spray way more dangerous.

And the timing? It hinted at dark currents of cruelty, verging on sadism. Sy had made it to Friday morning, halfway to the four-day break you earned by surviving graveyard. Now he'd have to report back on swing the following day, only to earn a measly three days at the end of the week. After that they could easily move him again, and again after that, so that his four days remained just out of reach. He supposed they could do this forever.

When he got home he popped another ventricle to stay up past dark, the better to get his biorhythms straightened out. Drifted off anyway. Woke up when the phone rang. It was after five.

Harold had got wind of his transfer.

"Friendly heads-up," he said, straining to sound casual. "Laying low's gonna be trickier now. More people, more managers, more activity. So loose lips, if you get my drift. Don't let on you know me. In the interests of prudence. Same for Dwight and Lencho."

Sy got his drift. Bad for the cause if he blew his cover. Fine by him. He *didn't* know them. They'd met once for lunch, a meeting notable for the absence of food or drink. Why would he incriminate himself on the basis of a lunchless lunch, a passing acquaintance with his lunatic brother, some nebulous kinship with Naldo Galvan? Still, no harm in playing along. No need to advertise his affiliations, tenuous as they were.

"Cool with me. Converters, though. What am I in for?"

"Hard to explain. They'll show you. Tougher than anodes. More than twenty-two cents an hour tougher. A lot more if you're stuck with the wrong skimmer. We were hoping to get that fixed in the next contract."

"The wrong skimmer."

"Don't sweat it. Smelter jobs are all"—he paused, chewing over alternatives to *fungible*—"pretty much the same. From the standpoint of alienation, I mean. The main thing is converters are closer to the action. More later, got a meeting."

He promised to stay in touch. For now Sy had twenty-three hours to himself, He spent the evening browsing travel brochures he'd found at the depot. He'd been thinking about his four-day post-graveyard break, now deferred for another—what, five weeks., was it? He spread the brochures on the floor near one of the swamp coolers, where they rustled gently in the mechanical breeze.

"Blessed by an average three hundred fifty sunny days each year, Tucson is surrounded by majestic saguaro forests and five magnificent mountain ranges."

"A drive from the valley floor to the summit of majestic Mount Lemmon traverses seven of the world's nine life zones."

"Dress tends to be casual."

"During monsoon season, travel is ill-advised when rain is expected, as people, pets, and even automobiles can be swept away by high water levels."

He'd never heard of life zones before. He'd read that rainfall totals were well below normal—notwithstanding the previous day's Old Testament lightning storm—and that some meteorologists feared a drought. He'd always thought a lack of water was the point of a desert. But then he'd always imagined deserts as settings for movies about the Foreign Legion, infinite sweeps of sand and camels. He made a mental note to check out life zone seven as soon as he got the chance, and to make inquiries into number nine.

Then it was late morning, the apartment on simmer. Fueled by three cups of instant coffee he drove to Ronstadt's, where he bought a twelve-inch Japanese portable TV and a pair of electric fans. Watched the Watergate hearing ghost-free and in less-than-living color—pea green, for the most part—in his underwear. Shuffled off to the kitchen when Senator Sam gaveled it to a close.

It hadn't dawned on him to stop for groceries. His cupboards held a bag of Ruffles and the last of the Rainbo bread. In the fridge were a couple of stranded beers, some iffy slices of luncheon meat, and a sad black banana.

He fixed a potato chip sandwich and settled in with a bottle of Dos Equis to watch *I Want to Live!* in progress. Susan Hayward still planning to go straight. He drifted off before she went to the gas chamber. Jolted back by another lightning crack, a thunderstorm of epic proportions. He'd missed most of that too. The clock said one fifteen. His shift started at four.

He switched off the TV, showered, and drove to the only place he knew that served breakfast all day. The sign atop the Bank of America said ninety-three. Flashes of sunlight caromed off cars and storefronts, reflected up from the bone-dry pavement. Brilliance from all directions, everyone seemingly in white, a sweaty parody of heaven. The waitress brought him eggs and buttered toast and an urn of coffee and he gave her his thermos to have filled and waiting when he was ready to leave.

He lingered absently over a Times, gazing out on the gleaming city and milking, for as long as he could, the laminated air-conditioned hospitality of the Copper Penny.

* * *

It was a long drive north, his second in daytime, stickier but less arduous than navigating mountains by the moon and stars. He left the radio off, opting instead for the subway roar of the wind through the windows. Hoping the steady blast might calm his nerves, take his mind off the gnarl in his gut.

Shpilkes, the Jews called it. Only this was a distinctly *goyishe* form of agita, born of copper and open spaces and foreign, surely, to even the most dyspeptic of Talmudic scholars. His unease grew as he rounded the curve where the twin stacks came briefly into view. A glimpse told him something was wrong. Not till the picture was gone from his line of vision, when all that remained was an after-image, did he manage to solve the puzzle. The smoke was missing.

Two four-hundred-foot, twenty-four-seven epic exhaust pipes, and not a puff rising from either one. This was something he'd never witnessed. Least of all on day shift, when the brass made their presence felt in the name of maximizing production. No smoke meant no production. No production seemed impossible.

As he turned east the straightaway afforded a better view. There they were, two slate-gray obelisks, shotgun barrels aimed at an unaccountably crystalline sky. The sun behind him, so dazzling he had to angle his rear-view toward the cliff side of the narrow road. Thirty-four hundred feet above sea level, not so much as a cyclone fence, nothing between him and a tin can grave but crag and cactus. Still this was the mellow stretch, beyond the dead man's curves, and induced only mild vertigo. His *shpilkes* were another story.

The wave of dread he'd felt on first beholding the stacks—when he knew an interview was the worst that could happen, and he'd likely advance no deeper than Freako's perimeter—returned with a vengeance, That had been more of a field trip. Now he'd seen inside the belly of the beast. Even so he hadn't *been* inside, really. He hadn't gone near the underground mine, which he conceived as a crude capitalist twist on the Grand Canyon. He'd barely survived a week on an anode wheel, and only thanks to motivation from Dr. Hernández. He was still a tourist, a dilettante. This was what worried him.

Ordinarily the stacks, smoking under the moon and stars, were a disquieting vision of end times. the planet burning, dissolving into malignant vapors of sulfur dioxide and God knew what. They'd also become a regular sight, a familiar station of the cross en route to his secular, second-rate martyrdom. They loomed now like the ruins of a lost civilization, some buried city on a planet where time had stopped.

Which was, he supposed, another way for the world to end.

He eased past the trailer and into the lot. Fifty yards or so from the locker room entrance, near one of the giant garage doors that opened out from the smelter's shell, hundreds of men clustered in small groups, coveralls gone or dangling at their waists. Some were standing, others lying on bare ground or using their hardhats for seats. A handful were shirtless, glistening in the sun. It might have been a disorderly line at the Fillmore East, save for the work clothes and industrial boots.

He wandered over and took out a cigarette.

"Yo, new dude," somebody said. "Spare a square?"

Sy tapped the pack so a Kool poked out the top. The speaker was a hard-looking Chicano with a missing tooth and a Fu Manchu mustache and a cobra tattoo on his right forearm. It wasn't the company cobra. Sy sheltered a flame with his cupped hands and they took long, meaningful drags.

"Simon," he said. "Second week. First on swing."

"Simon, right on. Everyone calls me Snake." Streams of smoke fled from his nostrils. "So this is some crazy shit, right? Couple of white dudes start walkin' out, like, two hours ago. They're like, 'We're walkin' out.' Wavin' their arms and shit, like 'join us,' and a bunch of dudes did, and then furnaces are shuttin' down, comin' offline, and pretty soon that's all she wrote, we're all out here diggin' the sunshine. Like our own little Woodstock. Because, y'know, fuck it. Six-hour shift? Speakin' my *language*, little brother, *¿me entiendes?*"

"Anarchists," somebody said. "Commies and agitators. They don't like it here, can't blame 'em for that. But you can't strike till the contract's up. That's the law."

"Wildcat," Snake said. "Not strictly legal. But they can't shitcan everyone, 'less they want to ditch the plastic hats and put their own asses to work. Which you *know* they don't. *Pinche pendejo* whitecaps. So, y'know, fuck it."

Sy scanned the horizon for Harold.

A doper in a bandanna shuffled over. Or a biker. Or both. Burly and bearded, a latter-day Orson Welles who drank no Thunderbird before its time. He took a last pull on his smoke and flicked the burning butt in the direction of a man in a plastic hat. The hat, the color of milk, signified front-office. The whitecap—as Sy now knew to refer to him— was taking pictures using a zoom lens, keeping a safe distance. Some of his subjects flashed peace signs. Others turned their backs or went on with their business, or whatever it was they were doing.

"Smile," the bandanna said. "You're on Candid Camera."

He lit a joint he retrieved from behind an ear, like a pencil, had a toke and passed it around. Sy begged off, reasoning that getting high was the polar opposite of laying low, especially with the brass taking photos.

"Thanks, man," he said. "Next time."

People in street clothes, scheduled for swing shift, were milling around now, mixing and talking with the men they were there to relieve. No way to know if he'd be working or not.

A scratchy, disembodied voice, the kind you'd hear at an airport, spoiled the party. It was a different whitecap, this one with a megaphone instead of a camera. He stood on a loading dock wearing a necktie. The men in ties were the only people in hardhats.

"This is an unlawful work stoppage," he said into the megaphone. "Your local union has not authorized this action, and joins us in ordering you to immediately cease and desist. This is your final warning.

"If you are reporting for swing shift, clock in and proceed directly to your work station. Those of you who have abandoned your posts will be subject to disciplinary action. Do not clock out, your timecards will be adjusted accordingly. Do not shower. We need you to depart the premises. Those of you arriving for swing shift, proceed immediately through the change room and report to your posts..."

The crowd thinned and he spotted Harold, in animated discussion with Dwight and Lencho and several others he didn't recognize. Sy caught his eye and Harold shot him a small, barely perceptible nod. Sy took this to mean comply with the megaphone.

He punched in for his shift, then went in search of his new foreman. Found him by the salt dispenser, chewing on a cigar. He'd been expecting him.

"Bussbomb?" He extended a hand. Grip like a vise. "Leonard. That's my family name, for the record. But don't let me catch you calling me that. Call me Sarge."

Sarge was U.S. army, retired, same as a dozen other flunkies too low in the pecking order to merit a plastic hardhat. Competition for this particular handle had to have been stiff. The man had juice.

He was short and soft and had mean, beady eyes. Deep South, Alabama or Mississippi. One of those places where, when Sarge was a sprout, a tree was less a poem than an instrument of torture.

"Hope you ain't scared of a little work. Forget that foolishness out there. Every man here got a job to do, and mine's to see he does it. That's it. I don't care what a man's color is, what creed, Catholic, Church of England, don't make no nevermind. Wherever he pokes his pecker in the privacy of his home I leave to the almighty. Long as he puts in the work.

"Give me a fair day's work for a fair day's pay, we'll get along. That's it. Good crew here, mostly. They'll show you the ropes. Everything down now, someone payin' for that. But we'll have these bad boys runnin' again quick as a hare with its tail on fire. Ever punch a converter before?"

"'Fraid not."

"Follow me."

They walked to the side of an enormous furnace, then up a few steps to a platform. Two men bent idly over a railing, contemplating a wide canal in an attitude of anglers over a creek. Above them three black cranes hung like bats from a trestle at fifty-yard intervals. The men heard their approach and gave Simon the once-over.

"Chesney, Wickburn, this here's Bussbomb. He's replacing Morales. Bussbomb, this here's Wickburn. One of our best slag skimmers. Chesney, he's Wickburn's puncher.

"Son," turning to Chesney, "long as we're down, go and give Bussbomb a quick education on how we do things hereabouts."

He rested his hand on Simon's shoulder.

"Bussbomb, once you're straightened out you hunt me down and we'll go see Bullock, over on Three. Chesney here used to punch for Bullock, ain't that right?"

Chesney acknowledged this by scrunching his mouth and averting his eyes.

Chesney, though, was a talker, seemingly grateful for the quiet that came with a comatose smelter. A red-faced man in his thirties, he'd worked as a puncher for three years. He planned on graduating to skimmer, could name all the dials on the big dashboard by heart, had even spelled Wickburn once or twice on graveyard to prove his readiness. He guessed it would be an hour or so before they'd be making copper again.

"So, Bullock."

He was wedged inside his punchcar, a doorless, brick-red cab with a hydraulic rack in front. The rack held two thick silvery rods. Four slots were empty.

"He's a good skimmer," Chesney told him. "So there's that. Makes punching easier. We just had, what do you call it, creative differences. You'll be fine."

Chesney sat with his hands on a radio-sized dashboard, behind what Sy hoped was a plexiglass window, barely big enough to see through. Sy stood on the tracks to his right, the open side of the car.

"Back off a sec, watch this."

The car slid to the far end of the converter, then returned to its starting place. Chesney got out and tossed the bars from the rack onto the floor behind them, the clang of metal on concrete the loudest sound in the smelter. "Let me show you how this works, then you can give it a test drive."

You pulled a lever to go left, pushed to go right. There was no brake. You stopped by reversing direction, as gently as possible, or just letting your momentum die. The hydraulic rack you launched with the press of a button. The idea being to ram the rods into several dozen flapped openings everyone called tweers—but turned out to be *tuyeres*—which spanned the length of the furnace. This allowed compressed air to rush through the pipes and churn the metallic gumbo as it was being cooked, giving the iron and anything else that wasn't copper the time it needed to separate and rise to the top as slag.

Slag was what skimmers skimmed. If a puncher took too long getting the tuyeres unplugged the pressure dropped and the rods got sucked into the furnace and the puncher had to whale on them with another rod till the punchcar could work them free. Sy had seen punchers whaling. It did not look like fun.

"You get your rods stuck in there, you're bangin' away with all these sparks raining down from the mouth—the mouth's facing the crane aisle now, being out of the stacks, but when the converter's rolled in the mouth's just above us—and more shooting straight at you, and hard, from behind the flaps. So if it's bad you want to cut back to one or two rods, tops. Keep some fresh ones handy, 'cause when they finally come loose—and this thing's got a serious kick to it, so watch your hands—those steel axe edges will be soft as marshmallows. Also hot. So keep your gloves handy."

Simon nodded, expecting to take his place in the car. But Chesney had more.

"Marshmallow rods you can chuck under the furnace, into the crane aisle. An end loader will scoop 'em up and they'll get dumped into some converter, along with different ingredients, mostly lower-grade copper, maybe seventy percent, from the reverb furnaces across the way, but also chunks of cooled matte and silica from that chute up there, empty soda cans, whatever. This whole operation is basically digging ore out of the ground that's like one percent copper, and getting rid of whatever's not copper—sulfur dioxide, molly—that's molybdenum— probably gold. Like Michelangelo, the sculpture's already there, you just chisel until you find it. Process of elimination. Anyway, the converters give you copper that's ninety-eight, ninety-nine percent pure. Then it's made into anodes, and then it goes to the refinery.

"Long as it's selling for ninety cents a pound, Freako turns a profit. Lower than that they'll shut us down. Skimmers are like the chef, they say what goes in the oven and when, how long to cook it and so forth. That's what the gauges are for, if they're working. You don't want a skimmer who depends on the gauges. That's how converters get backed up. Slag sloshing from the mouth, air pressure's dropping, skimmer's all freaking out. Only way to get the oxygen flowing is open the flaps. The catch being the lower the pressure, the harder to punch. All that thick mess clogging the tweers. Your fresh rods, they'll bend like a bitch or jump right off the rack, probably both. You want your tips melted down into points. Like arrowheads. Or enemas. You know, for constipated converters."

He paused, finally, in case Simon had any questions.

"Go ahead, take her for a spin."

Sy hopped in and fondled the dashboard. Hit the button and the rack lurched forward. The recoil felt like a head-on. Chesney laughed and he tried it again, tapping the button to blunt the collision with the front of the car. This prompted a thumbs-up. Moving along the track was simple enough. The trick, Sy thought, would be finding a rhythm. You'd want to hit your targets, withdraw the rods, move laterally to the next set of flaps, and get to the end of the track before the first tuyeres seized up again.

Float like a butterfly, sting like a bee.

He coasted to where Chesney waited and crawled out of the car. There was a jangle of bangs and motors, a loose dystopian rumble that rattled his bones. A crane heaved above them, a pair of anchorlike hooks plunging and dangling in its wake from the kind of thick, braided cables that held up the Brooklyn Bridge. A man inside, peering down from an open window a hundred feet or so in the air—Sy pictured a top-floor room in an eight-story building, twelve feet per floor—guided them to a massive coal-black ladle that might have been cast from the liquefied iron of a thousand skillets.

The craneman bounced a hook against the pot till it collared an ear—ladle ears were made to be grabbed—and tipped it slightly so gravity would hold it in place. Then he lassoed the other ear and the ladle levitated a few feet and sailed to the end of the aisle, where it thudded to rest. A front-end loader scooped great doughnuts of congealed metal off the floor and dumped them into the pot, and then the crane released its grip and sailed away down the aisle.

"Fun's over," Chesney said.

"Got that right," said Sarge, who'd materialized out of the dust. He clasped his hands together in a show of something like high school spirit. "Bussbomb, let's put your ass to work."

He led Sy past another furnace, then up a few steps to a platform where a red-bearded man stood streaming tobacco juice over the railing.

"This here's Bullock," he said, though Bullock hadn't bothered to turn around. "Bull, this here's your new puncher, Bussbomb."

Bullock arced a parabola of tobacco juice into the aisle. When at last he showed his face he appeared more anthropoid than bovine, more a Kong than a Bull. Or a distant, less corpulent relation of Haystacks Calhoun, the six-hundred-pound hillbilly professional fake wrestler his father watched when Sy was a kid.

Bull was a more obvious handle than Kong, given his surname. But it wasn't fury in his eyes so much as indifference, some natural talent for cruelty. You wouldn't want to get on his bad side. That he had other sides wasn't entirely clear.

"'Bussbomb. How d'you spell that?"

Sy spelled it.

"So, Irish. My people were English, mostly. We're natural enemies."

This was a joke. But he thought it best to correct the record.

"Bussbaum. Jewish."

"Ah, a Chosen Person. College boy?"

"Some."

Bullock stroked his beard, spit some juice over the railing. "Well, shit, just do your best. About all we can ask, right, Sarge?"

Sarge laughed, the kind of deferential laugh that told you all you needed to know about the pecking order.

"Bull's the best we got," Sarge said, speaking into the back of his hand in a sort of stage whisper, as if anyone besides Sy and Bullock himself could hear over the hum and the clamor of irresistible forces battering immovable objects. "Man can read a flame good as anyone ever skimmed a converter."

"Name of the game," said Bullock, "read the flame."

This referred to the gauges, how you didn't want a skimmer who needed them. The converter platforms all featured banged-up banks of cockpit instruments, dubious oracles of redlined disaster. Pride of place went to dinnerplate-size dial thermometers that topped out at three thousand degrees, at which point the furnace would presumably self-destruct and the gauge dissolve in a puddle. It took temperatures of twenty-three hundred degrees to skim enough slag to produce so-called blister copper. This was around ninety-nine percent copper, roughly as pure as Ivory soap.

Bullock could tell the temperature of his ingredients by the color of the flame rising from the mouth of the furnace. Once he'd judged it ready to skim he cut the air, blasted his railroad whistle, and rolled the converter out, belching fire. He poured the slag into a waiting ladle and wolf-whistled a crane to haul it away. Then he picked up his platform phone and had the craneman return with another kettle of molten matte from the reverb furnaces, plus whatever else might be lying around the crane aisle.

There but for fortune, Sy thought, went Michelangelo.

The general rule was three rounds for copper to reach the blister stage. This was the pinnacle of skimming success, a sort of smelter nirvana. Skimmers proved the quality by pouring the lava over the lip of the furnace and catching some in a sample spoon with a long handle, reeling it in like a flounder. Then they'd dip the spoon in a bucket of water to cool it off, and pull back a half-sphere topped by a squiggly outcropping called a worm. A worm meant you had blister copper. Old-timers smuggled the samples out in their lunch buckets.

Simon learned most of this later. His first day he understood nothing of these dark rituals, save what he'd gleaned from Chesney. Bullock was no help, in fact took no notice of him once Sarge had left the platform, only deigning now and again to poke the air with two fingers in a gesture which brought to mind the Three Stooges, but which Sy interpreted, correctly it turned out, to signify the act of punching.

Bullock, who mainly perched on a high stool at the back of the platform, made a practice of wandering periodically to the opposite corner for a better look at the flame in the furnace's mouth. When the color told him the pressure was dropping he'd glance in Sy's direction, nod, poke. Sy would dash to the punchcar and give it his best shot, neither butterfly nor beelike but slow and methodical and well enough, evidently, for a virgin puncher. That Bullock was indeed a connoisseur of light, as advertised, made the task manageable. Bullock, though, never said a word about how Sy was doing. Once the oxygen was flowing again he'd materialize at the end of the track and pantomime a knife slicing his throat. This was Sy's cue to cease and desist.

When he wasn't punching, he hung around aimlessly weighing whether to cease and desist altogether, to hop in the truck and drive till he reached civilization. The smelter was hotter on swing than on graveyard, and converters were noisier and more chaotic and far more nerve-racking than anodes. Bullock hated his guts, but without passion, the way you'd hate a mosquito. You just want it to go away.

Only Sy couldn't go away. He was semi-committed. His greatest fear, other than burning in molten metal, was turning up MIA at a moment when Bullock needed him. This fear compelled him to sit in the punchcar, smoking and waiting, except when he needed to stretch his legs. Then he'd stand beside it, like some uniformed chauffeur on Fifth Avenue, chained invisibly to his limo. He only took off for lunch, or dinner, when Sarge told him he could.

He had his usual cold burrito in his usual spot on the loading dock, among the forklifts and end loaders. There was the hint of a breeze—it was after sundown, the less excruciating portion of swing shift—and he stopped worrying, briefly, about Bullock and furnace punching.

His thoughts drifted back to the walkout. Harold and his apostles had triggered it, this much was obvious. Was this how it began, then, the return of Naldo Galvan? That seemed unlikely. Given the lack of popular support—gratitude for a shortened shift didn't qualify, surely, as solidarity with a workers' movement—the spark, if that's what it was, might already have flickered out.

Bullock was rolling in with a fresh load of matte when Sy finished with lunch. He was up and down the rest of the shift, alternately punching and desisting on cue. He'd just reached the end when his new relief, less friendly than Dr. Hernández, waved him off. Bullock had already left, as had Chesney and everyone else on swing. They had all been relieved, per custom and common decency, ten minutes before the shift changed. Meltzer showed up at five past midnight.

Sy changed his clothes in an empty locker room and drove home in the glow of a magnificent moon, unsullied, once he'd slipped the reach of the smokestacks' plumes, by the light of buildings or motor vehicles. It was a dreamy ride, so much so that he forgot to turn on the radio till he was almost to Tucson. When he remembered he found it was dead.

And so, at one in the morning, was Tucson, the only signs of life being the neon ones proclaiming the names of shops and restaurants that had shuttered hours before. Tucson was a cowtown minus the cows, and now, sixty minutes past midnight, minus humans as well. Even the bars were dark.

One a.m. Tucson time was three in New York, a full hour from last call. Except for Indian land, which it didn't control, Arizona didn't believe in saving daylight. Different world, different time. He wasn't in Queens anymore.

Night in the desert belonged to the snakes and Gila monsters and whippoorwills.

They were out there, somewhere.

* * *

The phone rang at seven. Lady Liberty read seventy-eight degrees. He waited for the ringing to quit and went back to sleep.

After a minute or so it went off again. He placed the receiver on the pillow, listening with his available ear.

"Simon," urgently.

"I'm on swing, Harold. Have a heart."

"I know. That's why I'm calling now. I want you to meet some folks before your shift."

"Some folks. What happened yesterday?"

"Things happen. Tactical error."

"Things."

"We've been terminated. Me, Dwight, Lencho. A few others you don't know."

"Tactical error."

"Right. Foreman told Lencho to dump wet matte in a converter. Wet matte can blow a converter sky high."

Sy knew the legend about the rookie cleaning a reverb furnace.

Weeks on the job. Just married, kid on the way. A converter exploded across the aisle. The rook had to be medivacked to Texas with third-degree burns. Never came back. Not a peep from the union. Then it happened to someone else.

This was soon after the Steelworkers drove out Mine Mill.

"So Lencho refused. Took guts. You have a right to refuse an unlawful order. It's in the contract."

Lencho, evidently, had brandished his pocket copy, pointing to the clause in question. Or a page opened at random. In any case the foreman suggested he stuff his contract. Lencho, first in Spanish and then in English, said he'd be delighted to stuff it.

Then he said where.

"That's Lencho," Harold said. "Should have demanded to see his shop steward. Which is me. *Was* me. Anyway, here we are. Like I said, tactical error."

"So a wildcat."

"That's what they're calling it. We're talking to lawyers. We tried to make lemonade, turn a mistake into an opportunity. Started waving our own contracts, marching toward the exit. Chanting 'yoon-*yun*, yoon-*yun*.' Everyone followed us, even the deadbeats who won't join the union."

He sounded weirdly excited. There was a long pause.

"But they only fired twelve of us, the people they pegged as troublemakers. Which of course."

"And the local?"

"Local's doing zip. They're in on it. They want us gone worse than the company. Already put out a press release. Two strikes and you're out, that's the grievance process. You can file a grievance, then appeal if you lose. Once you lose your appeal—and you always lose your appeal—the contract says you can go to arbitration. But the union won't pay for arbitration. So it's two strikes and you're out. The union's already turned us down. That's why people don't join the union. It's a joke."

They'd rounded up the usual suspects, then. Harold and Dwight and Lencho were now, like Trotsky, nonpersons.

"We're meeting this morning. We need you there, brother."

Brother. He was needed.

Harold gave him the particulars. Sy agreed to go, though he couldn't quite see the point. The troublemakers were terminated. No troublemakers meant no trouble. No trouble meant no redeeming social value. So much for *la lucha*.

All he was doing now was making copper. In a smelter. In the desert. In the Southwestern, drought-stricken summer. For five dollars and fourteen cents an hour.

Harold, with help from his apostles, had ruined everything.

* * *

The place had the look of an unmarked squad car. One of those low-slung Spanish colonial jobs, parked on a corner so still you could hear lizards shed. Inconspicuous as tumbleweed. Sy had to squint to make out the name, "Vanguard Books/Libros," on the awning and storefront window. Pale gold stencil washed out in the glare, backed by a white curtain. Not a book in the window, just a plain white curtain arranged to let in light at the top, like a hospital room. The mid-morning sun seared the back of Simon's neck, rivulets of sweat salting his face. Summer in Tucson was nearly as hot as the smelter, even without the space suit and steel-toed boots. And now skies were threatening.

He dug a Kleenex out of his cutoffs and mopped his forehead. Opened the door to a jangling of hand bells, soft and Christmassy. They put him in mind of Donna Reed, Jimmy Stewart. The little girl, Zuzu. Angels getting their wings. The store had only a few rows of bookshelves, indifferently stocked, labeled by subject: labor, civil rights, slavery and Reconstruction, the Soviet Union, the Spanish Civil War. There was a modest display with biographies of César Chavez, Paul Robeson, Helen Keller, the Hollywood Ten. But no bestsellers, no bodice-rippers, no self-improvement or children's books. Anyone could make the place for a front, if anyone ever came in. But there was no reason to come in. There was nothing, really, to buy.

Also, he realized, there wasn't a cash register.

He was gathering the warm breeze from a plastic gyrating fan when he heard a door open behind a curtain. Harold emerged from the other side. "Simon," he said, his voice and bearing that of an undertaker. Sy nodded in a way that affirmed the solemnity of the occasion.

Behind the curtained-off door was a sort of efficiency apartment. Sy wondered if there was a Murphy bed in one of the walls. Mini-fridge, dining room table, love seat. In a corner were stacks of folding chairs. Others were set up at a table bearing a box of graham crackers, a tray, and a pitcher of ice water. All but two of the chairs were taken.

In the middle were Dwight and Lencho. The group's leader, a den mother of sorts, was an elfin woman with aviators and frazzled white hair she wore in a longish ponytail meant to convey youthfulness, Sy supposed, but which only accentuated her age. He clocked her at sixty or so. Beside her sat a large, unkempt man of similar vintage wearing an engineer's cap. At the other end of the semi-circle was an elegant old Chicano, silver hair crowning his face like an alpine peak. He sat quietly at attention, straw Stetson in his lap.

No one was smiling.

The woman offered a china-doll hand. "Joyce Campbell," she said. Trace of a New York accent, seasoned with notes of Middle American. "This is Edgar, my husband. Pedro Ruiz—everyone calls him Pete— worked side by side with Naldo Galvan. You were in some of the crowd scenes in *Ciudad de Esmeraldas*, weren't you, Pete? And I think you know Dwight and Lorenzo—Lencho—from the smelter?"

"I do," Sy confirmed, the words hitting his ears like a wedding vow. "Glad to meet you."

"Thank you for coming. Short notice, I know. But that's the nature of crisis, isn't it."

He shrugged. He'd never given much thought to the nature of crisis. Anyway, she didn't seem to need his opinion.

Harold took one empty chair and Sy took the other. Joyce leaned forward, as if to share a juicy morsel of gossip.

"Ed and I own this place. It's one way to keep doing our part. Ed's basic-industry days are behind him. And I can't pass the ThreeCo physical, if you take my meaning."

Sy wasn't sure he did.

"Wrong gender."

Right. Females were *verboten* in copper mines. Restricting women to office jobs was a matter of doctrine at Freako, like the casting out of menstruating women under Jewish law.

"Well, you probably wouldn't like it there."

Joyce gave him a look straight out of the Bronx. Dwight plucked a graham from the serving tray, broke it carefully along the perforation, and munched one of the halves. The unmunched half he slid into the pocket of his work shirt, a short-sleeve Ben Davis model in navy blue. Everything paused while they waited for him to settle.

"Here's the thing," Edgar said, once Dwight was back. Edgar was as gruff as Joyce was affable, the business end of the partnership. "These men need their jobs back. For everyone's sake. Meanwhile they need someone inside the plant, someone to be our eyes and ears. Someone to take the temperature, so to speak, up at the smelter."

He removed his engineer's cap, kneaded it with his big paws. The pinstripes oozing between his furry fingers.

"This is bigger than three individuals," Joyce put in. "They gave in to adventurism, they've learned their lesson, time to move on." She glanced at Lencho, who looked at his shoes, and then at Harold, who appeared duly contrite. "Harold tells us you were inspired by *City of Emeralds*."

"That's true."

"Are you aware Naldo Galvan, the real José Castillo, is still on the frontlines, still leading the fight for democracy in the workplace? Just out I-10 a ways, in Mineral City?"

He assured her he was.

"So here's the thing," Edgar again, pushing on. "These three boys—these three young men—are the next generation, the sequel, you might say, to *City of Emeralds*. They stood up to the bosses, so the bosses had them eliminated. Or so they think. That's where you come in. You can rewrite the ending. So the bastards don't win."

"Rewrite the ending."

"Exactly. You've heard the working man's golden rule? 'Them that's got the gold, make the rules'?"

Sy nodded appreciatively.

"Well, don't believe it. Cynicism is their secret weapon. Because here's the thing. The gold standard's dead. Nixon killed it. Bretton Woods, convertibility of currency to gold? Gone. The 'Nixon shock,' they called it. Now it's 'fiat money,' quote unquote, backed entirely by the 'full faith and credit' of the U.S. government."

Jake lived for this stuff. Simon wasn't following.

"It's a trick of the light, is the point. It only has value if you *believe* in it. This is the fatal flaw of a plutocracy. The bosses get what they want—slavery, open shops, speedups, pick your poison—because we let them. But what the people giveth, the people can take away. The plutocrats and kleptocrats and all the rest of the rats will find that what goes around, comes around. The wheels are in motion. See what I'm saying?"

"I think so. You're saying the emperor has no clothes."

"Exactly."

"Like Wile E. Coyote."

Edgar gave his mouth a few thoughtful taps with a forefinger. "Lost me there, sorry."

"From the Road Runner cartoons. What goes around, comes around. Wile E. Coyote's the predator, done in by his prey. His schemes backfire, his equipment blows up in his face. He's no match for the Road Runner's speed and cunning. It's a parable of the underdog."

There was a long silence. "One of my profs wrote a book about it."

Whooshes of traffic mixed with the whirr of the swamp cooler, which worked no better than the ones in his windows. At length Pete was beset by a coughing fit, brief but tubercular. When the worst had passed, he took a final drag on his smoke, then snuffed the butt in the Coke bottle by his feet. It made a small hissing noise. He pulled some tobacco and papers from his overalls and set to rolling another one. Hunched over his cowboy hat, using the crease as a work table.

"Those cartoons are reactionary." Dwight now, rising uncertainly to a point of personal privilege. "Wile E. Coyote's an assassin. Ruthless. But we're supposed to pity him. Poor Coyote, his weapons of war keep blowing up in his face. Meanwhile the Road Runner, who Coyote's trying to kill, is portrayed as some kind of terrorist. That's no 'parable of the underdog.' It's a narrative of the state as Keystone Kops, comically inept and nothing to worry about. It tells kids the real threat to societal order comes from the people. No wonder they grow up to be Republicans."

Everyone looked to Joyce, a Greek chorus of five heads swerving as one. She removed her aviators, bowed her head, massaged the bridge of her nose. "Well," she said. "This is all very interesting, this explication of sacred texts. Rewriting endings and whatnot."

Outside were thundercracks, rain pummeling the roof and sidewalks. The apartment felt like a bunker. Thanks to the black curtain Sy couldn't see what was happening in the streets, much less in the skies. These storms were glorious, his favorite thing about Arizona. And now he was missing another one.

Joyce deferred to the thunder, then went all Sarah Bernhardt, declaiming to the balcony.

"Yes, it is bread they fight for. But they fight for roses, too." More thunder. She paused again. "Lawrence textile strike, nineteen twelve. Immigrant women, mainly. Everyone wants fulfillment, a better life. But first things first. What Ed's saying is, the workers don't realize how strong they are. They need these men to show them. The women in *Esmeraldas* were real. Think about that. Think about those miners' wives, impoverished, uneducated, fingers worked to the bone, how they put themselves on the line and carried the day in Mineral City. Think about Lawrence, Massachusetts, about Rosa Parks. A fire starts with a spark. Stand up for Lencho. And help your union brothers stand up for themselves."

"I'm no Rosa Parks," Simon protested.

"We don't *want* you to be Rosa Parks," Joyce said, mildly exasperated. "We just want you, Simon, to work with us. To be our eyes and ears. Our man in Havana, so to speak."

He'd seen the movie. "Not really a spy, either."

"Look," Edgar said, stepping in for his wife. "Just hang onto your job. That's all we ask. Head down, eyes open. ears to the ground. Keep us apprised. Meet with our little group from time to time. As we develop a strategy."

"What kind of—"

Harold cut him off at the pass.

"It's not just the fight for our jobs. It's the larger fight. The one you came here for. Naldo's fight. We lose our jobs, we lose our union membership. We lose our opportunity for leadership. Our best hope is for you to stay on the job under the radar while we work on a strategy."

"It's a lot to digest," said Joyce. "Sleep on it. No need to make a commitment."

Sy agreed to sleep on it. He would have agreed to anything. He could definitely sleep on it.

"And stay in touch. We're always open, day or night. Figuratively speaking. Don't be a stranger."

Harold walked him out, through the curtain. Pete, somehow, was already at the door. Sy hadn't noticed he'd slipped away.

"*Mijo*," he said, whiskey voice barely audible. He smelled like tobacco. "A word, please, before you go. You have questions. For now, just remember. We're all here for a reason. We struggle. Or we wither. Struggling is better. Take it from an old Mexican."

He took a pull on his hand-rolled. "Worked in that goddamn smelter myself, years ago. Hate that *pinche* place." He started to laugh. Then he was coughing again.

When the coughing stopped, they shook hands goodbye, accompanied by the jangle of Christmas bells. You didn't linger in doorways in Tucson. Not in summer. The sun was out, between the clouds. Smell of bygone rain. Everything freshly rinsed, from the squat adobes and Lego office blocks to the asphalt and dust, too baked even in monsoon season to yield anything much but copper and cactus.

Sy sat in the truck for a while. Pete was right. He had questions. His first semester, when they'd forced him to live on campus, a rump caucus of red-diaper babies referred to his dorm as Gus Hall. They'd had to explain to him that Mr. Hall was the top dog of the Communist Party USA, which he'd taken for dead. Even now, at close range, you could barely detect a pulse. But was the party just mimicking rigor mortis, possum-like, till conditions improved? Could it be that decades after Stalin was denounced, by Khrushchev no less—after the Beats, the FSM, Abbie Hoffman, Tim Leary, Martin, Malcolm, Bobby and Huey, the Beatles and Dylan and Janis Joplin and Gracie Slick—people here in America still pledged secret allegiance to Gulag Joe and his joyless proletarian wet dream? Joseph Stalin, "gardener of human happiness," who led the Great Purge of the revolutionary party, who condemned millions of peasants to excruciating deaths by forced labor and famine? Who sent Trotsky into exile, and severed his skull with a pickaxe?

Simon hadn't met many radicals over thirty. A few profs, like his corduroy lecturer. But even the older ones were New Left. These young ones, Harold especially, screamed Old Left. They disliked Mao and Trotsky. They weren't Wobblies. Who did that leave? Fidel? Allende? Gus Hall? Were the elders of this mini-cabal, here in Tucson, Arizona, in 1973 A.D., a secret cell of officially licensed Bolshevik hangers-on, relics of the antediluvian, Kremlin-bankrolled American Communist Party? Living, breathing, card-carrying Reds in the land of white belts and bolo ties?

And, if so, how many were FBI?

He stopped for lunch at the Copper Penny, vowing to try some other place soon, and browsed a Times. Independence Day, it appeared, had come and gone. He'd slept, or possibly worked, through the fireworks. He read about Alexander Butterfield, the "surprise witness" who told Sam Ervin's committee Nixon had bugged the White House. The White House later confirmed the existence of tapes, reported the Times, but "declined to say whether recordings of crucial conversations would be made available to the Watergate investigators."

God bless the Times. "Declined to say." That was rich.

He left his waitress a hefty tip, grabbed his thermos, and pointed the truck north to continue, for now, his career in converters.

* * *

Swing was a convection oven, temperatures so high management made sure the salt-tablet dispensers, at least, were reliable. Salt, in a copper smelter, was life. Even suits got dehydrated. The hottest part of the smelter was the converter department, in the middle of the facility. No hope of even a wisp of sunbaked, hundred-degree oxygen.

Sy was assigned to converter Number Three, the middle of the middle.

It was a long shift. Bullock spent most of it leaning back in his folding chair—a perk reserved for skimmers, punchers having to settle for stools—hands on hardhat, teeth bared, squirting splendid effortless arcs of charcoal saliva that sailed past the raised drawbridge of his red mustache, across the platform, and clean over the guardrail. This might go on for thirty minutes, till he stood and walked to the rail and expelled what remained of the dip. Then, using the nail on his pinky, he'd dig a fresh pinch from the tin of Red Man he kept in his lunchbox.

He did know his flames. The converter hummed. As a puncher Simon was anything but a natural. But Number Three made relatively few demands. Wurtzel, the skimmer on Four, was a gauges man. His puncher, Renfroe, aka Special Ed—he'd left important parts of his skull in Southeast Asia—remained in a more or less constant state of readiness. Same for Gutiérrez, the skimmer on One, who had families in Chihuahua and Durango and would sooner be found by *la migra* than by either of his wives.

Chesney laid this out over lunch. A font of information. Dago and Sahagun, the skimmers on Two and Five, were thirty-year men, ogling retirement. All but checked out. Dago, real name Cicciarelli, typically slept through graveyard, and—once the brass had gone—B shift as well. Had to be roused at key points in the conversion process. This responsibility fell to his puncher, Gabby, a skinny Jehovah's Witness who left Watchtowers in undisturbed stacks in the lunchroom every few weeks. Also, once a month, a companion rag called Awake!, which Chesney said would do more good for the world rolled up and administered upside Dago's head to stave off apocalypse.

They didn't talk about the wildcat.

Meltzer, his relief, was late as usual.

* * *

He phoned Harold next morning.

"Simon," said Harold, though Sy hadn't yet said a word. "How's converters?"

Sy ignored the question. He'd be asking the questions here.

"What was that yesterday? Felt like a central committee meeting."

"Study group. Marxist-Leninist study group."

"A study group. You're telling me you're a study group?"

"That's all I can say now. The phones are tapped. That's why we met at the bookstore."

"Your phone's tapped. You're telling me Nixon wants to take you out, on account of he's scared of a Bolshevik revolution led by six unemployed people in Tucson, Arizona."

"You saw what happened to Howard Hunt's wife? Went down in a plane crash? Nixon's capable of anything."

"Maybe. But Hunt's wife knew where the White House bodies were buried. She was Nixon's worst nightmare, her and Dean. Way bigger threat than a handful of, what, Marxist-Leninists."

"But they *knew* she was ready to talk. The point is the CIA is everywhere. The point is the phones are bugged."

"Jesus, Harold. It's 1973. Everyone's phones are bugged. The *White House* is bugged. But in case anyone's listening: My *brother's* the Marxist in the family. I don't have a theory on the workers of the world, how they contain the opium of their own destruction and the negation of the negation, whatever that even is."

Harold sighed. "Right, well, that's what study groups are for. But you don't have to, y'know, join the group. No contracts to sign, nothing to tie you down, no long-term commitments. Just stick with it awhile. You didn't come all this way to punch a converter."

This was true.

"Joyce said she sees something in you."

"Uh-huh. What would that be, exactly?"

"She wasn't specific. Potential, maybe. She's big on potential."

"Maybe she's big on me still having a job."

"Lots of people have jobs at Freako. Not many have potential. At this historical moment."

"Not anymore."

"Look, we screwed up," Harold said. "We, the three of us. But Naldo didn't screw up. Neither did anyone in the rank and file. Remember that José Castillo speech, about fighting for 'the salt of the earth'? Don't punish them for Lencho's mistake. Seize the moment. You're part of the solution, or you're part of the problem."

"This machine kills fascists."

"Woody Guthrie."

"The quality goes in before the name goes on."

"Who said that?"

"Nobody. John and Yoko. Forget it."

"Okay. Anyway. Sorry for the ambush. We just *really* need your help. Think about it. I'll be in touch."

"Homing pigeons, maybe," Simon replied. "Even Nixon can't bug a homing pigeon."

* * *

The days dragged on. Bullock mellowed with age. On two separate occasions he addressed Sy as Bussbomb, a welcome nod to his existence. Invited him to hang out on the platform. Midweek he enlisted his help with "mudding the lip," a ritual that entailed grabbing fistfuls of mud from a bucket and heaving them onto the mouth of a newly empty converter. This protected the lip, like Chapstick for furnaces. You didn't want lava flowing over a naked lip.

Once the lip was mudded, Sy's main job was to wait. He had to be ready to punch, but was otherwise free to wander. It was skimming that demanded attention. A converter was a boiling kettle that had to be watched. Skimming was more like killing time in a laundromat, only with molten lava instead of sudsy water. When he grew tired of sitting and spitting Bullock roamed his cramped platform like a tag-team wrestler caroming off the ropes, Haystacks Calhoun in a jumpsuit.

Other times he jawed with fellow skimmers, either in person—he was the only skimmer, Sy noticed, cocky enough to abandon his post for more than a minute or two—or via semaphore. Or he'd signal a craneman to pick up a two-way house phone to confer about sports or the state of his payload. He amused himself with seriocomic play-by-play accounts of spills and overflows. These he broadcast mock-solemnly over the public address system, which was intended for work-related announcements but which anyone could access just by pressing a button. Occasionally he rose from his chair and strode to the edge of the platform to check his flame. Then he'd nod and give Simon the sign to get back to work.

Bullock reigned, by unspoken acclamation, as BMIC, big man in converters. He sold canned hams on the cheap, and boasted a customer base that spanned the entire Freako complex. Sarge was a regular. The hams fell off a truck every couple of months. Also available in season were duty-free cigarettes, Cuban cigars, the odd specialty item. Bullock bragged that he earned more moving merch than making copper. Nobody doubted it.

Once Simon had proved his worth Bullock gave him a steep discount on a nice Hormel. But first he had to swear on his mother that lots of Jews ate cloven-hoofed beasts. Sy suspected Bullock thought Jews *were* cloven-hoofed beasts. Perhaps he'd demand to see Sy's naked feet sometime in the locker room. That would be just like Bullock.

Sy didn't want his hot hams. But it didn't feel like an offer he could refuse. Bullock had his own enemies list, and telling him "no" rocketed you to the top. There wasn't a man alive who could keep his ears to the ground from the top of Bullock's enemies list.

What Simon heard, mostly, was bitching. People bitched about everything, their jobs, their wives, the state of the world. Bitching was a language of common prayer, a shared vocabulary of rote, ceremonial riffing. You bitched, therefore you belonged. Just like family.

Freako's family tree was a cactus, long and spiky. People's fathers had worked there, and their grandfathers. Dago's son worked underground. There was no telling if the fathers and grandfathers, back in the Mine Mill era, bitched about the union. Nowadays, though, bitching made up the lion's share of discussion about the Steelworkers. Not that it came up a lot. Arizona was a right-to-work state, which meant the right not to join whichever branch of Big Labor staked a claim to your interests. You got union wages and benefits whether you joined or not. So no dues equaled bigger paychecks. All you lost with free agency was what members knew as a feckless, fruitless grievance procedure. You didn't lose any friends. No one cared, really, about the union. They especially didn't care about Harold and his apostles.

As a rule, in fact, caring was as unlikely to crop up at Freako as a maternity ward. This was the place's dark, depraved beauty. Freako reeked of a musty maleness that gave rise to a loose-knit, shambling esprit de corps, wrapped in a kind of casual racism so expansive, so deeply rooted, it had started to feel—Simon being not of this world, and without standing, perhaps, to judge his co-workers' cultural values— like just another flavor of assholism.

The only black man in the smelter was a craneman. Lanky and soft-spoken, he exuded a quiet confidence that made Bullock, for one, wonder openly if he might have friends in the Black Liberation Army. He answered to Ozell, the name his parents had given him, or Big O. Last name Payton. That's all anyone dared to call him. Everyone else was fair game. Dago, for instance. Everyone called him Dago. Nobody ever objected, Dago included. This was the Freako way. There was a single Indian on the crew, a slag skimmer, and everyone called him Chief. Had three Indians worked in the smelter, they would all have been Chiefs. You didn't win points for originality.

Which is why, when he was finally given a smelter handle, they settled on Philly.

Simon Bussbaum, born and raised in the borough of Queens, New York.

Philly. For Philadelphia Jew.

* * *

He had a nickname in college. He was christened the Buzzard by a flannelly freshman from someplace near the Canadian border—Watertown maybe, or Plattsburgh—owner of a bespoke hash pipe in the shape, so he claimed, of his family jewels. Insisted on calling him Buzzbaum. One night they were sharing a bowl or two— using an off-the-shelf pipe Sy had remembered to bring—and the kid out of the blue called him Buzz, the serendipity of his glassy-eyed wordplay so delighting him he nearly coughed up a lung. Next time they met he declared Sy should forevermore be known as Buzzy the Crow, an old cartoon knockoff of Rochester, Jack Benny's TV butler. A gravel-voiced racist crow, gone the way of Amos 'n' Andy.

The kid, Kyle or Calvin, introduced him to friends as the Buzzard. Sy didn't care for his friends. But he liked the moniker. It had a mythic quality the kid would have regretted if he'd had any inkling. Sy soon ditched him and his stoner friends too. But he held fast to the alias. As though it had once been his rightful name, a title bestowed upon him in the cradle, before the palace was stormed and his parents beheaded and all order and majesty and history lost to the ages.

The name was meant as a chummy slander, a strained feint at intimacy, buzzards being the trailer trash of the avian world. In the Old World, though, the word didn't refer to turkey vultures and chickenhawks. It referred to what Americans knew as straight-up hawks. Everywhere but America, it seemed, buzzards were magnificent, avian predators, the great birds you saw sometimes on Channel 13 riding a thermal, blissful and otherworldly, spiraling up and up.

Simon made it his secret identity. Never told a soul.

Definite article. The Buzzard.

* * *

After swing they went back to graveyard. Forward actually. The sociologists at the community college had reconsidered their mental health assessment, and now believed single-week shifts caused less deleterious quality-of-life impacts, after all, than two-week shifts. They had also determined that progressing alphabetically—A to B, B to C, C back to A—made for a more productive workforce. It was this second finding that sealed the deal.

Sy scored some No-Doz at a Circle K and another nickel bag from Dr. Hernández, dreaming of four days in Mexico.

He and Bullock were mudding the lip, the predawn creeping in through the doors and cracks in the walls, when Bullock invited him to join the crew for a beer. Locals mustered at the Wagon Wheel, a company-owned bar on a two-block strip—gas station, barber shop, hardware store, greasy spoon, Salvation Army, obligatory Circle K—in the heart of the company town. The town, all but nameless, appeared as Pueblo de Cobre on a map taped to the Texaco's window. Sy had no more wish for beer at eight in the morning than he'd had for cut-rate hams. But no, once again, was the wrong answer. He made a point of telling Bullock he'd show up late, owing to his relief, a man he now thought of as Fucking Meltzer. It was, in its way, a plea for help. Bullock did not take the hint.

The Wheel was shabby and dark, redolent of suds and sweat and testosterone. Streamers danced from the windows, powered by legitimate air conditioners. A muted TV over the bar sent squiggly green images of Senator Sam into the void, and Merle Haggard and Charley Pride took turns on the jukebox. Hot dogs simmered in one of those countertop rotisseries native to movie-house snack bars, as near as the town got to a theater. They looked like the desiccated leavings of a chihuahua. They were selling like hotcakes.

He ordered a Bud—planning to drink no more than the situation demanded—and made his way to a horseshoe-shaped booth toward the back, where Bullock was holding forth. Chesney was there. Also Renfroe, Dago, Sahagun, some others he barely knew.

"Philly," Renfroe greeted him. Sy shot him a sideways look. "Philly," he said again, as if Sy hadn't heard him the first time. "For Philly Jew."

Simon looked at him, puzzled but cognizant of the plate in his head.

"That's what Sarge calls you."

Bullock found this hilarious. "Philly Jew. Only kind Sarge ever heard of, I guess." Then, tapping Sy with a spoon on the top of his head: "I hereby christen you Philly."

Sy shrugged.

"Or PJ, maybe."

"Suit yourself," knowing he would anyway.

"Alright then, down to business," Bullock clinked his christening spoon on his beer bottle. "So. Dumb fucks finally did it. Went and hired a skirt."

Sy, it seemed, was the last to know. Bullock noticed, stroked his mustache in a significant way.

"I have this on good authority. She starts on the anode wheel, graveyard tonight or tomorrow. Any day now they'll be putting a Kotex machine in the crapper."

"Maybe she'll burn her bra." Renfroe, animated again. He was endearingly dim, which was why nobody called him Special Ed to his face.

The others slurped their beers, peered into their bottles.

"They can't make you use it," offered Salcedo, a craneman he'd only seen up in his crane before. "The Kotex, I mean."

That, as smelter wit went, was more like it.

"For real, though," Salcedo continued, addressing himself to Bullock. "My mother, she worked up in Morenci like eighteen months. During the war. Anodes, reverbs, all kinda shit. Her friends too. So the men could go kill Nazis."

"But that was *war*time." Bullock's tone said he shouldn't have had to say it. "Anyway, this ain't Morenci. That what you want? Your old lady working at Freako?"

Salcedo locked eyes with Bullock. He wore a Black Sabbath T-shirt with the sleeves cut off and "Paranoid" printed across the front in purplish letters. Biceps the size of coconuts. "Bro," he half-whispered, all bonhomie drained from his voice. "Leave my old lady out of it."

Bullock held up his hands in a gesture of peace. "Hey, *amigo*. Wasn't me who brought her up."

"Yeah, it was. Don't be talkin' about my old lady or my mother."

Dago leaned across the table and rested a hand on each of their arms. "*Amigos, hermanos,* fellow wage slaves. I tell you this from my heart. I've got three daughters, and any one of them is a better man than any two of you dipshits combined. So lighten the fuck up."

"Easy for you," Bullock said. "You've put in your papers. We'll still be here while you're going to seed in a hammock, shooing flies and living off Social Security. We're the ones stuck with the curse."

"Curse, horseshit. Navy used to keep women off ships, too, on account of them being bad luck. You make your own luck, my friend. Look at yourselves. Big macho men, scared of a little snatch."

Bullock eyeballed the cross dangling from the older man's neck.

"Dago, no offense, but there's more evidence women cause mining disasters than there is Jesus rose from the dead."

Dago slapped his palms on the table. He definitely took offense.

"Bullock?" More challenge than question. "As a gentleman and a God-fearing Christian, I suggest you go fuck yourself." He stood to leave, not waiting for a response. "I'm gonna hit the head."

The rest of them sat there, fondling their beers.

Sahagun looked at Bullock. "So," he said. "What do we do now?"

"Nothing *to* do but suck it up."

Bullock blew across his empty bottle, absently, sad as a distant foghorn.

"I bet she's a lesbian," he said. "Fuck it. I'm having another beer."

* * *

"Philly," blurted Bullock the next night. It was their last graveyard shift this go-round. He'd been sulking about the new employee, "the skirt," pumping Sarge for intel. She hadn't shown up after all. Sarge thought maybe the brass aimed to give her a fresh start on days, when the whitecaps could keep watch. But this was a stab in the dark. He was out of the loop.

Bullock streamed a gusher of Red Man into the crane aisle. "Philly, c'mere. Something I want to show you."

The converter was blowing high, nearly ready to skim. Bullock wouldn't need him to punch again. Sy followed him to the far side of the furnace.

"All this heat," Bullock shouted, over the din. "Shame to see a man eat a cold sandwich."

They gazed at the face of the giant cylinder, quartered by narrow, crisscrossed metal planks jutting out from the surface.

"We're rolled in, heat your lunch right up here on the ledge. Four, five minutes. Sandwiches, burritos, cheeseburgers. Chicken legs. Chicken soup, hell, matzo balls. Cook it right the fuck up. Converter's under control, go and have yourself a picnic. Get lost. It's the goddamn catacombs, this place. Forget underground. Judge Crater could be up there somewhere, shit, nothing but nooks and crannies, dens and lairs and sanctums. You know the drill, when to be standing by. Don't go AWOL on me, we're good."

Simon wasn't sure they were good. But they were better. Which, for now, was good enough.

* * *

Days off came with asterisks. Only the footnotes changed.

Sy had got used to graveyard starting at midnight of one day and ending the next morning. You clocked out of your last C shift the morning of what the rest of the world called Monday, but Freako deemed Sunday. Then you'd need to sleep it off. You'd lost a day before you changed out of your jumpsuit.

Now the sociologists were squeezing you at the back end. Instead of returning after four days off to Friday's B shift—which at least gave you part of a day—post-graveyard workers would be due to return on A shift, eight hours earlier than under the old regime. Which basically shot Thursday night.

They had you coming or going.

He slept most of Monday. He couldn't tell if he'd tuned out that day's lightning storm, or incorporated it into his dreams. But the monsoon rains were already receding. So the sun may never have left. He opened his eyes briefly in mid-afternoon to find his thermometer had cracked the century mark, a literal red mark on the small glass tube. These readings were imprecise, the souvenir's value being more sentimental than meteorological. But objective metrics weren't the point. The heat was stifling.

You didn't need a weatherman to know which way the wind blew. Dylan said that.

The thermometer was a memento of a childhood trip to Liberty Island. He and Jake had climbed to the crown, the highest point still open to tourists, while their parents browsed the gift shop. The copper-plated statue had arrived from France brown as a shiny penny, but had turned green over time. This mutated pigment, the result of oxidation, was called verdigris. Sy's souvenir version featured a mouse-gray patina—intended to signify silver, probably, by well-meaning artisans in some Taiwanese *chotchke* factory—except where the plastic peeked out from under the flaking paint. The plastic was sort of an off-white. As if her armor were slowly crumbling, and Lady Liberty would someday stand naked before the world.

He rousted himself around seven. Swigged some caffeine from a can of flat Dr. Pepper. showered, and scarfed a sandwich while he checked the movie listings. Tucson was bad for movies. He smoked a joint and watched TV for a while, expecting Harold to call. Then he went out to dinner, smoked another joint, and crashed in front of the set.

Two days down.

Next morning he grabbed some breakfast at a bohemian-leaning café on Fourth, then headed south on I-19. There was nothing to see till he glimpsed, on his left, a cattle-skull-shaped cantina. The sight of it—the ghostly cranium pallid against the mountains, longhorns white against the cloudless sky, cars and trucks waiting by its mouth like sacrificial offerings—rekindled his sense of the limitless desolation of the desert landscape. It was kitsch. But it was magnificent.

It reminded him of that poem, how so much depended on a red wheelbarrow. William Carlos Williams, no ideas but in things. He tried to remember the rest of the poem—something about chickens and rain—and wished he'd remembered to fix the radio. Soon the horns vanished into the distance and the view was all scrubland, an endless brown patch of nothingness, no ideas or things either.

He cruised for an hour or so, windows down, scorched air pounding his face. Then, at last, Nogales. He parked in a Safeway lot on the U.S. side and walked the few blocks to Mexico. Beyond the entry station loomed a vista of low green hills dotted with orange-roofed houses. In minutes he was south of the border.

On the other side was a sign, *Bienvenidos a Nogales*, and beyond that the city itself, the real Nogales, gateway to Mexico. Worlds away from the drive-in churches and focus-grouped climate-controlled shopping environments and culture wars and peace with honor and all the rest of the hideous, familiar comforts of home. Like walking into some pre-Columbian painting. There was music everywhere, literal music but also Mexican *español*, more lilting and lyrical than the Tommy-gun Spanglish of subway-riding *puertorriqueños*. So not quite pre-Columbian. A time after Spain conquered the Aztecs, but before sitcoms and Dow Chemical conquered America. Before America.

Bienvenidos.

He roamed the tourist district, weaving through the waves of pedestrians spilling under the storefront awnings, the honking trucks and broken-down buses. Burros hauled wagonloads of gringos in sombreros and gift-store T-shirts. Sidewalk vendors hawked brightly patterned rugs and shawls and picture postcards and *fotonovelas* and jewelry and vases and oil and plaster-of-Paris renderings of *la virgen* and baby Jesús. It was exhilarating, all this crazily untamed life, a wonderland of curio shops and *farmacías* and open-air hot dog and taco stands. And depressing, too, to think of his own crabbed existence, his sweaty apartment, his arranged political marriage, his thankless and pointless job. It was pleasant to think about ditching the truck in the Safeway parking lot, a lot indistinguishable from the one in Tucson where he'd bought it from Frank, before he'd even begun at Freako. The symmetry of it.

Across the tracks was a restaurant, La Roca, built into the side of a cliff. Simon was lighting a cigarette when a man stepped from behind a great rock wall, a wall *de roca*, accompanied by a girl Sy hoped was his daughter but could see she was not. He was a Tucson business type, a paunchy, middle-aged Anglo sporting a bolo tie. She was pretty and blonde, well-tanned. A poster child for Sweden or Los Angeles.

The man thrust an Instamatic in Sy's direction. Asked him, in pidgin Spanish, to snap their photo. Dark ruddy races being, in Harold's word, fungible, and Simon sporting his best summer tan. The pair struck a pose, the gold on the man's simian finger twinkling, through the viewfinder, against the girl's bare shoulder. He handed the camera back and the man slipped him a crisp dollar bill. Sy felt a twinge of outrage, suddenly, on behalf of the brown people he represented, embodied even, in this *turista*'s ignorant eyes. He wanted to crumple the bill and make him eat it, to crush his smugness with a few well-chosen words. But couldn't come up with the words. Not in American English, not in the Queen's English. Not even in Queens English. He pocketed the cash. His mood had turned sour.

He trudged back to Obregón, the main drag. Took a seat at the bar of a taquería, near the window. Tourists streamed past in waves, maybe the sons and daughters of tourists Sy and his friends had laughed at as kids, clutching their maps and their shopping bags, blocking the sidewalks to gaze up at the skyscrapers. Maybe the same ones, older and slower.

He longed to be someplace else, farther south, Mexico City, Oaxaca, Guatemala. Embraced by the locals, a simpatico Anglo medicine man, say, like Walter Huston after the treasure has blown away, returned by a sandstorm to the bosom of the Sierra Madre. The chimichanga was disappointing. He finished his beer, had his smoke, left the smug businessman's bill plus one of his own under a small pile of change. Mexicans, he'd been advised, preferred American money.

He bought a Day of the Dead skull in a nearby emporium. He envisioned it as a conversation piece, should he ever have any visitors. Not till he got back to the border station did it hit him that possession of a plastic *Homo sapiens* head by a Mexican-looking Jew might raise questions, in the minds of U.S. border police, about his fitness for life in a civilized nation.

An agent looked him up and down, oblivious to his shopping bag.

"Name?"

"Bussbaum. Simon Bussbaum."

"Simon Bussbaum," he repeated. "Are you a citizen of the United States, Simon?"

"Yessir."

"ID?"

He produced his New York license. The agent studied the photo, had him remove his shades. "What brings you to this part of the world, Simon Bussbaum?"

"I live here now," he said. "In Tucson. Working at ThreeCo. Cobra Copper?"

"ThreeCo." A kind of melancholy crept into the agent's voice, as if visited by an inkling of distant disaster, the Hindenburg or the wreck of the Hesperus. "You're going to need a local license, son. Once you establish legal residency—this includes working in any occupation other than seasonal agricultural labor—you're required to have a state-issued driver's license. That's the law. You'd be surprised how many folks don't realize that."

He indicated the bag at Sy's feet, its contents peeking out of the space at the top. "Death's head, huh?"

Sy nodded.

The guard waved him through. "Welcome home, Simon Bussbaum. You get that license now."

* * *

The Girl, as everyone called her, was assigned to an anode wheel. This suggested she had upper body strength, and this, in Bullock's mind, confirmed she was a lesbian. But he still wanted proof. It was tricky to leave the platform on days, with the whitecaps making the rounds. So Salcedo, in the southernmost crane, volunteered for aerial reconnaissance duties.

This produced little actionable intelligence. In her hardhat and jumpsuit and the rest of her spaceman costume she looked like anyone else on the anode floor. Salcedo did make one notable observation: It wasn't just her foreman spending suspicious amounts of time in her company. The suits buzzed around her like drones to a queen. It was unclear whether this was due to her being female or simply a new hire in need of special attention. Bullock regarded this as a thousand percent rhetorical question.

"You know somebody's bonin' her," he said, cradling his phone after hanging up on Salcedo. "Only way she gets the gig."

Sy, gently: "If she's a lesbian, though."

This prompted a side-eye from his skimmer.

"Don't talk stupid. Lesbians—it's like this giant smorgasbord, all you can eat. No limits. Women, men, whatever."

Bullock grew suddenly reflective—daydreaming, or remembering soft-porn flicks at the drive-in—and just as abruptly snapped out of it.

He dug out a chaw of Red Man and stuffed it into a cheek. In time he stood up and spat a black loogie into the crane aisle.

"Plenty good men," he said, "been ruined by lesbians."

* * *

Simon was lying on top of his sticky bedsheet, having dozed through the brief morning window of tolerable temperatures, when the phone went off. He knew it was Harold. Harold was the only caller he'd ever had who wasn't a wrong number.

He set the receiver next to the pillow. "Day off."

"I know. That's why I didn't call yesterday. We'd like to meet."

"Harold."

"Won't take long, honest."

"It's already eleven."

"You won't regret it."

This was surely a lie. But Sy hadn't made any plans. He agreed to a meeting at two. He showered and lounged in his underwear and had pretzels and coffee and watched The Mike Douglas Show. There was nothing else on the tube but daytime soaps and a sci-fi flick he'd have to be bedridden to watch. He missed Senator Sam.

Zuzu's bells announced his arrival. There were voices behind the curtain. A copy of *Ten Days That Shook the World* caught his eye. He'd seen Eisenstein's movie in film class. *Ten Days,* called *October* in Russia, was a tour de force, surreal, jarring, and masterful. Ironic montage and crazy angles. A silent picture from 1928, a year or so after Al Jolson started singing—sometimes in blackface—on American movie screens.

Howard Hughes tried to strangle *Emeralds* at birth. Stalin let *October* live, but not until scenes with Trotsky, like Trotsky himself, had been purged. The Russian film took other liberties with history. The storming of the Winter Palace in 1917, coming as it did in the dead of night, was both unphotogenic and unphotographed. The Bolsheviks solved this PR problem by staging a spectacular daytime re-enactment worthy of Cecil DeMille. It was this choreographed, Hollywood-style overthrow of the Mensheviks that Eisenstein captured on film. And it was this version of history the masses would tell their children and grandchildren. The Bolsheviks, they would say, relishing the memory. In broad daylight the Bolsheviks toppled the bourgeoisie, and without help from the likes of Lev Davidovich Bronstein, a Jew who called himself Trotsky.

Sy took the book from its shelf and blew a thick layer of dust off the cover. The dust hung suspended in a shaft of sunlight. He was a sentence or two into the liner notes when Harold pushed through the curtain. He flashed Sy a thumbs-up when he saw the now-legible cover.

"John Reed, hell of a writer. Soft on Trotsky, but still. First draft of history."

"I liked the movie. I should probably read the book. Too bad there isn't a cash register."

"Heavy-handed imagery. Montage and all that. Artsy, I mean. Give me *Emeralds* any day. A *movie* movie. Something regular folks can understand. Just my two cents."

He led Sy into the back. The scene was identical to the first time, except for the absence of graham crackers. Sy prided himself on his talent for spotting continuity errors.

"The local's refusal to arbitrate is good news," Edgar announced. The decision left the committee free to act, he explained, no longer in thrall to the union and its pathetic grievance procedure.

"We're exploring our legal options," added Joyce. "But it's murky. The union sacrificed its right to sue on the altar of arbitration. But it doesn't believe in arbitration. I call that unilateral disarmament."

"Except we're not in the union anymore," Harold said.

"So we're not bound by the contract," Edgar said. "We get three strikes."

Pete dropped a butt in his soda bottle. There was a low hiss and a puff of smoke. "And *then* we're out. Like Casey at the bat." He shot Sy an avuncular wink. "But Casey, you see, is still famous. He struck out, okay. No joy in Mudville, okay. But Casey today is a bigger legend than Babe Ruth, Willie Mays, Jackie Robinson. This is the long game."

When they'd talked enough baseball they got down to business. Sy had been summoned—on one of his two days off—to shed light on the new employee. But Sy demurred. No one had seen much of her, he explained, save from above. She didn't use the locker room or the cavernous *hombres* room, obviously, so only a few rank and file workers, all in anodes, had made contact. She supposedly took lunch in the foreman's office.

"We think she could be an ally," Joyce said. "Down the road. Her father was a lifer, literally—had a heart attack underground, pronounced DOA at the hospital. Name of Tanager. Regular union, followed orders, typical contract miner. They think of themselves as entrepreneurs. Better than wage slaves. The more they work, the more they earn. Company men, most of them. Anyone pushing for safety is picking their pockets. That's the attitude."

"Bad blood with the daughter," Edgar said. "Or so we're told. But blood's blood. You can see why she'd have a leg up when the company decided to go co-ed. She's a legacy hire."

The daughter had been away. No one knew where, or why. Or why she'd come back. But Freako's interests were clear. Mother Mongoose hoped to remediate the PR damage from a recent dam breach at the tailings pond. The resulting river of toxic sludge was proving as toxic on Wall Street as it must have been there in the neighborhood.

Workers and villagers were also grumbling about sulfur dioxide emissions, which were peeling the paint off their cars and trucks. Freako had trumpeted plans to build a profitable plant to scrub the toxins from the acid released by the stacks. But this would take time. Ditto for mollifying, if not compensating, disgruntled vehicle owners. Cue the corporate imaging team. Sprinkling some women into the workforce, the PR mavens hoped, would send the message that Freako was changing its ways, accommodating itself at last to the demands of the latter half of the twentieth century.

"Haldeman let his sideburns grow," Edgar said. "Now Freako's hired a female. Lipstick on a pig."

Not that the revolution couldn't do with a makeover. Even if they did land a lawyer—and no one thought this was likely—there wasn't a judge in the territory dumb enough to rule for the Terminated Twelve, much less Lencho, Harold, and Dwight. So they couldn't count on the courts.

Tanager was the long game.

Tanager, the committee agreed, would put a new, simpatico face on the struggle for labor rights. The goal was a united front, a movement led by relatable, plain-speaking working folks. People for whom materialism implied cars and self-cleaning ovens and new shoes for their growing kids. Real people driven to fight not for a cause, not for some abstract *ism*, but for their rights and dignity. People who led by example.

Like the heroines in *City of Emeralds*.

"Remember," Joyce said, "when the sheriff got an injunction to lock up the strikers, it was the wives who took their place on the picket lines. The men resisted, the women persisted. In the end, it's Esperanza—wife of José Castillo, the character played by Naldo Galvan—who rallies the community, and leads the miners to victory."

"*Esperanza* means hope," said Pete. "We hope this young woman can play such a role at Freako."

A duel with Freako, then, for the maiden's hand.

It was Simon who'd have to bell the cat. Sy being the only human they knew, or nearly, still on the Freako payroll. They were willing to look past his dubious motives, his half-assed commitment, even his probationary status at Freako, which compelled him, per previous instructions, to keep a low profile for months to come. But what were a few months in the scheme of the long game?

Joyce turned to Lencho. "Show him the picture."

Lencho produced a Xeroxed sheet of mugshots, the upper half of a page of what a small insignia identified as the 1966 Pueblo de Cobre yearbook. At the top were the words "Go Cobras." Below that were two rows of thumbnails of graduating seniors, including—sandwiched between a couple of kids in ill-fitting suits and ties, one with a trace of a mustache—a striking, dark-haired girl looking confidently into the camera, amused by some private joke. This was Tanager, Samantha O.—Chorus, Folk Song Club.

The three other girls Lencho fit on the page wore their hair in sculpted styles their mothers must have insisted upon, unnatural flips and bobs and whatnot forged with rollers and aerosol spray. Tanager's was long and straight, much of it draped behind her left shoulder—which was turned ever so slightly forward—in a way that veiled the corners of her eye and eyebrow. The rest fell gently across her right shoulder and vanished out of the frame. There was no evidence of makeup. She had on a V-neck blouse, modest but not conservative. A perfect fit for the Folk Song Club.

Sy rolled up the sheet, tapped the tube a few times against his palm to convey thoughtfulness. Lencho showed no sign of wanting it back.

"This is all theoretical," Edgar said. "Maybe she's her father's daughter, politically speaking. That would be unhelpful. Maybe she's plotting revenge. We can work with that. Maybe she's open to new ideas. That's good too. We're hoping you can get to know her a little, pick her brain, learn something about her attitudes and opinions, what she's been up to during her years in the wilderness, so to speak. Don't rush it. Take it slow, work to gain her trust. Let's see how it goes."

Simon couldn't see it going terribly well. "Some of the men hate her already, just on principle. They say she's a curse."

"On principle," Edgar repeated.

"Plus I barely know my own crew. Not sure how I'd manage this."

"Who better than you," Joyce said. "Middle-class Jew from—Brooklyn, is it? College-educated. Not exactly a poster child for copper miners. No offense."

Wrong borough. But otherwise on the money.

"*Use* that. This girl, she'll feel isolated, not just alienated but all alone, especially now, while she's still the only woman on the floor. You saw the picture. She's pretty. She'll be hounded mercilessly. So she'll *feel* alone. But they won't *leave* her alone. Which will make it worse.

"Like Edgar says, there's no rush. Pick your moments. Look for opportunities to show some empathy, some understanding. Show her you're there if she needs you. As a friend, I mean. Someone to lean on. A shoulder to cry on. Don't force it. We don't want to spook her. If it happens, great. Then give us your honest assessment. About her feelings toward the company, the union. Her thoughts about social justice. No judgments, no wrong answers. We want to know if she's approachable."

Sy said nothing. The group took this as assent. The plan made him uneasy, recruiting an asset for a network—or whatever this outfit was—whose nature he still didn't grasp. But this mission seemed harmless enough. What was so wrong with making himself available to a newbie in need of connection, a practitioner of the musical arts, someone who might, in fact, be a kindred spirit?

Anyway, as Edgar said, this was all theoretical. Sy's chances of meeting her—much less gauging her willingness to front a struggle for workers' rights directed, for all he knew, from Moscow—were microscopic at best.

Joyce slapped her hands together. "Outstanding. We knew we could count on you."

He checked his watch. Day one of his two-day weekend was slipping away.

"One more thing," Edgar said. "We're planning a trip to Mineral to huddle with Naldo and a few of his union brothers. We thought you'd be interested."

Sy told him he was.

"You'll like him," said Joyce. "We'll let you know."

Harold escorted him out. "That'd be cool," Sy said, aware suddenly of his sodden armpits. "José Castillo, live and in person."

"Naldo, right. Fair warning, he's not big on discussing the movie. Just so you know. If you do get to meet him. Anyway, stay tuned. Meanwhile holler if you get anywhere with Tanager."

And with that Harold retreated into the sanctum of Vanguard Books, the store that put the "front" in "storefront." Sy left to the jingling of Zuzu's bells.

* * *

He saw by the paper it was his birthday. Twenty, no big deal. He was already legal to drink in both of his states of residence. He decided to celebrate modestly, treating himself to dinner at an Italian joint near the campus called Fat Mario's, housed in a white stucco structure he could now identify as Spanish colonial. Across the top were horizontal stripes of red, white, and green. A cracked marquee overhanging the terra cotta roof boasted New Jersey-style hoagies and cheesesteaks, plus pizza by the slice. He had three pepperonis and nursed a bottle of Dos Equis while he browsed the entertainment listings.

An ad promised "live jazz under the stars" at a hotel a few miles away. By the time he was back on the road the sun had dipped behind the mountains. The sky flooded his side-views, swirling tie-dye patterns of blues and pinks and yellows. Soon he spotted the hotel's neon sign, the blinking green arrow directing him to the visitors' lot. From there he followed the twangs of a Wes Montgomery-style guitar to the swimming pool. Patio tables, most of them empty, lined the perimeter, and there was a bar near the kiddies section, by the entrance. Beyond the diving boards, on a shaky homemade bandstand, the guitarist plucked a hollow-body rigged with a pickup. The combo included vibes, a clarinet, and a bare-bones drum kit, and wore matching uniforms of Haggar slacks and fedoras. They looked like a goyish bar mitzvah band.

The night air was still and tolerably warm, and the band was doing its level best with "Girl From Ipanema." A couple of tables were occupied by open-faced girls in gaggles of two or three, all drinking and deeply tanned and young and as lovely as the girl in the song. One was looking at him.

He offered a toast with his plastic cup. The motion sent his scotch sailing over the rim, through the metal grates of his table, coming to rest finally in his lap. He sponged the mess as best he could with a stack of cocktail napkins. When he looked up he found she'd taken a seat beside him, leaning in, summer dress catching the starlight, an unlit Virginia Slim hovering a whisper away from her perfectly moisturized lips. He pulled a matchbook from his pocket—still dry, thankfully—and cupped the flame against a phantom breeze. Admired her slender fingers, the downy blonde fuzz toward the back of her face. He lit a Kool for himself.

The band was butchering "Just the Way You Are," which deserved it.

"I'm not always this big of a klutz," he said. The table was damp and littered with crumpled napkins, the scotch invading his underwear.

"Jesus, my shorts are soaked."

A white wreath of smoke streamed from her lips. "Don't go changin'," she said.

Not an original line. But Bacall had writers. Bacall was the gold standard. A movie star's movie star, voice like a smoky scotch.

The song limped along, leaden and endless. But Billy Joel was onto something.

The girl from Ipanema, or wherever, would do nicely.

* * *

She was rustling beside him, grunting small satisfied grunts. Wrapped in one of his T-shirts.

He couldn't recall her name. Layla? Lola? Lucille? Nancy? Melanie? Audrey? Betty Jo Bialosky?

Starting to panic. Not sure if she'd even told him.

Too late now.

He slipped out of bed and into the shower. Flipping through his mental jukebox.

Sweet Jane, Sweet Melissa, Sweet Caroline. Sweet Marie. Lovely Rita. Sugaree, Suzy Q, Peggy Sue, Mary Lou. Nadine, Maybellene, Jolene. JoJo. Loretta. Rosalita. Rhiannon. Sexy Sadie, Ruby Tuesday.

He was still getting dressed when she opened her eyes.

"Hey," rubbing them with her knuckles. "You're leaving?"

"First day of swing shift. I'd stay if I could."

"Swing shift," she repeated. "It's the crack of dawn."

This was true. It was also true that he wasn't due back at work till the following day. And now it was moot. She was snoring lightly, grunting her little grunts again. He had an overpowering urge to get moving. Decided to leave her a note.

"Sorry had to run. Write down your number? Cab fare's attached. Door locks—just pull shut behind you. Thanks. Peace, Simon."

He left it on the toilet seat lid with a five-dollar bill, using the toothpaste tube for a paperweight. Snuck into first light like a burglar.

An unmemorable night, then. But no regrets. Any port in a storm. Or a drought.

Which was pretty much, the realization dawned, how the cadre must have felt about him.

* * *

He spotted a car stereo store and parked in the back. The guy was just opening up. Sy picked out a no-name radio and cheap speakers and the guy said to give him an hour. He walked to a busy breakfast place which featured endless windows and a bottomless cup of coffee. Watched the traffic go by on Speedway and pondered a map.

The new radio did the trick. The radio was AM-FM, but there was nothing but talk and classical on FM. He punched in a top forty station the installer had created a preset for. Blather and ads, interrupted occasionally by a pop tune. He drove a few miles west to Old Tucson, a popular set for horse operas starring John Wayne and others of similar ilk. He watched a costumed man pound horseshoes awhile, then joined a group of Japanese tourists to observe a gunfight. From there he took the scenic highway to Mount Lemmon, traversing seven of its nine life zones. Once back at the bottom he headed east, in the direction of Mineral City, then south to Tombstone. There was the Boot Hill cemetery, for outlaws who died with their boots on, and the O.K. Corral, site of the celebrated shootout with Wyatt Earp. There was a reenactment of that, too, but they charged to go in the corral. One gunfight was plenty.

He decided to spend the night in Bisbee, a copper town turned artists' colony where Phelps Dodge was wrapping up operations. The town was cooler than Tucson, temperature-wise, surrounded by low forested hills. The main attraction was the shut-down Lavender Pit, an iridescent arena with strata that rose to the rim like bleachers. Voices in telephone receivers at intervals along the fenced-off perimeter told the history of local mineral excavation. A skull-and-crossbones sign read "Stay Out! Stay Alive!"

He got a decent rate on a ground-floor room at the Copper Queen, a turn-of-the-century beauty that looked like a cathouse, with its western décor and grand wooden staircase. "Urban legend," insisted the desk clerk. John Wayne had stayed there, he added, as if that proved his point. Sy had dinner and cocktails in the Spirit Room and Saloon. The room was air-conditioned. He slept almost till checkout time.

The death's head greeted him on his return home. The skull, accessorized now with a spare respirator and a leftover college-insignia watch cap, occupied a place of honor atop the swamp cooler, the nearest thing in the flat to a mantel. He'd hooked the respirator straps to the shuddering contraption's underside to keep it from shimmying off, and covered the eye sockets with a pair of shades that were missing a temple. Scuffed-up lenses the color of pond scum. The thing looked like some hipper-than-thou, highly flammable smelter worker.

His note was gone from the toilet lid. A new one, on floral-print stationery, was Scotch-taped to the medicine chest.

His eyes went straight to the bottom. Courtney.

"Hey you," the note said. (Had she forgotten *his* name?) "Thanks for the cab fare! My friends thought you were cute! Don't go changin'! Toodles, Courtney."

She'd written her number beneath her name, double-underlined and clinched with a boatload of exclamation points. The O's in "Toodles" were cat faces. Tiny whiskers and kitty ears. If they ever did this again, he might have to see some ID.

He showered, hit the Copper Penny, girded himself for swing. Mundy, the guy he relieved, was punching when he arrived, so he took his place in the car at the far end of the track. Bullock appeared as soon as he made it back. His mood was foul.

"They're keeping her on days for another week," shouting over the din. "Cowards and cocksuckers."

He shook his head in something like disbelief.

"Alright, we're done. I'm rolling out."

* * *

Swing now bought you two days off, down from three under the old, two-week rotation. The light at the end of the tunnel of graveyard, a nominal four-day weekend, had dimmed to three. Day shift earned you twenty-four hours and change.

Every few months—no one was clear on the formula—your turnaround time would shrink by another day to ensure your total downtime matched the era of two-week shifts. A palpable gloom hung in the air, mixed with the heat and dust and sulfur fumes. The psychic weather at Freako, under normal conditions, was a comfortable blend of hostility and indifference. This fog of malaise was flat-out dispiriting.

And the latest rumor had Freako planning to shut down, temporarily, if copper prices dropped any lower. Old-timers had seen it before. Supply and demand, rudimentary economics. Chilean workers had just ended a two-month walkout at *El Teniente*, the world's biggest underground copper mine. Workers had been rebelling against the workers' state. Now Salvador Allende, a Marxist, had nationalized the industry.

So much copper re-entering the world market would have a deflationary impact, Bullock explained. Commodities being, yes, fungible. Copper at less than ninety cents a pound made it unprofitable for Freako to mine, and—more to the point—suicidal to keep paying its workers around the clock. And Allende would love screwing with Nixon, whose CIA was already there, hatching plots with the generals. Next move was Allende's.

Meanwhile the girl, weeks after hiring on, remained in the shadows. Some day shift workers had crossed paths with her, exchanged a few words. Mostly she was a phantom. The novelty of her arrival, and the danger she posed to the public weal, seemed to wane as the week wore on. For everyone, that is, but Bullock, who sulked and simmered, glaring at Dago or whoever dared scoff at the curse. To Bullock, injecting estrogen into the workforce—upending its delicate hormonal balance—posed a bigger threat than Allende. Freako was planting the seeds of its own destruction.

Courtney called the morning after his last swing shift. He'd lied about his start day, so she shouldn't have known he was off. Possibly a coincidence. Or maybe she knew he'd lied and forgave him, as she'd forgiven his klutziness at the pool. Or maybe she planned to hold the lie over his head for the rest of their natural lives.

This did seem a tad on the Machiavellian side for someone who made O's into little cat faces. Unless little cat faces were a ruse, part of a long con. He couldn't let down his guard.

She wanted to meet for dinner. But he was in a mood. He felt hung over from an especially dreary week. He wasn't at all bothered by the radio silence from his voluble family. But he found his apathy as depressing as the knowledge that it was reciprocated. He had nothing to say to Courtney. It was all he could do to keep from calling her Toodles. He repeated her name to himself: Courtney. Courtney. Courtney.

She felt like Italian.

"Hold that thought," he told her. "There's a bug going around at work, nothing too serious. I should probably keep to myself for a bit."

"Well, phooey. You're no fun."

"Sorry. Rain check?"

"Rain check," she said. "Haven't heard that in a while."

"Still rains where I'm from. Back east I mean. But it's unpredictable. I'll call you, okay?"

"I guess." She was pouting over the phone. "No kidding, you're no fun at all."

He'd thought this was self-evident. He spent the next few hours smoking pot in the balmy crosswinds of the swamp cooler and an electric fan. Eventually he made coffee and found a movie on TV about two guys who get whisked off by a comet. It was set in the nineteenth century, and this happened during a duel. Somehow the comet plopped them down on the moon, which was populated by cavemen and gorilla people and monsters portrayed by an assortment of bugs and reptiles. He dozed off and never found out if they got back home.

He wasn't sorry he'd missed it. He felt sorry for Courtney, sorry he'd lied, sorrier still he'd agreed to recruit this Tanager person. A straight-up bribe, Galvan for the girl. It made his stomach hurt.

Nonetheless his appetite had returned. He felt like Italian himself, but you never knew—of all the spaghetti joints in all the world, etcetera—so he cruised till he found a Chinese place that wasn't part of a shopping mall. The place was empty save for the kitchen help and the waiters. A man in red and gold made a sweeping motion to indicate the emptiness, and Sy settled on a booth under a speaker hooked up to a country station. Everyone wore sweaters against the air conditioning. Except for the spicy soup he'd ordered to warm his insides, the food was bland and unsatisfying. He nibbled a bit and had a few beers and asked for a carryout box.

He pushed through the swinging doors to the parking lot, where a rat was rummaging in the garbage. The rodent paused, fixed Sy in its beady-eyed gaze, and went back to its business. It was a puny western rat, not the kind you saw in New York, the kind children mistook for pussycats and which, in league with the local cockroaches, would eventually rule the world. Possibly these western rats would be servants, tending to the needs of the master-race rats. But it wasn't bothering anyone. Sy tossed it an egg roll and hopped in the truck.

The days were shorter now, the evenings mercifully milder. He watched the sun slip slowly behind the mountains, endless granite and firmament, the sky on fire. One saguaro in silhouette in the middle distance, bending and turning, adapting itself to the vanishing light.

Riveting as any wheelbarrow.

Dusk turned to night in the rectangular frame of his windshield. He stepped out of the truck. Stars and planets, a memory of mountains, the saguaro now no more than an outline. The glow of the waning moon revealed the indistinctness of things, his own body and soul an aggregation of atoms doing business as Simon Bussbaum, a speck of matter under the illusion that it did, in fact, matter. The illusion—the *delusion*—of purpose. God spoke to Moses in the voice of Charlton Himself. Had the celebrated *critique de cinéma* ever plumbed the implications of *that* little detail?

Only at the planetarium had Simon seen so many stars. The sole constellations he could make out, still, were the dippers. Failed as always to connect the dots of the mama and papa bears, the ursas of outer space, their unseen lines constituting the bones. He nevertheless felt a bond with the ancient astronomers, contriving mythical creatures from this infinity of celestial objects. Beyond the invisible bears, lost in a riot of gaseous pinpricks, sat Cassiopeia. A queen on her throne, supposedly, in the form of a *W*. After a while he gave it up, turned his gaze to the spot where the cactus had been. But he couldn't make out the cactus either.

From the void came, first, an unfathomable silence, a sonic oblivion so profound it might have been—could *only* have been—the soundtrack to the universe. And then, taking shape before his planet-sized pupils, a freeze frame: a long shot of a broken man, a lonely *hombre* at frontier's edge, hungry and horseless and out of luck, dumbstruck at finding himself, as the credits begin to roll, with a gun to his head, reaching prayerfully for the sky.

2.

Simon was polishing off a roach when he heard the knock at the door. You never wanted to hear a knock at the door, in those days, with weed in the air. Especially in Arizona.

He was just back from graveyard. He warbled "Hang on" and crept to the bathroom to flush the evidence. As if any narcs or drug-sniffing dogs could miss the lid in his underwear drawer. He fanned the fumes in the bedroom with yesterday's Times, which did nothing at all. He was about to light a Kool for the minty aroma when his visitor's patience ran out.

The front door seemed to be made of balsa wood, its only lock one of those doorknob levers useful, mainly, for bathroom privacy. In Arizona home security meant shooting intruders, not keeping them out. The landlord had promised to get him a deadbolt. Sy hadn't noticed, till now, the lack of a peephole.

A voice claimed to be Jake. This was hard to believe. But it clearly wasn't a cop. And it wasn't the landlord. He cracked open the door. It was Jake.

He'd had some kind of a makeover. His Jewfro was gone, kinky hair now shoulder length, lashed to his forehead by the kind of red and white paisley bandanna favored by Irish setters. He wore a Navajo-style bracelet, silver and turquoise, where his Timex had been, and a leather necklace embellished with brightly colored stones. His face, drawn and deeply tanned, had a faint, greenish glow about the eyes— the light through his flip-up shades—a hint of the Lone Ranger which accentuated, by contrast, the indigenous motif. He'd ditched his wire-rims for regular plastic frames, and no longer resembled banished Bolsheviks or renegade Beatles. He looked like a Jew who wanted to look like an Indian.

"Jake," he said, "Jesus."

"I know, right? Dad told me where I could find you."

Sy had updated his entry in his parents' tattered spiral-bound address book after he signed the lease. That was how Jake would have gotten it. He wouldn't have asked, not wanting to divulge his plans. Sy doubted he'd been in touch with their parents since hitting the road.

"Well," he said, "you found me."

Jake slid past the door and out of his backpack, which featured an upside-down American flag patch. Seeing no chairs in the living room—décor was Day of the Dead minimalist, more from negligence than intent—he settled cross-legged against the wall. His legs, dark and sinewy, ended in hiking boots.

Sy lit the Kool in his hand and offered one to Jake. Set a plastic ashtray next to him on the floor.

Jake nodded, belated affirmation that he had, in fact, tracked Simon down. "And I guess you found Howard."

"Harold."

"Harold, right. So you're at that copper mine, Creepo?"

"ThreeCo. Affectionately known as Freako. I work in the smelter. Just got off graveyard. I'll need to crash soon."

Jake shrugged. "Been up in Navajoland. Support work."

"Navajoland."

"Indian Country. Big Mountain. The Diné, last of the traditional Navajo. *Diné* means 'the people.' They're about to have their land stolen, again. Black Mesa, this patch of dirt the great white founding fathers considered worthless, turns out to be the mother lode. Twenty billion tons of primo coal. Next stage of the genocide. You never heard of it, I bet, and it's right in your backyard. Peabody's been strip mining there forever, poisoning the water. But that's too slow. So they're pitting Navajo against Hopi, buying off tribal leaders, trying to clear the elders off a place they believe they're duty-bound to protect. They say it's Mother Earth's liver."

He was right. Sy had never heard of it. Genocide no longer made the news. Or maybe Jake, awakened from his proletarian fantasy, was plagued by a whole new set of delusions.

Sy was monitoring his brother's ash, which hung precariously over the carpet. "So you're, what, relocating to Arizona?"

Jake flicked the shaft into the plastic tray. "Up north, Four Corners. Sharing a teepee with some righteous heads. We do things for the old ones, heavy lifting, tending sheep. Whatever they need. The younger ones, the few who haven't split yet for Flagstaff or California, feed us stew and fry bread. Weed too. Do what you can, take what you need. I'm learning Diné, check it out. *Yá'át'ééh.* That's hello."

Lazy fastball, down the middle. "And goodbye?"

"*Hágoónee.*" Three syllables, more sung than spoken.

Sy repeated the word, haltingly, steering clear of the intonation. But Jake made no move to leave. "Okay, here's a plan. Shift starts at midnight. Come back around seven, I'll stake you to dinner. You can crash here tonight if you want."

He handed Jake a ten and a couple of cigarettes. "So, Trotsky. Dustbin of history?"

"Hell no. He's still the man. Trotsky said the dialectic could change from country to country. Stalin had him killed for that. But he got it right."

Sy was sorry he'd asked. He sensed a lecture coming on. And this wasn't the time.

"Say you've advanced to monopoly capitalism, you've invented Pong and electric pencil sharpeners, put men on the moon. Richest country in the galaxy. And you still have people subsisting on reservations. Diné, for instance. Their whole way of life is based on sheep. Same country as J. Paul Getty and Howard Hughes. Development's uneven.

"Like the blind man and the elephant—you feel the tail, I feel the trunk, we figure it's two different animals. Unless we're Stalin. Stalin would feel the trunk and say, *Da*, animal. An animal's an animal, a country's a country. That's what he got from Marx. But America's not China. It's not Cuba, or Mexico. And development's not the same in Tucson as it is on the rez, or in Queens. This is beyond obvious. But too subtle for Stalin."

He took some care snuffing his cigarette, glanced up to see if Simon was listening.

"So Trotsky says *nyet*, revolution's not one size fits all. The process can skip a stage or two. Stalin thought the stages were carved in stone, like the Ten Commandments. So he wasn't just a murderer. He was a moron. Russia proved primitive cultures can lead the way. Which they pretty much have to here in Ameri-kay-kay-kay, where the proletariat's too busy buying new cars and boats and timeshares to worry about class struggle.

"He didn't say that, exactly. But it makes sense. Nobody knows better than Indians what a shitshow capitalism is. Not even people descended from *slaves*. This whole country, really, is Indian country. If anyone's vanguard, little brother, it's Indians."

Simon's grasp of doctrinal disputes among the disciples of Marx, Engels, and Lenin was feeble to nonexistent. Maybe Jake knew what he was talking about, maybe he didn't. Maybe it didn't matter. Marxism was a religion. Adherents believed what they wanted to believe.

"And that's what you're doing up there? Leading the revolution?"

"Nah. I'm mostly tending the sheep. Doing chores. Black Mesa's not Pine Ridge. Everyone's heard about Wounded Knee. They've got Brando, Jane Fonda, movie rights. Diné have us. Did you know Mormons claim Indians are one of the lost tribes of Israel? Ever compared our profiles? You can hardly tell us apart. Diné believe the Creator put them on Big Mountain to defend Mother Earth. The grandmas are armed, some of them. White-haired Indian *bubbes*. They're refusing to leave. So, you know, maybe I *am* there for a reason.

"Anyway, they're beautiful people. Beatific, is what. That's the word. *Beatific*."

Jake, it occurred to Simon, should have been a Talmudic scholar. Jews got to argue with God.

"And what about you? Been welcomed into the working class?"

A fair question. Sy didn't feel welcomed. The cell deemed him acceptable. And he did have a paying job in a smelter. But this just meant he was present. He didn't *belong*. Not like Jake. Next to Jake he was an impostor, a dilettante. Their father called them a matched pair of subversives. But they didn't match at all.

He was still, for better or worse, Simon Bussbaum, even here in the desert, even decked out in a silver hardhat and fire-resistant coveralls. As for Jake—was he even called that, anymore? He'd probably taken an Indian name. Maybe invented one for himself.

Jake had always been a chameleon, changing colors according to need. Now Jacob Bussbaum, his brother, was no more. They'd both escaped Queens. Only one of them had escaped his biography, his history, his nature. Shed his skin like a snake. It shook him, seeing Jake so completely, cosmically unhinged. How was this fair? Jake was beyond lost. And yet, owing to some not-quite-Christian strain of amazing demented grace, seemed now to be found. He belonged, in his mind as well as his heart, to an Indian nation he believed—on the word of the Latter Day Saints—was one of the lost tribes of Israel.

Jake was bonkers, certifiably batshit crazy. But he was all in. He owned his delusions. This was the difference.

* * *

Pop tunes and deejay chatter got them to Miggy's, a Mexican place with a marquee that read "Elegant Dining Elsewhere." The food was good and the servings, by any measure but Jake's, plentiful. Jake ate with the ferocity of a feral dog. He was the antithesis of elegant dining, an advertisement for elsewhere, except that he used utensils and didn't talk with his mouth full. He barely said a word, in fact, other than ordering more food, till he'd laid down his knife and fork and swigged the last of his third Corona.

He'd had a reason for knocking on Sy's door. He'd come to say *hágoóneein.*

This wasn't the reason he'd come to Tucson. He just happened to be in the neighborhood. He'd borrowed a truck to pick up supplies from local supporters. He might make follow-up runs in the future, but Sy shouldn't expect to see him. *Ever.* Jake renounced the Bussbaums, renounced the very idea of the nuclear family, a form of social organization the Bolsheviks had judged obsolete and the Bussbaums had done their utmost to prove them right. Diné were his family now, Big Mountain his home. The only way he would ever leave, save for resupply missions, would be in a squad car or a body bag.

Simon had always assumed being a Bussbaum was a permanent condition, something you learned to live with. But he wished his former brother the best.

Jake fondled the stones on his necklace. "Nobody's sure what will happen. Congress is gonna redraw the boundaries, declare Diné illegal, basically. So they go to sleep on their own land, wake up in Hopi territory. Maybe the feds build new houses somewhere they can relocate to. Some might go. But more won't. Because the Creator put them there. They live in hogans, these sacred dwellings. Their *houses* are sacred. They'd rather die than live in the suburbs. So there could be a shooting war, another Wounded Knee. Meanwhile the feds are waging a war of attrition, restricting their herds, starving people off the land.

"All I know is I'm not leaving without the grandmas."

He stared off into the restaurant, addressing himself to empty tables and a dwindling crowd of indifferent, inelegant diners.

"Big Mountain," he said, "is the hill I'm ready to die on."

He asked for another beer and Sy waited for him to drink it. Sy told him about the wildcat, how Harold and the others had lost their jobs. It was the first time he'd seen him laugh in years.

"So you came two thousand miles just to work in a smelter?"

"Not just," he said. "I might get to meet Naldo Galvan."

Jake finished his beer and pushed away from the table. "Galvan, right. He's alive and kicking, then."

Sy dropped him in front of his building, gave him a duplicate key, and took off for work. He felt sure Jake would leave before he got back, just as he felt sure he'd forget to drop the key in the mailbox after letting himself out. He held out the slimmest glimmer of hope he'd remember to lock the door.

But he wasn't shocked on his return to find the key gone and the apartment unlocked, less secure, even, than usual. Jake might morph with the seasons, might see himself as a Bolshevik or a Navajo, part of a lost tribe, but he'd always be partly Jake.

Whether his failures stemmed from forgetfulness or hostility— passive acts, that is, versus passive-aggressive—Sy had no way of knowing.

* * *

She was in the building. Everyone felt it. Even Renfroe, who didn't know what was up. No mistaking that something was in the air.

Bullock was in a lather. Nearly everyone else regarded this development as mildly diverting, a faint note of birdsong amid the mechanical din. In the same league as whispers that Cary Grant slept with Randolph Scott, or Cher had quit sleeping with Sonny. Maybe true, maybe not. No skin off anyone's nose either way. It eased the tedium, was all.

Tanager had been sprung from the day shift, where the whitecaps were on hand to protect her. Her handlers had devised a scheme to keep her safe—from what wasn't entirely clear—even on graveyard, a shift whose defining trait was a near-total absence of supervision.

Freako, in its corporate wisdom, had posted her to the reverb crew. Reverbs were smallish furnaces that hung over the crane aisle like castle balconies over a moat. They faced the converters, which Harold told him were apt to greet infusions of wet rock and matte by blasting large irregular holes in the smelter's roof. This was why Lencho sparked a wildcat.

The rookie who got medivacked to Texas, never to be seen again, was cleaning a reverb furnace when he lit up like the Fourth of July. Sy believed the story might be apocryphal, a cautionary tale. Also a sort of eulogy for the waking dead, those hapless creatures sentenced to hard time in reverbs. Cleaning the spouts was hazardous duty, orders of magnitude dirtier and more dangerous than dropping a sledge on a slow-moving wheel. That was Tanager's concern, though, not the company's. The company had its own problems.

From a corporate perspective, somebody needed to do these jobs—if not Tanager, then some other misfortunate soul. Workplace accidents were fully indemnified. What Freako couldn't bear was the risk of unpleasant publicity—"First Woman in Smelter Raped, Pillaged by All-Male Labor Force"—while Mongoose labored to rebrand itself as forward-looking, the mining company of tomorrow. Stashing her in reverbs was a form of business insurance. It was nothing personal.

Bullock saw Tanager's admission into the sanctum as sacrilege. An affront to the Code of the Working Stiff, Nonferrous Division. A matter of principle. Simon found him grasping the guardrail, a ship's captain in search of land, staring across the aisle at the idle spouts. Bullock may or may not have registered his presence.

"Goddamn fucking cocksuckers," he said. "Fucking goddamn cowards." His voice had the icy calm of a hitman. You thought he might whack someone. Sy felt he should say something, jolt him back to his senses. Only he feared he might be the someone.

Bullock rolled the converter in. Sy slunk off to sit in his punchcar. Now and then during the shift, standing on the platform, he could make out the darkened shapes of jumpsuits up in the spouts, wielding wands that resembled swords. One of these shapes was the girl, a slight, androgynous figure, attended always by a larger, lumpier one. The pair would blast awhile, pause and discuss, blast again, disappear, repeat. The historic nature of their exertions, hers anyway, not lost on the converter side of the aisle. With each sighting came a new round of leering and play-by-play, generically lascivious, as impersonal as Freako's approach to troop deployment. She was another body, a blank slate, faceless and close to anonymous. You only knew she was a girl because she was *the girl.*

Tanager was Freako's Venus. She was the brightest planet in the solar system. But you had to look hard to find her.

Bullock's eyes were burning holes in the sky.

By week's end he was losing it. He buttonholed some friendly suits when they came on in the morning, no doubt offered them hams and cigars. But they wouldn't bite. He smelled a conspiracy to sneak the girl on and off the premises. She didn't use the lockers, the shower facilities, or the *hombres'* room—management had made special arrangements of some sort—and flew the coop before the earliest birds hit the lot. His best potential intelligence asset was her partner, a geezer Bullock had known and disliked for years.

Bullock disliked everyone in reverbs. He just didn't know most of them.

He was late to the locker room, trying to squeeze one last whitecap. Sy had had to wait for Meltzer, as usual, and still got there first. Amid the macho wit of the locker room today was some desultory chatter about the girl. Bullock said nothing. He undressed and stowed his boots and coveralls in his locker. Then he parked on a bench in his underwear till the geezer stepped out of the shower.

"Hey, Krinsky," he shouted. "Let me ask you something." The man halted mid-step, naked and suspicious. Took refuge behind his towel.

The room grew quiet, save for the white noise of showers in progress. A toilet flushed.

"How does she pee, our new colleague? Standing up or sitting down?"

Krinsky considered the question. "Probably," he said. He turned away, showing Bullock his butt cheeks.

"That's good. You're all right, Krinsky. Nice ass. Seriously, though. Man to man. What's she like, under that jumpsuit?"

Krinsky scrubbed his pits.

"Hey, you know what, forget it. Just give me a name. You must call her something. Or did Freako swear you to secrecy? I get you're a company man. But you can tell me her name, right?"

Krinsky whirled around, still naked. His face closed in on itself. Eyebrows like snow-laden eaves. A middle-aged Walter Brennan, crusty, well on his way to grizzled. He'd extracted his union card from his locker and now, exposed and defiant, palmed it alongside his temple like a TV pitchman hawking deodorant.

"Member in good standing. More than I can say for you."

Bullock waited a beat. Working the room.

"And a lovely member it is. Do us a solid and put it away now."

Krinsky pulled on his boxers. The towel around his neck gave him the look of a broken-down pug.

"Tanager. Samantha Tanager. Goes by Sam. That's all you get."

"All I wanted," Bullock said. He surveyed his audience, its numbers and attention waning now that the storm had passed. His mouth curled into a rough facsimile of a smile. Then he shuffled off to the showers.

"Sam," he was saying. "She goes by Sam."

Sy passed on a shower and made for the exit. Friday morning. his first day of freedom. By the time he reached the lot cars and trucks were merging from all directions, jockeying to join a slow, unstately procession toward the one open gate. He switched on the radio. Pimply wah-wah angst about a white boy, Louie, who falls for an unidentified black girl. He sat on the running board, half-listening, smoking a cigarette, and admiring the powder blue sky, a few random wisps of feathery cloud. The sun was up over the hills, and thick black smoke rose from the stacks, drizzling sulfur dioxide and peeling the paint off the vehicles below. The line of traffic kicked up small billows of dust as it nosed its way to the gate, a caravan so sluggish it might have been standing still.

Only the girl, Tanager, hurtling into the weekend.

* * *

He was a full-fledged resident of the Grand Canyon State. But his license said otherwise. And he still hadn't seen the Grand Canyon.

He was due back Monday morning. If he planned it right he could squeeze in a quick trip to the South Rim, get the lay of the land, scope it out for a four-day weekend.

But first he had to do laundry. What few stitches of clothes he had he'd brought from Queens. And even Simon Bussbaum couldn't wash his underwear in the sink forever.

Harold didn't call. Courtney did, wanting to get together. Sy begged off, explaining that his brother was in town. His brother was unstable, he said, and he was worried about him. Some of this was true.

"Tell me you're not seeing someone else."

I wish, Simon thought.

"Just my brother."

Jake would be leaving soon, and he, Simon, moving to day shift. He'd have evenings free. He promised to phone her then.

"Swear you're not seeing anyone else."

He swore on his brother's life, which seemed to cheer her a bit. Jake wouldn't have minded. He wasn't seeing anyone else. He wasn't sure he was seeing Toodles, for that matter. And how had a lone lost night, a night sucked straight into the memory hole, turned into the present participle? He *saw* Toodles. He *had seen* Toodles. But was he *seeing* Toodles? Hard to say.

He stuffed his wardrobe in a Hefty bag and drove to the Launder-Eez. The A/C was set to blizzard. Experience suggested Fridays were a sort of laundromat Sabbath, a day of rest for the pay-laundering hordes, and he arranged his schedule accordingly. A grungy tie-dyed couple were sitting cross-legged, somehow, in their molded plastic chairs. They were eating grapes, tossing one now and again to an Irish setter sporting a bandanna. Against the opposite wall was a frazzled mama with a baby on her hip and a pair of toddlers she kept yelling at in Spanish to sit down and be quiet. The kids squealed whenever the dog caught a grape. By the time Sy had popped his quarters into the washers the tie-dyes had left, and soon the kids and their mother had, too, and it was just him and the Muzak.

He spread an auto club map over a folding table, names, obscenities, and lewd drawings carved into the surface. He calculated the miles. Six hours to the vicinity of the canyon, and who knew how much longer to park and walk to the rim. He couldn't do that today. He still hadn't slept, and the thought of navigating forests and hinterlands by the moon and stars filled him with city-boy dread. Even Flagstaff looked too far to get to tonight.

But waiting till tomorrow to leave Tucson would kill most of the day, even without bathroom breaks, blowouts, or the sundry mechanical shocks '49 Chevys were heir to. Better to aim for Phoenix after dinner, find a Motel 6, and head out early enough next morning to soak in the view from the South Rim, maybe cruise the lodge and the souvenir shop before heading home. Sunset fell later now, even without Daylight Savings. By then he'd be back in civilization, or at least the outskirts of Phoenix, where he guessed the highway was better lit.

He tossed his stuff in a dryer and searched for something to read. On a small table connecting the plastic seats was an undisturbed stack of *Watchtowers*. He felt a twinge of respect for Gabby and his fellow witnesses, sending their deepest beliefs into the void on a regular schedule. Beside the *Watchtowers* were rumpled newspaper sections with abandoned crosswords and dog-eared magazines of various vintages, *Peoples, Sports Illustrateds, TV Guides*. A recent copy of *Time* featured Nixon and Agnew. The cover asked, "Can Trust Be Restored?"

He was checking the dates on the papers when the door swung open. A gust of desert air swept in, a happy respite from the arctic cold. A girl stood in the entrance, backlit, propping open the door with an elbow as she maneuvered her shopping basket over the fluted threshold strip. Her eyes were hidden behind sunglasses. But he sensed it was her.

The face was more weathered than her yearbook mug. She'd swapped her flowing hair for a shorter cut, a cut-rate Klute, befitting a different breed of working girl. Dangly earrings, plaid shorts like boxers, and an oversize Laura Nyro T-shirt, a dramatic black-and-white pose from the cover of *New York Tendaberry*. The picture looked like Louise, the girl who'd dumped him. Actually vice versa.

The girl—or woman, now that he saw her close up and out of uniform— caught him checking her out. He pretended to read for a while. When he guessed it was safe he stole another look. She'd removed her shades. It was definitely her. He had eyes on Tanager.

She loaded her wash and fed a bill into the change machine. A motorized whirr of rejection pierced the calm of the Sabbath. She smoothed the bill on the changer's surface, tried again, whiffed. Fished another out of her purse. Pulled it taut, considered its crispness. Tried again. The bill came back.

She stared the device down, arms folded.

"Laundry goddesses in a pissy mood, apparently."

His pockets were bulging with coins. He'd never been lucky with change machines.

"Your money's no good here," he said, regretting it instantly. "Paper, I mean. I'd be happy to trade."

He laid two parallel lines of quarters and dimes on the table. She took what she needed, slapping down one of her flabby bills whenever she'd scooped up a dollar's worth. Her face was lightly furrowed, laugh lines around the eyes. Under the yellow fluorescent lights she seemed not so much pretty as striking, swarthier than her yearbook photo suggested. He knew her father was Anglo from the cadre's attitude, their zeal in excommunicating him from the brotherhood of the righteous, writing him off as a tool. Anglos—Simon, by dint of expediency, being the exception—were deemed unworthy of slack. Plus Tanager didn't sound Mexican. His daughter did look Chicana, though. Probably Aztec blood on her mother's side.

She thanked him for the coins and they retreated to their separate corners. Sy was pairing his socks when she got up to tack a flyer to a bulletin board inside the door. He focused on his socks, all of which were identical. He paused at the flyer on his way out.

"Kittens," he announced, eyes on the board.

A shirtless blood donor, sleeping it off in a plastic chair—Sy hadn't seen him come in—grunted to life.

"Kittens. Know anyone needs one? Sister? Girlfriend?"

Sy shook his head, pondered the Xeroxed photo. "I might. Need one, I mean."

"You don't look like a cat person, no offense."

"No, I am. I mean cats are cool. I've just never had one. My parents wouldn't let me. They were allergic to living things."

He'd got her to smile. Mouth like a toothpaste commercial.

"That a problem?"

"Depends. Little guys need homes. Got one of those?"

"Apartment. Not far from here." It dawned on him this was her neighborhood, too. Nobody drove more than a couple of blocks to the Launder-Eez.

She gave him a thumbs-up. On her thumb was a Hopi-style ring, silver with black inlay, like the ones flower children sold from card tables on the sidewalk on Fourth.

"They're eight weeks old, still suckling. Mom's a stray. But a sweetheart. Can't vouch for the father. They'll be ready to wean in a week or two. If you'd like to meet them."

"I might do that."

She went back to her laundry. The flyer showed four kittens with black-and-white markings—though this was possibly the Xerox— huddled together in what looked like a bureau drawer. Along the bottom edge were tear-off strips with her name, Samantha, printed lengthwise in capital letters. Beneath the name was a phone number.

Simon tore off a strip, waggled it to get her attention. She glanced up from her magazine and bobbed her head goodbye.

When he got home he smoked a joint and took a nap, dreaming of kittens, Tanager, and the Launder-Eez. Then he showered and treated himself to dinner at a Mexican place with an outdoor patio. It was too late for Phoenix by the time he remembered his plans.

The Grand Canyon would have to wait.

* * *

Toodles came over Sunday. He'd promised her dinner. But she'd missed him, and was eager to show it. He'd missed her too, in a way. But not nearly as much. They smoked part of a joint and flopped onto the mattress and stayed there till the sun went down and the room was tolerably cool and dark except for the glow of their cigarettes. He called for a time out. Then he called for a pizza.

They showered separately—she'd brought a change of clothes—and ate in front of the TV. She vetoed his first choice, taped excerpts of Senator Sam. Another channel was showing *Casablanca*. He'd seen it dozens of times, more often than he could count. Even Toodles had seen it more than once.

She wanted to go back to bed. But he wanted to watch the movie.

She saw herself out. The door slammed shut just as Ingrid Bergman was saying how she and Bogart hadn't known each other that well in Paris, and how if they left it like that maybe they'd remember those days and not Casablanca. Sy drifted off, stirring awake again to the musical stylings of uniformed Nazis in Rick's café. Then Victor Laszlo had the band strike up *La Marseillaise* and he was good till the end, Rick and Louis strolling like lovers into the fog.

He Saran-wrapped the leftover pizza and threw a clean sheet over the mattress. He finished the joint and stared a long time at the ceiling, thinking they'd never have Tucson. They hadn't shared a meal, really, or watched an entire movie together. She owned Carpenters records. Politics bored her. He could barely remember her name.

Tanager, though, was another story. Whatever fate had in store for them, they'd always have the Launder-Eez.

* * *

The brains behind the new-look Mongoose, meanwhile, had been rocked by a revelation. It was like Dr. Strangelove said of the Russians' Doomsday Machine: Keeping Tanager under wraps defeated the whole point of hiring her. A PR strategy, it turned out, required publicity.

Word came down Monday. Sarge made the rounds. A local reporter would be on the premises. Employees were to steer clear of the anode department, where, in the interests of access and photo angles, Tanager had been temporarily reassigned. They were to be on their best behavior. The reporter and a photographer would be accompanied at all times by company brass. Employees were to speak to no one unless instructed otherwise by said brass. They were to understand this would never happen.

Bullock had done some sleuthing over the weekend. He lived in town, surrounded by Freako families. He'd hung out at the Wheel, knocked on doors, made some calls. The few adults who remembered Tanager knew her second-hand, mainly, via classmates from high school. They described her as different, a loner, words that applied to artists—she was, in fact, a folksinger—and serial killers. She wasn't known to date much, and had a reputation for being "stuck up." Some old-timers recalled her father, but vaguely, and only if they'd worked with him underground. The family had lived in Pueblo Heights, a pancake-flat tract favored by contract miners but too pricey for wage workers. Only a few had interacted with him, and most of them couldn't stand him.

"First-class prick," Bullock said. "Guys on his crew hardly noticed he'd croaked. Neighbors held a damn block party."

No one, Bullock included, believed this.

According to Bullock's sources, Fred Tanager worked at Freako for ten, twelve years. Roughed up his wife when he was in his cups. The sheriff would come out, settle him down. There were rumors about him diddling his daughter when she was a tot. But the sheriff told Bullock these were the kinds of rumors people spread about pricks like Tanager. He'd never seen any evidence.

Samantha, in any case, wasted no time flying the coop. Escaped the week she got her diploma, didn't return till Daddy was in a casket. She stayed for the funeral, which was private, then helped her mother pack her belongings. And then they were in the wind. Fred Tanager died of natural causes, not in an industrial accident, a tough break for his widow. Possibly he'd had life insurance.

This was the sum of their intel the first few days. The promised article appeared in Thursday's papers, after the shift was over. It took up most of a page in the women's section. There was a photo of Tanager on the shop floor, in full battle gear, clutching a sledge. Another had her seated in an office, hatless, looking much as she had at the Launder-Eez, minus the earrings. The caption described her as a "reluctant trailblazer in what has been, until now, a man's world."

She was a single mom, four years older than Simon.

A Hot Job, But CoCoCo's 1st Female Laborer
Cool As a Cucumber
By Shirley Colfax, staff writer

Pueblo de Cobre— *Jackie Robinson smashed baseball's color barrier. Neil Armstrong walked on the moon. And just this month*

Samantha Tanager, a fetching copper miner's daughter, broke the ban against distaff laborers in Arizona's No. 1 industry.

But Tanager, the first female ever to don a hardhat at the Cobra Copper Company's sprawling complex north of Tucson, doesn't see herself as a civil rights pioneer. And she doesn't want any special treatment from her new employer, the state's largest.

"All I want is to do my job," declared the svelte, sinewy 24-year-old, clutching a sledgehammer on the anode floor of the CoCoCo smelter. "A fair day's work for a fair day's pay."

An area native who relocated recently to Tucson—she graduated Pueblo de Cobre High School in 1967—the lean, muscular Tanager said that while smelter work is hot and dusty, she is confident that she has what it takes to succeed in the day-to-day business of producing the malleable red metal.

"Raising a kid, that's my idea of a challenge," stated the trim, tomboyish single mother, making a fashion statement for modern womanhood in her yellow jumpsuit, silver gloves, thick black safety specs and aluminum hardhat. Affixed to the hardhat is a green decal that signifies membership in the United Steelworkers of America.

Lithe and graceful, Tanager is hard to miss in the otherwise all-male facility. She is even more so when, in an office a hundred yards or so from the dangers posed by molten copper, she removes her gear to reveal a deeply tanned face framed by short brunette tresses.

But while a pretty face might launch a thousand ships, it won't smelt copper. According to a spokesman for CoCoCo's parent company, Mongoose Mining and Metallurgy, the real key to Tanager's admittance into the corporate family was her determination to succeed in a traditionally male occupation.

"Smelting copper ain't for sissies," declared Bradley Dinsmore, a public information officer visiting from Mongoose's Phoenix headquarters. "Samantha has copper in her blood, and she hit the ground running. She's tough and smart. That said, we encourage all young, able-bodied women to consider pursuing career opportunities with Cobra. Samantha's example will point the way. She's a born leader."

The story went on to say Freako would soon build a women's locker and shower facility, enabling Tanager to (a) stop using the whitecaps' bathroom and (b) start taking showers. There were a few more random facts, how long she'd worked in the smelter, how much copper her department sent to the refinery (200,000 tons a year), etcetera. The photos were large. You could tell the reporter hadn't spent much time with her, or got her to say much of anything, and that this was how Tanager wanted it.

Bullock brought his paper to work Friday, brandishing a rolled-up copy as if he'd hit pay dirt on a longshot pony. "No special treatment my fat ass," he said more than once. "She's using the *executive crapper*."

Hardly anyone had seen the story, and those who read Bullock's copy were mainly intrigued by the crapper. Bullock said it was fishy how little Tanager had told the reporter. Most of his crew didn't know if Bullock himself was married, if he had kids or dogs, if he'd ever done time. But nobody thought *that* was fishy. Nobody had a clue how he turned out to be Bullock.

He settled down, eventually. But the gears kept turning.

"Somebody's bonin' her," he said, blank-eyed, lost in his flame. "Guaran-fuckin'-teed."

* * *

Harold had a brainstorm. Simon suspected it was the cadre's brainstorm, actually, and he'd been keeping it under wraps. But he unveiled it with what, for Harold, qualified as a flourish.

"You should go to a union meeting. There's one Monday. I doubt she'll be there. No one goes to these things. But you should go. Set an example, establish your bona fides. Lay the groundwork."

This was Plan B. In case Tanager didn't pan out.

The local met once a month at a VFW hall in the heart of the no-name town. Two separate sessions were scheduled to accommodate workers on different shifts. This month's were Monday, Sy's only day off. But bench players had to be ready.

He went to the morning session. An American flag waved from a pole outside the building. Another hung on a wall behind the podium.

A chaos of folding tables took up the back of the room, and behind them a broken vending machine, a hand-scrawled out-of-order sign over its coin slot. In the front were uneven rows of folding chairs, most of them unoccupied. Portable fans nudged gusts of hot musty air toward the center of the room from the corners behind the podium. The place was thick with sweat and tobacco smoke.

A clock on the wall said "Drink Hires Root Beer—Roots—Bark—Herbs." At a little past ten the business manager checked his watch and called the roll of officers. This took barely a minute, the roll consisting of the business manager, the treasurer, and an officer whose title Sy didn't catch. The business manager, who served as the meeting's chair, was a pudgy man in a short-sleeved shirt, dress white, pits already drenched. He declared that a quorum was present.

Next up was the treasurer, a lanky Chicano in a polo shirt that matched the business manager's. The general fund continued to show a positive balance. For this the treasurer credited the outstanding leadership of the officers present, as well as the local's members—some of whom he was happy to see today, including a few new faces—in negotiating a new three-year contract. Hard bargaining had preserved both the local's strike fund and individual brothers' savings. This news was greeted with polite applause from the smattering of brothers in attendance.

"I would also call your attention to our unanimous vote not to pursue mediation for employees who were terminated due to an unlawful strike," he added, eliciting dutiful cheers and whistles. "This was a big savings, as they could not have prevailed in defending an action that went against our own contract."

"Good riddance," blurted the business manager, the sentiment amplified by his handheld microphone.

There was new business. Several brothers had complained of missing guardrails and other safety issues, reported the unidentified officer, and stewards were making inquiries. Some had suggested the local organize a touch football team as a way to boost esprit de corps and recruit new members, once the fall weather returned and outdoor activities were feasible. The officer proposed that the business manager canvass the membership to gauge interest, and, if warranted, see if the machinists, electricians, and brothers of other locals might wish to field competing teams. The treasurer inquired about potential costs, given the need for uniforms and so forth. The business manager replied that while the treasurer raised a valid question, some community-minded firm, the Wagon Wheel for example, might be persuaded to sponsor a team. He expressed confidence that nonbudgeted expenditures would prove modest.

A guy in a cowboy hat asked if the team would be co-ed.

"In your dreams, Orville," replied the business manager.

The motion was seconded without amendments and carried, in the opinion of the chair, by voice vote. Somebody raised a point of order to the effect that a formal motion had never been made, but he was ruled out of order.

Finally the business manager opened the floor to questions and comments, and, hearing none, made a formal motion to adjourn. The nameless officer seconded, and the meeting was gaveled closed, according to the root beer clock, at 10:23 a.m.

The business manager caught Sy on his way out. He introduced himself, pumped Sy's hand. Sy told him his name and said he worked in the smelter.

"The smelter, good for you. Always glad to meet a new union brother. You coming off graveyard or working swing?"

"Day off, matter of fact."

The man's face brightened. "Wow," he said, stretching the word to something like slow motion. "Above and beyond. Living in Tucson?"

Sy told him he was.

"Good for you," he repeated. "Nice to see members take an interest. Thank you for driving all that way, and on your day off. Good luck in the smelter. Five-fourteen an hour, not bad for a starting wage."

Sy had just reached the truck when he heard the voice again. "Simon," the man shouted. "Find out if our new sister can catch a football?"

They both laughed, Simon regretting it right away, sorry as much for himself as for his popular new sister.

* * *

Management had reversed itself. Decided to keep Tanager on days after all. The crew found this out when they came on swing. Hardly anyone had seen or spoken with her, still, a separation which compounded her aura of mystery. Having her face in the papers had lent her an aura of myth.

Maybe they wanted to make her the hardhat Garbo. Or maybe they just wanted to keep her away from the drooling multitudes. Either way the upshot was that she and the multitudes wouldn't be in the same place at the same time for at least another week. Possibly longer.

Nobody took this harder than Bullock.

"Fucking goddamn motherfucking cocksuckers," he said. Screamed in fact.

* * *

The airwaves thrummed with forecasts of doom for Allende. Chilean women, especially, wanted an end to shortages and rising prices. They wanted change.

Freako was rooting for a coup. The president's ouster, went the consensus, would stabilize copper prices. Stable prices meant the company could keep operating into the foreseeable future. Ninety cents a pound was mission critical. No Allende equaled no shutdown.

The overthrow of Chile's democracy would be a godsend to Freako shareholders. But what about those Chilean women? They reminded Sy of the women in *Emeralds*. Not the images but the flesh-and-blood women, the ones who lived in Mineral City, who went on living there after the cameras were gone. How did they view their sacrifice, their victory, now that the Steelworkers had made strikes obsolete, dissidence futile, now that a motley band of bookstore militants was pinning its hopes on Simon Bussbaum, of all people, to save the franchise, lead the way to a workers' paradise? What would they tell themselves, now, to make sense of that?

His heart ached for them, for the women of Chile, for women everywhere.

* * *

After a decent interval he dialed the number on the paper scrap from the Launder-Eez. It was impossible to know Tanager's schedule, what with her cycling through crews instead of shifts. Amid thousands of rotating workers, Tanager was a fixed star, consigned to perpetual days and granted time off according to some exotic algorithm that applied only to her. He guessed she was due for a break. He still had a few nights to go on graveyard.

"Simon, of course," she said, after he'd identified himself. She sounded surprised. It was around eight, a few hours before he'd have to leave for work. Dinner dishes clattered in the background. "You're our third caller. Proud owner of a brand new kitten."

This caught him up short.

"Any chance I could meet them first?"

"You're not ready to commit," she said. "I get it."

She suggested he drop by next morning, after work.

She lived in the western half of a small duplex, north-facing, set off by a colorful pebble lawn with a modest cactus garden. The kittens were mewing from inside a fruit crate she'd placed in a corner of the living room. Every few seconds a nose or paw poked through the slats. Across the room, a toddler in overalls struggled to escape from an older woman, presumably Tanager's mother, who shooshed and whispered to her in Spanish.

"*Gatitos*," said the girl, pointing and squealing. "*Gatitos*."

The crate held three kittens. Only one looked like the Xerox. One was white and brown with a Rorschach test on its head and a swirly coat that called to mind Yodels or Devil Dogs, one of those chocolaty-creamy confections Sy had missed since leaving the East Coast. The third was a tabby with dark stripes that seemed to be dripping into its eyes.

"You're just in time. Already gave one kitty away. And I'll have to keep one, I guess," directing this toward the toddler.

"Kitty," the toddler said.

The little girl dashed toward the crate, Grandma in pursuit. Tanager scooped her into her arms. "So this is my mom, Rosa García Tanager. Elena's the wriggly one. Mama, this is, uh, Simon—"

"Bussbaum."

"Simon Bussbaum," Tanager said.

Her mother nodded. *"Mucho gusto."*

"Mucho gusto," he said.

"Can you say *'mucho gusto'* to Simon, Lainie?"

Lainie went on wriggling. "Kitties," she said, reaching with both hands toward the box. Tanager passed her back to her mother.

His kitten was black and white, as advertised, only cleaner, satiny, its ebony fluff interrupted by silvery inlaid patterns, stripes and circles and an upside-down heart that started near its rabbity ears and looped south to its whiskers. Imploring brown-green marbles for eyes. A white triangle covered its chest.

It mewed with a ludicrous urgency, a puny, incongruously willful squeak toy.

"She still wants her mom," Tanager said. "But mom's had enough."

He lifted her out of the crate and up to his cheek. Purr like a baseball card in bicycle wheel spokes.

"Full disclosure, tuxedos aren't the brightest bulbs on the tree, usually. But they're sweet."

The kid was losing it now. *"Dios mío,"* said her grandmother, crossing herself and hauling the child away. The only sounds now the mewing and purring.

"Kid's crazy for kittens," Tanager said.

"This one likes me, I think."

"Hate to tell you, they're not that picky."

He placed the kitten back in her crate, where she was set upon by her siblings. There was freshly brewed coffee, and Tanager brought him some in a souvenir mug from the Painted Desert. He sat on the sofa and she pulled up a chair.

The girl was two. Grandma babysat while Tanager worked. Lainie's dad had been killed by friendly fire before the baby was born. Tanager indicated the small table to his left, which held a framed photo of her husband in uniform. On a matching table to his right was a shot of them together, posing at what was likely the South Rim.

"Nixon sends me checks. But it's the three of us now. I needed to work. Just took a job in a copper smelter, believe it or not."

"Freako, right," he said. Grateful for the opening. "I saw you in the paper. Recognized you from the laundromat. I'm in converters."

She noted the smallness of the world. He nodded agreement.

"Not sure how long I'll last. Management's worried about me. Like I might get shanked in the prison yard. I mean, I know what they say about me. Behind my back. Big macho mining men. Junior high schoolers are less scared of girls."

"Most don't care. A few think you're a curse."

"Men," she said and sipped her coffee.

"Not all."

"You're different, I'm sure. You're all different."

"Well," he said. "You never know."

"Sometimes you do."

Grandma and Lainie came in from the kitchen. Lainie worried a sandwich, her face smeared with peanut butter and jelly.

"We've been calling her Tux," Tanager said, meaning the kitten. "But that's just a placeholder. Tell you what. You drive her off the lot today, I'll throw in the naming rights for free."

"Deal."

He rose and went to the crate. Tux seemed wrong. With its silver on black swirls, his new kitten looked more like a negative image of Hopi jewelry. He didn't know any Hopi words, though. And he'd forgotten the Navajo ones Jake had taught him.

Tanager brought him a small litter pan and a paper bag with enough litter to fill the bottom. She put two cans of cat food in the pan. "I'll lend you a carrier. To get her home."

"*Gatito*," Lainie said, arms waving, her grandmother reclaiming the sandwich as a preventive measure.

Something stirred in him then, seeing this family, these three generations of close-knit females. Nixon had taken the toddler's father, her mother's husband. Sy thought of the scene from *Emeralds* where the miners' wives, mothers, and children take their places after an Anglo judge, a low-rent Millhouse, shuts down the picket line. He tried to recall the Diné word for *hello*.

He reached into the crate, lifted the kitten to his ear, her motor at full throttle.

Lainie laughed and pointed, "Kitty," she said.

"She's a nice kitty," he said. "What should we call her?"

He nestled the creature in the crook of his neck, listening, an insistent purr like the roar of the ocean in a furry seashell.

"Kitty," Lainie said.

"Kitty needs a name," he said, dropping to a knee so she could touch the animal. "Like Lainie."

They were at eye level now, Sy, Lainie, and the kitten. He broke the news in a conspiratorial whisper.

"Esperanza," he said, exultant. "*Se llama* Esperanza."

* * *

She spent a long time reconnoitering. At last she curled up on the bed and he went shopping for cat food, cat toys, catnip, a proper litter box, a box of litter, a litter box scooper. They spent the rest of the day sleeping. Tanager had told him cats mostly slept while their people were gone, too, so it was fine to leave them alone. But this seemed more faith than fact. He didn't see how you could know such a thing, absent a White House-style taping system. He was glad to be down to his last two graveyards.

Solitude did seem to suit her. After his final shift they had a snack in the kitchen. Then she followed him into the bathroom, and then to the bedroom again. He knelt and flopped backward onto the mattress, which was still on the floor, clutching her to his chest. She was fearless. Or possibly not too bright, as advertised. But playful and affectionate. They were playing when the phone rang.

"We should talk," Harold said.

Sy was rolling plastic balls with bells inside, trying to get her to fetch. She liked watching them roll, but lost interest the second they stopped. Fortunately he'd bought a dozen or so. "Okay, shoot."

"In person, I mean."

"Right."

"So can we meet?"

"I guess. The bookstore?"

"Enchilada's better. Just me and you. Got something for you."

"The Enchilada."

"The Enchilada. You're off now, right? One tomorrow?"

"One tomorrow. The Enchilada."

Esperanza was curled up on his pillow again. He threw another jingly ball across the room.

She opened her eyes, briefly, and went back to sleep.

* * *

The phone woke him up.

"Toodles. Courtney. Damn." He was zonked.

"Well, wake up, sleepyhead."

"I just got to bed. Coming off graveyard."

"Graveyard? I thought you were on swing. So you'd be up by now. Graveyard I did not expect. I didn't think you'd be on graveyard."

"Well, I am."

"News to me."

"Just right now trying to get to sleep."

The cat, rousted from sleep as well, sat at the foot of the bed, bathing herself.

"So," he said. "It's your nickel."

"So, I thought you might call."

"I wasn't sure you wanted me to."

"You're such a dope. 'Course I wanted you to."

"Well," he said. "You're the one walked out. Right in the middle of a movie."

"You like movies better than people."

"Depends on the people. And the movies."

Her breathing grew faint. She'd moved the receiver away from her face and he guessed she was crying. The clock made a sound like clicking teeth as a new pair of tiles tumbled into their slots. It was ten-twenty, police radio code for location. He'd heard Broderick Crawford say it a hundred times.

He stared at the clock, like some minor apocalypse might be triggered when the next tile tumbled into place.

"Still there? You okay?"

There was fumbling with the phone at the other end.

"I don't know," she said. "Not really." Her voice was soft and sad, like a whispered prayer.

"Not really," he repeated.

There was another pause.

"I got a cat," he said.

"A cat."

"A baby cat. A kitten."

"A kitten. When were you going to mention this?"

"Whenever I talked to you, I suppose. I'm mentioning it now."

"I'm allergic to cats."

"Sorry. I didn't know."

"You didn't ask. I can't stay at your place now, this means. I mean, like, ever. I get a rash just thinking about cats. I can't even stop by, if you've got a cat. So that's just super. I mean, you could have said something, you know? Why didn't you say something?"

"I can come over there, I guess."

"You guess?"

Esperanza squeezed her nose between his cheek and the telephone's mouthpiece. He may have addressed her as "sweetheart" as he relocated her to another part of the bed.

"Oh Jesus," he heard Toodles say. As if she'd dropped a vase, or chipped a fingernail. Her tone more panicked than prayerful. "Goddammit, Simon. Are you alone right now?"

He considered the question. He'd just told her about Esperanza. Literally, then, he wasn't alone. But wasn't everyone alone, cosmically speaking? This was the gospel of Sal Mineo, as Plato, who asked, in reply to the planetarium's godlike voice in *Rebel Without a Cause*: "What does he know about man alone?" It seemed a fair complaint, at least, and a saner response to the Almighty's voice than Charlton Heston's in *The Ten Commandments*. Though of course things ended badly for Plato.

He was about to reply to Toodles when she got tired of waiting.

"You know what, Simon? Forget I asked. Fuck you, in fact. See you around."

He didn't hear her hang up. He waited, unsure if the line was dead. Then a busy signal broke the silence.

Tricky to slam the receiver, perhaps, with a Princess phone.

"Ten-four," he said.

* * *

The rains had quit. The drought was official. One of the local TV stations aired a segment on the great drought of 1954, when the Austrian expat psychologist Wilhelm Reich showed up in Tucson to make it rain. Reich was known for inventing the orgone box, a machine he'd designed to tap the primal energy of the cosmos. He said this energy was blue.

Reich flogged his wooden box as a gateway to massive orgasms, which, beyond their intrinsic value, could pacify dictators, cure cancer and constipation. Reich had been banished from the German communist party, the International Psychoanalytic Association, and several Scandinavian countries. He relocated from Maine to Tucson to build what he called a cloudbuster on the back of a truck.

The idea being, more or less, to bring the clouds to climax.

Reich was unloved in Ike's America, much less this cowboy corner of it, and the cosmos proved no friendlier. He blamed his failure to satisfy the skies on the Tucson Mountains, which he said were disturbing the atmosphere. He loaded his wife and ten-year-old kid in the truck and headed west.

The rains did come the following March, serial kickass storms that launched the wettest monsoon season since 1921. Tucson got thirteen inches, more than double its average rainfall. Not long after that Reich was found dead in Lewisburg Federal Penitentiary, Pennsylvania, while serving a two-year sentence for shipping orgone boxes across state lines.

"And get this," said the TV reporter, speaking now to the anchorman. "When Wilhelm Reich and his family moved to Tucson they lived on *Wetmore Road*, at the northern edge of the city. And his ten-year-old son attended—"

"Don't tell me—"

"Wetmore Elementary School!"

"Can't make this stuff up, folks," said the anchor. "Thanks, Maureen, for that thought-provoking look at a forgotten chapter of local history. The Wetmores, of course, are one of Tucson's founding families, and Edward L. Wetmore was a meteorologist himself back at the turn of the century. We're just having a little fun here, folks, no disrespect intended, I'm praying for rain, I promise you. But right now, stay tuned for more news, coming right up after a short break..."

Too little sex and too little rain.

The Enchilada's A/C hit him the moment he cracked the door. The aroma of refried beans floated on crisscrossing currents. He lit a cigarette and scanned the room. Harold had claimed the gunfighter's seat, a banana-yellow linoleum-top table in a back corner. Only he wasn't watching the door. Anyone could have put a bullet in his brain and hightailed it into the desert.

He was hunched over a Times. "Chee-lay," he said, not looking up, stretching the syllables in a way that called to mind the shape of the country itself. "Fascists won't stop till Allende's gone. Kissinger, Nixon, the international copper industry. All one struggle. Why we keep fighting."

Sy snuffed his smoke in a plastic ashtray, its perimeter bedecked with cartoon enchiladas, the restaurant's logo. They were smiling but didn't look happy. Harold closed his paper. "But you know all that. Anyway, we're not here to talk about Chee-lay."

They inched side by side along the glassed-in counter, past the steaming bins of beans and rice and chicken and *carne asada*. Sy had the day off so he ordered a beer with his burrito. Harold paid for both of them. They didn't make eye contact again until they were back at the table.

"So," he said.

A grizzled man in a brown uniform came to collect their trays. All the employees, save for the manager, wore brown caps that said "The Happy Enchilada" embossed with a smiling, rolled-up anthropoid tortilla. The employees looked less happy than the cartoon enchiladas.

Harold waited while a gloomy human collected their trays. "Okay, here's the thing. Freako has neutralized the heart of the resistance. That was me and Dwight and Lencho, plus a couple of allies who've taken jobs out-of-state."

"A couple of allies."

"That was the stick," Harold went on. "Now they've cut a deal with the local to take back the others, but with enough conditions to keep them in line till the mother lode runs out. That's the carrot."

"So everyone, pretty much. Neutralized, I mean."

"That's where you come in."

He was un-neutralized. This was his entry ticket.

"And Tanager? Where does *she* come in?"

"They're feminizing the workforce. It's propaganda. The softer their public image, the harder they can grind their heels into the workers' necks. Bare-knuckles late-stage capitalism with a female face. They'll be putting her on a billboard before you know it."

He finished his taco and reached down into his bag. Popped back up with an unwrapped copy of *Ten Days That Shook the World*. "Gift from the group. Look inside."

Sy lingered over the cover, which featured an illustration of silhouetted figures lofting a black banner against a red background, the book's title in red block letters. The silhouettes, who marched clear around to the back, wore hats of various kinds, and seemed to be carrying weapons, though it was hard to be sure—the weapons, if that's what they were, had the shape of lightning bolts. A yellow half-sun with thick spokes, like a child's fingerpaint drawing, hung on the horizon, its direction also unclear. He looked inside. On the flyleaf, across from where "Vanguard Books" had been stamped in crimson, was a handwritten inscription.

"*En solidaridad*," it read, "Naldo Galvan." Beneath the signature, in parentheses, a different hand had written "(José Castillo)" using a ballpoint pen.

Harold was beaming, in his way. "We thought you'd like it."

This was the editorial *we*, a vague reference to unnamed others. These others did not, it was safe to assume, include Galvan. The inscription was generic, dedicated to no one in particular. Harold had warned Sy not to mention Galvan's alter ego, José Castillo, yet here it was in blue and white. His best guess, from the fastidious penmanship, was Joyce.

Even if Galvan had signed it himself, he hadn't done it for Sy. He'd done it for the sake of a sale, on the fantastical chance someone who'd heard of the film ever stumbled into the store. Of all the bookstores in all the world.

"How to think about this is we're rebuilding," Harold said once Sy had shut the book. This was the new-business portion of the agenda. "We have would-be allies all over Freako, people who know something needs to be done. They're just not ready to do it. Not on their own. They need leaders. And now there aren't any."

"And…"

"And that's where Tanager comes in. You and Tanager. Don't take this wrong, but you lack *authenticity*. Nothing personal. We look at it from an organizing standpoint. You've got no wife, no kids, no mortgage. You've been to college. You're from—Brooklyn, is it?"

"Close enough."

"No matter. You're East Coast, big city. A carpetbagger. You don't hunt or fish. You don't spend your weekends bowling or fixing carburetors. You don't speak Spanish. I could go on. Don't take this wrong. These things don't disqualify you from contributing to the struggle. But they do present challenges to your assuming a leadership role, even if you aspired to one. Which, let's face it, you don't."

"And you think Tanager does."

"Not at all. At least not yet. We'll have to bring her along. But she's a natural. Smart Chicana with an Anglo name. Presentable but not provocative. Single mom. We've heard she's a war widow. Been in the papers. Knows how to handle herself. If she speaks out about faulty equipment, health and safety, union collusion with Freako brass—if she stands up for workers' rights—she's an instant icon. She's already a pioneer. We need to make her a leader."

"People say she's a lesbian. People with influence."

"That's what people said about Joyce. Back in the day. Probably Rosa Parks and Mother Jones too. Ruling class slander 101."

"I'm not saying the ruling class. I'm saying the men. The hunters and bowlers and carburetor fixers. The salt of the earth working men. The ruling class seems to like her."

Harold scrunched his features into something like pity.

"Tell you a secret. Freako didn't want her. Did you know that? Wouldn't give her an interview. They wanted a girl. Just not *that* girl. Something went down with her father, we think, something they don't want to talk about. Heart condition or somesuch. Like he shouldn't have been cleared for work.

"Maybe they lowballed the widow, bought her off cheap. Tanager moved away after that, must have talked to a lawyer. Came back and threatened to sue, run to the papers. Don't ask how we know this. Trust me. They hired her with a gun to their heads. Now they're making the best of it."

"Lot of that going around."

"We just want you to talk to her. Sound her out."

Sy shrugged. He'd already agreed to this.

"Sooner than later, is my point. The sooner the better. We're losing momentum. Nobody wanted a shutdown. But it would have given us a chance to rally the men, build support for reinstatement. Now we're looking to the future. Tanager's the power hitter we can build a lineup around."

"If I can ever talk to her, that is."

"Just try," Harold said.

Sy promised he would. "I should get going. Plus I gotta take a leak. Long bus ride."

"One last thing. Road trip to Mineral City soon. Naldo's got some spare bedrooms, fold-out couch in the living room. His wife—his real wife, Teresa—will fix us dinner. Three-hour drive, give or take. You're welcome to come along."

Sy doubted he'd still be welcome if he whiffed on Tanager. And he didn't see how he could face Galvan—or his real wife, Teresa—unless he brought her into the fold.

"Let me give it a shot," he said. "Then ask me again."

They said goodbye and Sy made a feint toward the men's room. Once Harold was gone he wheeled and wound his way back through the bustling banana-yellow linoleum-top tables and emerged into the blazing, radiant daylight.

He hoisted the book, with its forest of Trotsky's men, to block the sun while he slipped on his shades. When he lowered it once again there were purple mountains in every direction, and beyond them the cloudless, untapped primal energy of the cosmos.

* * *

Tanager remained in protective custody, Freako's own princess hostage. The whitecaps shadowed her wire to wire. Her foreman, the sparkplug who'd given Sy his sledge and his walking papers, stalked her like a hungry stray. Nixon himself, holed up in the White House with Pat and a sullen posse of Secret Service, would have envied the isolation.

Millhouse, though, was an alien being, wooden and shifty-eyed, unfamiliar with human customs. Wore a suit and tie to walk on the beach. Tanager was flesh and blood. And treating her like some delicate flower—even as she pounded smoldering slabs of copper with a large rubber hammer—was no way to ease her into the ranks of the unwashed. Isolation affirmed her specialness. Which only made her more of a target for whatever horrors the brass feared might befall her when, at long last, they allowed her to mix with the general population.

Worse, from the cadre's standpoint, keeping her from the riffraff rendered their own plans, for the moment at least, inoperative. Galvan had earned his stripes as a homegrown champion of the working class. But how could you grow a grassroots leader who never put down roots?

Simon's challenge was more immediate. Management had her working his old station, Wheel Number Two. From a spot near Sahagun's converter Sy could get a glimpse of her before Sarge chased him away. This was as close as he got.

She still took breaks in a secret location, and the merest hint of unauthorized personnel on the anode floor would trigger a Mayday alert. But most of the men were content to spy on her from a distance, as circumstances allowed, comparing notes on her looks and proclivities after each new round of surveillance. Bullock bet Dago a box of Cuban cigars that if he, Bullock, asked her out, she'd turn him down in a heartbeat. This would prove her lesbian tendencies.

Everyone knew she'd say no—everyone, that is, but Bullock—on account of Bullock being fat, unattractive, menacing, middle-aged, and possibly married, not to mention she might be seeing someone herself. It was a sucker bet Dago was bound to lose, except that he meant to make Bullock the sucker by refusing to pony up, telling him instead to go fuck himself sideways on the grounds that the bet proved nothing about the girl, Bullock being fat, unattractive, etcetera. Anyway, Bullock, most likely, had no intention of ever asking her out, even if he could get within fifty yards of her. Just killing time until swing.

Only Tanager, when swing finally came, didn't rotate with the rest of them. They found this out at the start of their first shift. "They're keeping her on days," Sarge reported. "Timing wasn't right, I dunno. That's all they'll tell me."

Bullock let loose with a bestial moan that sounded like "Fuuuuck," but could as easily have been "fock" or "fog" or "far," the mystery vowel amorphous, multisyllabic, stretched to the breaking point. "What is wrong with these goddamn pussies you take orders from, Sarge? I mean what exactly the fuck?"

Sarge affected a tone of folksy innocence. "You know I'm just a pissant enlisted man, Bull, same as you. I just work here." This was an overstatement—foremen didn't do any work, and pulling rank seemed key to his very existence—but his powerlessness was real enough. "Y'all have a good shift now." He forced his mouth into a feeble smile and ambled off the platform.

Bullock did not have a good shift. He seemed on the verge of a meltdown. When he wasn't skimming or spitting he passed the hours twitching, vaulting out of his chair, belching profanities—his main targets being God and unspecified pussies—and, in moments of composure, venting his annoyance at Freako's collective failure to grasp the threat Tanager posed to the sanctity of a once-proud—and proudly male—institution.

He directed his rage at whoever was near at hand. This was usually Simon, who had no choice but to stick close when they needed to mud the lip. They alternated heaving their globs in silence, except that he could hear Bullock muttering under his breath as they crossed paths. When one of Simon's heaves missed its mark—clumps of mud, once aloft, had a tendency to disintegrate—he braced for abuse.

But they didn't cross paths this time. Sy turned to see Bullock flailing and gasping for air, his vexation over the state of things having caused him to swallow his chaw of Red Man and spiral into a red-faced spasm of coughing and choking. Fortunately for Simon Bullock couldn't discern his glee, focused as he was on clutching the guardrail, head down and wings outstretched like a seasick sailor, a pose he held till equilibrium returned.

Then he screamed at him to get off his fucking platform.

The next day Sy punched in early. Thanks to the latest schedule adjustments, Meltzer no longer relieved him. Now Sy was *his* relief. The worm had turned. Yet he hadn't taken revenge.

It was ten, fifteen minutes to shift change. Number Three was rolled out, Meltzer having a smoke in the car. Sy continued down to the anode floor, finding, surprisingly, the whitecaps gone, having jettisoned security to get the jump on their paperwork. Tanager's new temporary foreman—the sparkplug had rotated to swing, along with his regular crew—had his back to them, working out his production on a calculator. Sy crept over to where Tanager was parked, the very chair where he used to park his own bony butt, watching the anodes float by in the light of the late afternoon.

"Hey," he said.

"Hey," reflexively. She'd never seen him in his hardhat and safety glasses.

"The kitten's good," he said.

That's when she realized. "Oh, hey, *Bussbaum.*"

"Security's asleep at the switch, so. I'm due on swing, thought I'd say hi. While the coast is clear. They ever letting you out of your bubble?"

"Next week. I made them swear to it. Threatened to quit. Said I was done taking the hit for your raging hormones, your flashbacks and lousy childhoods and whatnot. Speaking generally, that is. I mean, I get it. They're scared that an incident—that's what they call it, an incident—will sink the company's stock. Which would sink their careers. Their best idea was house arrest. But no more. This is it. They swore."

Sy nodded, dubious.

"Anyway, everyone's been nice so far. Chivalry, I guess." She scrunched her face, amused by her own whimsy.

"I'm sure of it. King Arthur's court, this place."

Her foreman spotted him and started in their direction.

"And here's Rover now. Be seeing you. Congrats on your big liberation."

He saw her relief arrive. Shift change. He stopped in the *hombres'* room for a piss, enjoyed a cigarette, finally set out sauntering toward his converter. Meltzer's crew would be gone by now. And now it would be Meltzer cooling his jets, cursing *his* relief long after his crewmates had hit the showers.

Fuck you, Meltzer, he thought, unaccountably pleased with himself.

Only it wasn't Meltzer.

It was Bullock.

Sy waved to him from the platform end of the track. Bullock went on punching till he'd finished the run. Then he hauled his bulk out of the car and stalked off. Sy took his place and reversed course. The flaps offered no resistance, so the slag was ready to skim. When he looked up Bullock was right where they'd parted ways, slicing a finger across his throat. A minute later he was blowing his whistle and rolling the furnace out of the stacks.

Sy hadn't yet stowed his lunch, so he stayed in the car caffeinating and smoking while Bullock busied himself on the platform. The next batch got them to blister. Sy sat in the car and watched as Chief in Crane Number Two came and went three times, Bullock filling a ladle on each trip. When the crane retreated to the end of the aisle he knew the furnace was empty. He'd be needed on the platform.

But Bullock's expression told him he wasn't.

"You were AWOL. I told you once. Do not go AWOL."

"I fucked up, sorry. I never thought Meltzer would take off like that."

Bullock streamed a long, contemplative arc of Red Man into the crane aisle.

"Meltzer's a brokedick asshole. I'll deal with Meltzer."

The sound of one shoe dropping.

"Fuck Meltzer. And fuck you too, and fuck that lesbian bitch. Which, by the way, don't think I don't know why you were AWOL."

Bullock had spies everywhere. Such were the wages of years of discounted hams and Cuban cigars.

"I talked to her for, like, three minutes. It's nothing."

"Thick as thieves, what I heard."

"That's wrong. I met her once. Bumped into her at the laundromat. I barely know her."

"How do you even get on the anode floor, is my question. I mean nobody else can."

"Jesus, Bull, I snuck down there. For like three minutes, tops. They chased me away."

Bullock shook his head, slowly and sorrowfully. "Not sure I trust you anymore. Not that I ever did. But this looks bad. The brass all of a sudden diddling themselves, conveniently, while you play footsy with this *she-male*"—brief pause here, a mollusk admiring its pearl—"we're all supposed to welcome with open arms. Well, fuck that. My arms aren't open. You know how I feel about that shit."

They didn't speak again till the shift was practically over. Sy was asleep in the punchcar. Bullock woke him by thumping the top of the cab with a steel rod.

Muscle memory made him grab the controls. But the furnace was down. Bullock grinned menacingly and held the rod horizontally across his chest with both hands. He looked like a demented song and dance man.

"You awake?"

He couldn't not be awake.

"What'd you talk about anyway?"

"Who?"

"You and the skirt. You were talking. What'd you talk about?"

"Hello and goodbye. Like I said. She told me they're rotating her off days next week."

"Next week." The thought seemed to cheer him. "About fucking time." He was holding the rod vertically now, using it as a cane. He bounced it absently a few times on the concrete. Then he passed it to Sy inside the car and lumbered back to the platform.

* * *

Meltzer had screwed him again. Murder was in his heart. The next time Simon approached his punchcar Meltzer's feet were up on the dash, cigarette dangling off his lip. Life of Riley, everything but the hammock. He was out of the car in seconds. He glared as he walked away.

Sy had never realized how large he was.

Forget murder. Name-calling too. Sy settled for returning his stare as they crossed paths. "I talked to your daddy," Meltzer said, middle finger extended at eye level. "He's waiting on you."

Bullock had dealt with him, then.

"Meltzer hath come to Jesus," Bullock confirmed. "From now on you show up at least five minutes before shift change, That's it."

He said nothing more about Tanager. He said nothing at all, in fact, except to tell Sy when to punch and when to stop and, once, to ask him if lesbianism was acceptable in the eyes of the Hebrew god. Sy said he didn't think the Hebrew god was keen on women in general. He'd never heard of him being any less keen on lesbians.

Bullock stroked his mustache. "Your fags, though, whole 'nother story, am I right? I mean, Jews have a word for them?"

"Jews have a word for everything. My mother called them bachelors."

Dr. Hernández, his new relief, was right on time. Luckily he had a lid in his lunch box. Sy promised to pay him tomorrow.

* * *

He'd pulled the wrong cord when he shut the blinds and now the crack of dawn was streaming in through the slats. Esperanza nestled as usual in the crook of his left elbow, purring and kneading like he was her mother. This was not a responsibility he took lightly. He sank back into the pillow.

The knock on the door wasn't the first. He wasn't sure how he knew this. It wasn't the crack of dawn, either. It just felt like it.

Then another knock, louder, with a hint of belligerence.

Toodles perhaps. Or Jake.

"Come back later."

"It's Gil. Gil Willetts."

He had to think for a second. It was Willetts who'd sent him the lease and left the key in the mailbox. The man who'd promised him a deadbolt. They'd never met. Sy preferred it that way.

The cat was on high alert. Was she legal? He threw on some clothes and locked her in the bedroom, then padded in bare feet to the front door. The door lacked a chain, naturally, so he opened it roughly the distance a chain would permit.

"'Simon, Gil Willetts. Your landlord. I'd like to come in, please."

Sy widened the gap a bit. Stood in the doorway.

Willetts was a lanky man with a cockroach-shaped mole on his cheek and marbles for eyes. He had an oddly formal air about him, and Simon sensed he was happiest when collecting the rent. He tilted his head slightly and sniffed the air. His eyes swept the room before landing on Sy's.

"Sorry to come unannounced. I did call. There was a complaint."

"A complaint? About me?"

"About a cat. Is there a cat on the premises?"

"A cat? On these premises?"

"A cat, yes. On these premises." He spoke as one would to a young child, or an idiot. "I'm asking do you have a cat here?"

Sy mustered as much umbrage as he could.

"A cat? Who told you I had a cat?"

"Mrs. Hardwick, from downstairs. All hours she hears cat feet, claws scratching and running. Coming from here, she says."

Sy had never laid eyes on his neighbor, had only heard her daytime soaps and quiz shows floating up through the floor. Evenings were deathly quiet. She'd been a lovely neighbor.

"It's not a good time—Gil, right? I'm working swing shift, out till one or so. Maybe she heard me come home. I'd be happy to let you in some other time." He thought Tanager might cat sit for an hour while the landlord made his inspection.

Willetts reached into a briefcase by his feet. "Mr. Bussbaum, I try to be fair to all my tenants. So I remind you. There are no pets allowed." He brandished a legal-size sheaflet of paper, two or three pages stapled together. "See here. *'No pets are permitted on the premises at any time.'*" He stabbed the words with a forefinger. "No exceptions. I permit you to have a cat, I have to permit Mrs. Hardwick to have a cat. Soon there are cats everywhere. Animal smells are forever. So no cats. No dogs. No exceptions. This is only fair."

"Does Mrs. Hardwick *want* a cat?"

He shook his head. "Mrs. Hardwick dislikes cats," he said, instantly remorseful at letting slip a private detail. "She hears pittering, is all. Pittering. All hours, she says."

"Pittering." The certainty of an imminent scratching at the bedroom door, or a plaintive kittenish yowl, grew by the second.

Willetts peered over his shoulder for one last scan of the living room. "I'll leave you a copy of your rental agreement, in case you've lost the original. It lists your rights and responsibilities as a tenant. Word to the wise. Next time I'll have to have a look-see."

"Understood. Just call first, please. I work shifts."

He clicked the door shut. Checked the dial in the doorknob and went back to bed. Esperanza was waiting for him on the pillow.

When the apartment had turned too sultry for sleep he went off to buy some area rugs, to muffle the pittering.

* * *

Tanager's overlords, as promised, moved her to graveyard. They'd parked an ancient Shasta Airflyte by the loading dock for her exclusive use, an egg- and jaundice-colored dump the length of a VW Bug. Just looking at it induced claustrophobia. A porous crescent of rubber bollards served as a feeble warning to stay away.

The camper had rounded corners that gave it the look of a canned ham, and the joke was Bullock had bought it for Tanager as a welcome gift. Everyone but Bullock found this amusing. It likely belonged to a whitecap whose wife had banished it from the driveway. The crew dubbed it the brokedown palace, less a reference to a Dead tune no one had actually heard than to the paradoxical nature of Tanager's weird, uneasy celebrity. The most democratic of luminaries, she repaired to her private trailer as biology demanded, but took her breaks in the common lunch room, happy to hang with random peons.

By all accounts she mixed well with her fellow workers. She was not raped or pillaged. She showed no signs of being a curse. The rate of industrial accidents remained constant, and normal operation proceeded normally. Morale in converters, since Sy's arrival at least, had never been better.

Except, again, for Bullock. His sulked, glared, toggled between mean and malignant. Simon aside, Dago and Ozell were Tanager's only known defenders. But no one at all seemed up for a fight, a failure Bullock regarded as treason. He spoke only when necessary, which in Simon's case meant never. His bearing suggested the beefed-up ghost of Napoleon, or Nixon, or Adolf himself—depending on the quality of the light, and the intensity of Sy's mood—awaiting the end.

Bullock, though, refused to lose. The wheels were turning. His hours of brooding finally led to a revelation. Rather than punish the crew with silence—a sentence many were happy to serve—he would shape them into a hairy-chested militia, repel the invader with a phalanx of upraised schlongs. This insight occurred in the dark of night midway into the week.

Bullock was back.

"Top o' the morning, smelter workers and ships at sea," he bellowed over the PA system. It was a tick past four, when most of graveyard was asleep or wanted to be. "To all my Freako brothers"—emphasis on *brothers*—"I hereby summon you to an urgent meeting at the conclusion of this shift. We muster at the Wagon Wheel. Light refreshments will be provided.

"Our agenda, gentlemen, is (a) the good of the order, and (b) our individual well-being as men and Freako employees. This is all hands on deck. I repeat, this is an emergency. Your future hangs in the balance. And, as previously mentioned, free pretzels."

Blasting personal messages over the PA was a flagrant breach of smelter protocol, which was how protocol was generally observed on graveyard. Mostly it ensured that foremen would hear the news, and the news would percolate up the chain of command. Bullock focused the rest of the shift on retail lobbying, shmoozing the people he'd frozen out. Some he lured with the promise of goodies, some he bribed outright, a few he aimed to intimidate. Sy fell into the latter group.

But Sy didn't require convincing. Pressure was redundant. No way would he miss this.

He paid Hernández for his weed and hit the showers. When he got to the Wheel Bullock was stationed behind the bar. Tables were jammed against the walls and folding chairs added alongside the larger, more comfortable ones that usually went with the tables. The chairs were arranged in rows facing the bar. Country tunes rose from the jukebox as men filtered in. Some were still in their coveralls.

Sy took a seat toward the back. A long line formed at the bar, where Hank, the manager, and a bartender—her nametag ID'd her as Skye— hustled to keep things moving. When all the chairs were occupied latecomers slid into the booths or perched on tables. Hank and Bullock seemed pleased. Skye looked harried.

The last, dulcet tones of Merle Haggard's all-male backup singers were still in the air when the jukebox gave way to a murmur of low chatter and air conditioning. Bullock silenced the noise with a piercing wolf whistle, the same one he used to get cranemen's attention from his platform. He rapped on the bar with his bottle to gavel the session to order.

"Ladies and germs," he began. "I want to thank Hank here for letting us take the Wheel, so to speak, as it were"—Hank, his back to the room now, waved into the mirror—"and Skye for getting you all loosened up after a hard day's night." Hoots from the crowd, Skye saluting absently. "I'm Bull, purveyor of fine foods and tobacco and your humble and genial host." Good-natured boos morphing into a half-hearted chant of "Bull… Bull… Bull…" Then Bullock slashed a forefinger across his neck several times till the audience settled.

"I want to thank you all for coming—at least those of you who aren't here after every shift anyway, hassling Skye till she threatens to call your wives." More hoots, another salute from Skye. "Seriously, though, I think we all know why we're here today."

"Beer," someone shouted.

"Okay, right. But not just."

"Pretzels."

"Pretzels and beer, absolutely. Breakfast of champions. But man can't live on beer and pretzels alone."

"Poontang!" somebody yelled. This sparked a flurry of applause.

Bullock waited it out. "No respect, ladies and gentlemen, no respect. Alright then. Why we're here, my Freako brothers, is to stand up, to say how we earn our living is men's work. We're here because a copper mine is no place for a female. I don't care who her daddy was, how big her biceps are or who she rolls in the hay with. We're here, my brothers, to *take back the smelter.*"

Silence.

"Can I get an amen?"

"Can I get another beer?" somebody shouted.

"Prove you can hold the first one," Bullock said, "then ask me again." Skye gave him a high-five.

"Okay, dickwads, listen up." He scoured the room. "Is Dago here? No? Too bad. I see we have some geezers. Anyway, long as I've been at Freako—from the day Mother Mongoose hit pay dirt, matter of fact—this whole operation, office work excepted, all of it's been off-limits to women. This is for their protection. But it's also for ours. Because women in mines, no offense to our Jewish brothers, are bad juju.

"Everyone knows this. They know it in West Virginia. They know it in every coal and copper mine in every state in the union. It's only

Freako can't see it. They're blinded by ambition, trying to make mining sexy. Like we're in the damn hospitality business. They don't know shit about what we do, my friends. All they know is what kind of pictures they want in their annual report. And it ain't me, an overweight white dude with a big red 'stache. And, news flash, it ain't you either.

"They want Freako to look like a college, green and leafy. They want investors to think mining's pretty. They're ready to risk your lives for that. To boost their stock. Wall Street could give a fuck about you. Ditto the suits at Mongoose. This is just business to them, an experiment. Us lifers, we're the canaries in the copper mine. Human guinea pigs. We're the ones get fucked over."

Somebody raised his hand. "Shoot," Bullock said.

"Management can kiss my ass, totally with you there. But how's this the girl's fault?"

Bullock nodded appreciatively. "Great question," he said. "Nothing against the girl, per se. She's an instrument, the camel's nose under the tent, a hairline break in the levee. She's just one female. You hardly notice. But it's like that mole you never get looked at. Next thing you know it's stage five cancer and your kids are orphans, dressed in rags and scrounging in dumpsters.

"One female. Famous last words. We let her in, pretty soon you've got Kotex dispensers in the shitter, your wives and daughters are on the front lines in Hanoi, Da Nang, wherever the fuck. Our culture? Dead. Our traditions? Dead. Our manhood?"

Going for call and response. "Renfroe?"

Renfroe was somewhere else. Chesney, seated behind him, poked him in the back to get his attention.

"Yo."

"Brother Renfrow, are we gonna let Freako destroy our manhood?"

Renfrow looked more puzzled than usual. "No?"

"*Hell* no."

"Question," somebody said.

"Big O. Sock it to me, bro. What's your question."

It was Ozell, the smelter's black man. Lived in his crane. A few other black people were sprinkled around the complex like fugitive grains of pepper, underground mainly.

"You're tellin' me she don't deserve to work here 'cause she ain't like the rest of us. My question is this. You see anyone here look like me?"

Bullock scanned the room. Finally, his due diligence done, he turned back to Ozell.

"Everyone here looks like you, Ozell. I mean, more or less. Some of us may be lacking in, what is it, *melatonin*. Maybe we've got straighter hair, freckles, blue eyes. Whatever. But I look at you, what I see is a man. A black man, sure. Can't lie about that. But a man. That's the point, Big O. We're all the same, come right down to it."

"Uh-huh. One thing, though. I hear she's doin' the job. All I know. She's doin' the job."

Nods and shrugs. He'd said his piece. For what it was worth. The support of the smelter's only black man for its only female was the definition of a minority opinion.

Bullock finished his beer. "Ragsdale?"

A man in a muscle shirt rose from his folding chair. He had tattoos from wrists to shoulders, tattoos peeking out from his chest, suggesting a long prison stretch. Sy had seen him around once or twice. He was bald and nearly unrecognizable without his hardhat. He was older than Sy had thought and his tats drooped a bit.

"So say I'm on board. Say it goes against my grain, having women work alongside men, here, in this environment. Then let's say I also don't believe there's a damn thing you can do about it, short of walking off like them commies. You see where that got 'em. I'd sooner work with a qualified female than be out on the street."

This sparked nods and mutterings of approval. Bullock took it all in.

"Anyone else? Krinsky?"

Krinsky stared at his hands.

"So look. I don't want anyone walking out," Bullock said. "Matter of fact I don't want anyone doing anything you're not comfortable with. Shit, I'd handle this myself if I could, only I'm too much of a gentleman. Plus they're too chickenshit to let me and her work the same shift at the same time."

More chuckles.

"I called us together to take the temperature, test the water for how we can send a message, let this girl know she's not wanted here. Explain things. First Amendment stuff. I've got ideas, ask if you're interested. Not interested, that's cool, too. Man's gotta do what a man's gotta do, am I right?"

Simon eyed the door. But there was no escape. Whatever Bullock had in mind wasn't covered under the First Amendment. But neither was Sy. Free speech didn't live here, save for Bullock and his ilk, people with standing and physical heft. It didn't apply to probationary workers. And definitely not to him.

Still, speaking up had its appeal. The unarmed man standing against the hanging mob, the outraged citizen on the floor of the Senate. But that was delusional. Nothing Simon could say would turn the tide of public opinion in Tanager's favor. Bullock would turn the mob on *him*. Which would spoil any chance—already remote—of following, however modestly, in Galvan's footsteps.

He'd been told to lay low, A man had to do what he had to do.

"Philly. Bussbomb. Something you want to say?"

Lay low. Keep your powder dry.

"Right. What I thought."

They were adjourned. Some men helped move furniture back where it belonged, then sorted themselves into clusters at tables and booths. Bullock came out from behind the bar to work the crowd. Skye took orders. A few men made for the exit.

Chesney grabbed Sy's arm on the sidewalk. "You know he'll be gunning for you now, right?"

"But I didn't say anything," Simon protested.

"True," Chesney said. "But you *thought* it."

* * *

He grabbed a Times from a rack at the Copper Penny. His glove box brimmed with loose change. Loose change was how he'd managed to meet Tanager.

It was September 12. Today's paper, yesterday's news. "Allende Out, Reported Suicide. Marxist Regime in Chile Falls in Armed Forces' Violent Coup."

Banner headline, three rows of uppercase type, above large, side-by-side photos of Augusto Pinochet, the army commander, and the overthrown president.

He devoured the news with his scrambled eggs. Pinochet's military junta claimed it was throwing off "the Marxist yoke." Santiago police claimed Allende had shot himself through the mouth. A close adviser had also supposedly killed himself.

TV's Maureen said Wilhelm Reich was found dead in his prison cell. Sy wondered how many men in Nixon's prisons had officially shot themselves through the mouth, or beat their own heads to a pulp with a nightstick, without making it into the Times.

Freako had accidents all the time. Anything could be made to look like an accident.

Air force jets had bombed the presidential palace and Allende's residence. Scores of socialists and communists had been arrested. Others were ordered to give themselves up. Foreigners were to report to the nearest police station.

The Allende government's newspapers, its radio and TV stations, were to halt operations or be "assaulted by land and air." A state of siege was declared. Violators would be shot on sight.

A communiqué from the junta explained its aim was to "avoid violence and lead the Chilean people along the road to peace."

"The workers of Chile may be certain," assured the generals, "that the economic and social benefits they have achieved to the present will not suffer fundamental change."

Meanwhile, the White House said U.S. intelligence had known a coup was coming. The only question was when. The White House said it wouldn't have warned Allende in any case, as it strove to avoid "interfering in the internal affairs of another nation." The Times conveyed this without irony.

They called the Times the Gray Lady. This was ungenerous. The Times was next-level deadpan, achingly stonefaced as it went about chronicling the fall of the mortal world. It was this stubborn resistance to pathos, this godlike detachment from human frailty, which sharpened the ache. Readers supplied the color.

The Times, the old Gray Lady, was the Buster Keaton of daily journalism.

* * *

The ringing stopped before he'd worked the key into the doorknob. He was barely inside when it rang again.

Sy hoisted the kitten with one hand, grabbed the phone with the other. Esperanza tried to speak. He sat on the floor and she bounced onto his lap.

The next voice was Harold's. Wanting to know where he'd been.

"Stopped at the Wheel. Then breakfast. Just saw the news."

The news was why he was calling. The local angle was Joyce and Edgar had made a narrow escape from Chile. They'd been there a week, checking in on a daily basis. Then nothing. No one had heard from them till yesterday. They'd fled hours before the shooting started, and were unwinding now with friends in Cuba. The group wanted to meet as soon as they made it home.

The Campbells, whose bookstore might never have sold a book, hadn't scrimped and saved to mingle with penguins—Chile boasted a wide variety of penguin species, much beloved by tourists—in another hemisphere. They were not on vacation. Travelers to Chile now weren't your average tourist.

This was doubly true for Cuba. Triply even. Most high-profile American guests of Fidel were airline hijackers and Black Panthers on the lam. Less conspicuous visitors, Sy assumed, included Soviet-friendly camp followers.

So there it was.

The Campbells feared for the lives of colleagues they'd left behind, Harold said, and were awaiting updates in Havana. It took a second for "colleagues" to register.

"Jesus, glad they got out okay. But the others, fuck. Comrades, you said?"

Long pause. "I said *colleagues*. They'd worked together."

"Colleagues. Right."

"So anyway. We need to meet. All of us. Nixon's on the ropes, no telling what he could do. CIA's finished the job in Chile. Generals wrapping up in Vietnam. Idle hands. We need to go on the offensive. Plan is to meet at the store, then have a delegation head out to Mineral, confer with Galvan and his people. Time to get the train moving. How's it going with Tanager?"

A fair question. She hadn't been at the Launder-Eez. He hadn't managed to see her again at the smelter. He was thinking he might phone her for cat-related advice, maybe pay her a social call.

"Not great. Impossible to make contact. She's taking breaks in a trailer, getting a bit of a rep as a company man. I've heard grumbling. Doesn't seem promising, to be honest. I'm working on it."

"Well, keep at it. I'll be in touch."

"Regards to Joyce and Ed."

"By the way, what was that before? On the line. Sounded like a baby."

"Baby cat. Also known as a kitten. Named her Esperanza."

Long pause. "Okay."

He nudged the cat off his lap. He fed and watered her and scooped out her box. Then some fetching practice and off to bed. It was after noon and getting hot again, but he could only crack the windows an inch or two anymore because of the cat. He set the fans where she couldn't reach them, where they were as useless as ever.

She was asleep in no time, nestled in the crook of his arm, oblivious to the heat and sweat. He stared at the bulb in the ceiling till he finally drifted off, thinking how happy Tanager would be, knowing she'd found her a good home.

* * *

Bullock looked like the plague. He hadn't slept. Possibly he'd spent the day at the Wheel, bitching and pounding beers. Or maybe his wife or his squeeze had locked him out of the house and he'd passed the time in his truck with a cooler of Miller High Lifes.

Sy didn't know for sure if Bullock lived with a woman. He couldn't say with total certainty that he had a house. For all Sy knew he lived under a bridge. For all he knew it was London Bridge, now transplanted to a cactus ranch somewhere in Arizona. London Bridge had in fact been falling down, like the song said, sinking slowly into the Thames. An American oil tycoon snapped it up for a couple of million. The granite blocks were numbered, taken apart, shipped to the desert, and fitted together again at the ranch, now doing business as Lake Havasu City.

Sy had never seen a bridge over a lake. Anyone would rather see London than London Bridge. But London was an ocean away. The Atlantic was a continent away. The bridge was practically in the neighborhood.

Maybe Bullock had jumped off the bridge. Maybe he'd been fished out of the lake, kicking and screaming.

In any case the brash emcee from the Wheel was no more. Standing in tonight was this dead-eyed husk of a working stiff, soulless as Sy's pimped-out Mexican skull. Bullock had the vacant look of a sociopath. A hostile work environment was a foregone conclusion.

Sy was parked at the far end of the track. He saw Bullock's two-finger sign, faster than usual, more vigorous. He was shouting. But Sy couldn't make out the words.

He glanced up to see waves of lava lapping suddenly from the upturned mouth of the furnace, crashing down to the tracks. He bounded out of the car and the waves grew thicker and sloppier. Instead of separating from the slag, matte was settling at the bottom like cement, backing up the pipes that churned the mix and forcing a viscous mess out the top. It was the kind of convulsion common to other, more plodding skimmers, those who relied for guidance on unreliable instruments. It never happened with Bullock.

But it was happening now.

Bullock's gyrations had mutated now into a kind of hula dance, broad sweeps of his arms urging Sy back toward the car. Sy stood there, awestruck, imagining himself a sacrifice to the volcano gods. Never in his life, he realized, had he been on the brink of death. The prospect of immolation produced in him a profound rush of yearning, of wanting to live, to experience the joy and anguish of poets and martyrs, of doomed lovers, of Indians and outcasts and holy rollers. People, in short, who weren't from Queens.

The nature of this yearning eluded him, in the moment. What he felt was animal fear. He was terrified of dying, of drowning in liquid fire. He was willing to pray. Or beg. Dignity meant nothing. He did not want to die. Not dying was everything. He psyched himself to take off running, to harpoon anyone who tried to block his escape with a white-hot rod. Fight or flight, whatever survival demanded. Flight being the better option. He was twenty. He could outrun any sonofabitch in the plant, just about. But he never moved. He froze, there in the fiery rain of a boiling furnace, in the waning days of the desert summer.

And suddenly there was Sarge, too, flailing crazily in a cracker Kabuki with Bullock, still waving and dancing. Two corpulent jump-suited men, semi-hysterical, pointing and nodding and dancing him into the path of belching cascades of magma.

He hated them both. He put his head down. Then he was in the car.

There were two bars in the carriage. He aimed and fired. The rods lodged in the tuyeres, trapped between the furnace and the hydraulic rack. He eased out of the car, grabbed a fresh rod, positioned himself next to the carriage. A shotgun spray of metal pelted his arms and torso. He gripped the bar near the axe edge, choking up slightly, and brought it down on the stuck bars. He repeated this till the tuyeres let go and the carriage recoiled with so much force that the unstuck rods—their points melted to glowing stumps—went sailing over the track and down to the crane aisle.

Caterpillar operators salvaged these shiv-like rods for punchers' emergency use. This was clearly an emergency. Sy popped one of his rescued rods into the center slot. The carriage hung up again, then recoiled on its own, less violently this time. This allowed him to stay in the car, behind his plexiglass windshield. He repeated the maneuver, each time pushing the carriage a bit farther out, the spray and the molten waterfall finally ebbing. He saw Bullock tapping his fingers together, the sign for *more*.

The next leg was easier. Bullock gave the signal to stand down.

Sy scooted away. Bullock blew his whistle and rolled the converter out. The break would be brief. Sy ran to the bathroom and had a smoke and tried to compose himself.

These ups and downs formed the warp and woof of the rest of his shift. At last Dr. Hernández came to relieve him. As Sy passed the platform he saw Bullock consulting with Camacho, his own relief, and the whitecap Gilchrest, little blue plastic strips announcing his name from his plastic hat. Briefing them, presumably, on the sorry state of Converter Number Three. Gilchrest nodded in a supervisorial way, jotting notes on his clipboard. Camacho noticed Sy over Bullock's shoulder and shot him a look.

There was no mistaking the meaning.

It was Bullock. Not a damn thing wrong with the furnace.

* * *

He checked a folding map in a bookstore that actually sold books. London Bridge was north of Phoenix, closer to Vegas than Tucson. Another scenic wonder too far for a day trip. And overnights were out now on account of the kitten.

Also: Joyce and Edgar were back. The cadre had scheduled a meeting on Sy's last free day before A shift. So he wouldn't be going anywhere.

Slept through most of day one.

Next day he set out for Fourth. A riot of hair and skin, happy absence of white belts and Stetsons. Weed and women were everywhere. Tucson was a piñata of sun-kissed women—Nordic beauties in halter tops, bronzed *señorítas* speaking in song, a sprawling cornucopia of sweet, hormonal delights. Its bounty remained, thus far, more torment than treasure. But he had a good feeling about Fourth. Fourth teemed with women who liked weed.

Bearded men and horseless Godivas in bib overalls clotted the sidewalk. People sat cross-legged or stood idly or sang and strummed or banged on anything like a drum. A tie-dyed dude played a circus tune on a Woolworth's kazoo. Another beat on a colander with a large wooden spoon, keeping time to the cadences in his head. Panting dogs lay curled in patches of shade or wandered aimlessly, following their noses, sniffing the odd pedestrian and grazing on discarded candy wrappers or remnants of fallen sandwiches. Few were collared. Some shared his brother's taste in bandannas.

He paused to watch a man in a top hat doing tricks with a yo-yo. A dog yipped at the yo-yo throughout the routine, finally lunging outright when the performer "walked the dog." The trick, in which the yo-yo "sleeps" at the end of the string and instead of snapping back rolls forward, along the sidewalk—a dog on a leash—was an old standard, one Sy could do himself. What impressed him was the dog, how it saw only a spinning disk on a length of twine, a thing instead of a metaphor. This disdain for interpretation, it occurred to him, was why people loved animals.

He dropped some coins in the human's coffee can. But it was the dog who deserved them.

The heat rippled up from the sidewalk. Noonish. He felt woozy and must have looked it. A girl squeezed his arm, urging him into the shade. She steered him to a curb where a friend, or maybe her sister, sat with a cup of Italian ices. The second girl offered him the cup but he waved her off.

"It's a gift," the second girl said. "You can't refuse a gift. It's rude."

The first girl still had hold of his bicep. He accepted the cup with his free hand and slurped what was left of the ices, a thick, cherry-red syrup. Cold flavored water. The effect was immediate. The world returned, or he did. Cars and pedestrians, dogs, music. He wiped his hand on his sweat-sticky T-shirt.

The girl let go of his arm and held out her hand for the crumpled cup. She deposited it in a waste bin and sat down beside him. He was flanked by the girls. He scanned their faces, first one, then the other, their eyes obscured by matching red-tinted sunglasses. They both wore shorts and flip-flops, connected by well-tanned thighs and calves and ankles. He stared off at the mountains.

The second girl asked his name. She was his age, give or take, her brown hair tied back, like the first girl, who was blonde. They gave the impression of being twins. But he didn't think they were sisters. They just sort of matched. Their perfect skin lustrous, even here in the shade. Beads of sweat dappled their cheeks like wayward tears.

"Bussbaum," he said. "Sorry, Simon. Thanks. I work in a smelter. You'd think I could handle a little sun."

"No sun at all in a smelter, though."

"True enough."

"I'm Kelsey. This is Julie. So. Freako, huh?"

"'Fraid so."

"That's cool. My brother worked there. Didn't care for it. Woke up one night and decided not to report for graveyard. Next day he joined the army."

He couldn't help but laugh. "The army, damn. He *seriously* didn't care for it."

"Yeah, well. He died."

Sy waited to see if she might be joking. But she wasn't.

"Fuck. Sorry."

"Yeah, well. Thanks. Never made it back, not even his body. But, y'know, hey. Kev craved adventure. I don't guess it was what he expected."

"Nobody expects *that*," said the brunette, Julie. "Probably wishes he stayed at Freako. Although, y'know, then again."

They were all quiet then, staring into their palms. Traffic went by in the wide street, and pedestrians shuffled behind them. After a while the blonde, Kelsey, said, "I wonder if anyone's ever written a song about working in a copper mine. Have you ever heard a single song about a copper mine? I heard one about a coal mine. On the oldies station. Deejay called it 'Workin' in a Coal Mine,' I think. Made coal mining sound, I dunno, not so bad."

Simon nodded. "Lee Dorsey," he said.

"Who?"

"Lee Dorsey, the singer. 'Workin' in the Coal Mine.' Everyone thinks it's *a* coal mine. But it's *the*. Definite article. Anyway, that's his song."

"Lee Dorsey. I thought it was somebody else."

"Who did you think it was?"

"I don't know. Not Lee Dorsey. I never heard of Lee Dorsey."

"He did 'Ya Ya.'"

Nothing.

"Anyway. I work in the smelter. On the surface. Couldn't pay me to go underground, even at a copper mine. Coal's worse. Black lung, cave-ins. But even so."

"What's a ya ya?" Julie asked. It was a good question.

Kelsey shrugged. "Kev worked underground, on contract. Drove a '70 GTO. Fire-engine red. Three hundred seventy horses, zero to sixty in six. Crashed it into a guardrail. Walked away, nobody hurt. Lost his license though. Had to start taking the bus to work. I have his collection of copper ore. There's no coal in Arizona. Everyone knows that."

Sy thought about Jake and the Navajos. Jake was deranged, but Navajos knew coal from copper. Surely Jake had that right.

"No, there is. On Indian land, up north."

Dubious looks all around.

"Don't think so," Julie said. "I've lived here my whole life. Arizona's the Copper State."

It was not, in fact. Arizona was the Grand Canyon State. This was on license plates. But now wasn't the time.

"New Mexico's the Land of Enchantment," said Kelsey. "Nevada's the Lost Wages State."

"The One-Armed Bandit State," Julie said. "*El Estado Ban-dee-to*—how do you say 'one-armed'?"

Kelsey ignored the question. "The Gold Lamé State," she went on. "The governor is Wayne Newton. The state motto is '*Danke Schoen.*'"

"Gold lamé my butt," Julie said. "Gold *lame*'s more like it."

Kelsey laughed and called for a high-five, the girls' hands slapping in front of his solar plexus, their torsos brushing against his arms. It was the kind of move perfected by certain high school girls—*cocktease* was the technical term—and the years had done little to dim its power.

"Nevada's the Mineral State," he said. "Also known as the Sagebrush State." He'd meant this to sound playful, but it came off, even to him, as pedantic and professorial.

"The Mineral State, huh. And you're not even from there, I bet," Julie said. "Where *are* you from, Bussbaum, Simon?"

"Sorry Simon," Kelsey said.

"Simon's good. From New York."

"Thought so. Not many Bussbaums hereabouts. No offense. And here you are, working at Freako."

"Here I am."

"Is it, you know, rewarding? Working at Freako?"

"It's a living, my family would say."

"No, *rewarding*. For your spirit."

"I wouldn't say that, no."

"I wouldn't guess so," Julie said. "Kevin *hated* it."

"We're students," said Kelsey.

"On a spiritual path."

"A spiritual path." Suspecting they might be Moonies.

"Got a smoke, Simon?"

He pulled a flip-top package of Marlboros from his back pocket. There were five or six left, mangled but smokable. He passed one to Kelsey and another to Julie, cupping his hands over the Circle K matchbook as he fired them up. Then he lit one for himself with a separate match.

They smoked in the exaggerated way of teenage girls, taking small puffs and tilting their heads back to exhale. They struck him as not particularly spiritual. More physical than metaphysical.

Julie tossed her smoke into the gutter after a couple of puffs. Then Kelsey tossed hers. Sy went on smoking.

Julie removed her shades. She had big doll's eyes that made her seem younger still. "You look like someone who wants to make the world a better place, Simon."

Things had taken a turn.

"Do you, Simon? Want to make the world a better place, I mean?"

"Um, sure. I guess."

"I thought so." She put her shades back on.

"We're on a spiritual path," Julie repeated. "Why don't you take a drive with us, we can get to know each other better?"

He wasn't sure they were Moonies. It crossed his mind they were hookers, though he'd never heard of hookers working in tag teams. He didn't know much about hookers, really, other than the ones you'd see hanging on Lexington Avenue, streetwalkers in hot pants and heels and elaborate hair. Some of them had been pretty once, probably, but their faces had gone sad or mean or broken-down. Hookers on Lex all looked middle-aged, though they probably weren't. These girls looked more like movie hookers, which was to say not at all.

"A drive? Where to?"

"Big house in the foothills, beautiful. Great hiking. Communal living, you could say. Super people, super caring. Very spiritual. You'd like it, I promise. We have a car."

"Wait, you mean now? Like, right this minute?"

"Right this minute," Julie said. She extended a hand, as if inviting him onto a dance floor. "If you don't like it we'll bring you straight back. Scout's honor."

She was no kind of scout. If they weren't Moonies they might have been junior recruiters for EST, or Scientology, or Manson dead-enders who'd managed to stay out of prison—some had, he believed—and were looking to start a new band. Or maybe their kid sisters, the next generation of drug-addled murdering wack jobs.

They could have been Christians, or Jews for Jesus.

Anyway, he wasn't getting in any car with them.

"Not today, sorry. Not a great time."

"Sorry, Simon," Kelsey said.

"There's never a great time," Julie said.

"But now's really not good. Now's, like, bad."

"Now's all there is," Julie said.

"Maybe so. But my cat needs to be fed. Plus I'm a little wobbly. First day off graveyard."

"Maybe you could get someone to feed your kitty," Julie said.

"I can't, really. She's in hiding."

Kelsey arched an eyebrow past the top of her shades. "Your cat, you're saying."

"The Gestapo's after her," he said. "She's keeping a diary."

"You're funny."

"I'm here all week."

They'd lost the thread. "Well," offered Kelsey, "maybe we'll bump into you. Maybe you'll change your mind."

"Solstice is coming," Julie said.

"Huh."

"You don't know what you're missing."

"Story of my life. Anyway, thanks for the ices."

"The heart that gives, right?" Cryptic smile, seductive and gently mocking. "You look like you're wearing lipstick, by the way. Your kitty may not recognize you."

They took off down the street and he made for the truck. No sign of the yo-yo man or his literal-minded dog. He wiped his lips with his T-shirt. Cruised Tanager's house. A pickup, a beige Datsun, was parked beside a bright yellow Bug, a polished lemon on wheels. It was one of the newer Bugs, rear windshield big enough to see out the back. He stifled an urge to stop. She'd be rotating to graveyard tonight. Maybe trying to sleep.

He'd just reached his place when a song came on. It was in constant rotation, sort of a tongue-in-cheek cowboy tune. Honky-tonk piano, harmonica, high, hayseedy twang. A parody of a hayseed. A group of Juilliard grads, probably, students of Monk or Mozart or the Chicago Art Ensemble, earning their keep with corny lovesick shitkicker ballads about supernatural heat in places with names like Dragoon and Dripping Springs.

He wasn't sure these were real towns. If so they were the last places he ever wanted to go. He had no clue where they might be.

There was no telling about the foothills, either, or the house of super caring people. Tucson was ringed by mountains, foothills wherever you looked. But the girls never said which they meant. Following them demanded an act of faith.

That was the test.

* * *

He half-wished he'd taken the ride. Even the chance of a quasi-spiritual adventure. He stopped off to feed and water the cat, then grabbed a slice and a beer at Fat Mario's.

Mario's didn't serve booze. He wanted booze.

He cruised east on Speedway, a street as wide as the Hudson. He spotted a bar, but this being Tucson you had to drive a long way out of your way before you could turn around. He grabbed a parking spot near a derelict theater, the Palace. The marquee read "Coffy JC Superstar separate admission air cooled." It was barely twilight, the theater just now opening its doors. The bar could wait.

Coffy was in progress. Just him and the projectionist. He took a center seat close to the screen, where Pam Grier's cleavage loomed like a chocolate avalanche. A nurse by training, Coffy turned vigilante to avenge her sister's heroin addiction and rid the ghetto of drug-dealing pimps. A hero's journey, of sorts. Everyone in the movie wore Afros. The soundtrack from *Jesus Christ Superstar* bled through the walls.

The lights came on with the closing credits. An elderly man with a stick began wending his way through the rows of unused seats, searching in vain for Milk Dud wrappers and popcorn bags. The credits rolled over a freeze frame of Coffy strolling thoughtfully down a moonlit beach. She'd just offed her dope-pushing black nationalist lover with a shotgun blast to the crotch.

He still felt like a drink.

The bar was a cowboy saloon, drugstore variety, beards and boots and Western getups. C&W on the jukebox, pool table, couples on dates. A neighborhood joint, filled with regulars. He sat alone at the bar and sipped margaritas till just a handful of regulars remained. Only the bartender had acknowledged his presence, and only to ask what his pleasure was.

He drove home cautiously, signaling every turn and lane change. The lack of traffic made a '49 Chevy an easy target, and he was way overdue for a state-issued license. But he never saw any cops. Soon he was safe in bed with the cat, smoking a roach to smooth his tequila high.

He thought of the Moonie's brother, who never came back from Nam. How he woke up one night and decided, more or less, to give his life to his country.

The kid had worked underground, like Tanager's father. Hazardous duty. But to make him desperate enough to enlist—enlist!—in Nixon's demented, despicable war? It was beyond understanding.

Coffy's truth-and-soul war on smack, on the other hand, that was another story. *That* he could understand.

* * *

Whatever the Campbells saw in Chile—or did—debriefing was on a need-to-know basis. Simon had no need to know.

They were sitting around the table when Harold ushered him through the curtain. Joyce and Edgar looked recovered from their brush with the generals. Sy said he was glad they'd escaped.

"Well," Edgar said. "Others weren't so lucky."

Sy frowned sympathetically. Joyce urged him to take a seat. The body language around the table spoke volumes. Sympathy was misplaced, bourgeois sentiment unwelcome. The forces of reaction were on the march. The cadre was alarmed.

This was why he was here.

Pete drowned his butt in the dregs of his Coke. A dark plume streamed from the bottle, like bad news from the Sistine Chapel.

"*Mijo*, these are difficult times. Nixon will take the wrong lesson from his success in toppling democracy. The rise of the military will embolden him. The disgrace of Watergate will make him desperate. People of good will, who oppose tyranny—it's our duty to fight back."

People of good will. As if this cabal was a civics club, an earnest league of concerned citizens.

"Time to put our shoulders to the wheel," said Joyce, a new urgency in her voice.

Tanager was their dream, their redeemer. She could salvage the movement, and them in the process. This was the fantasy. And what else, really, did they have? There were instruments, and there were instruments. Tanager was a French horn, Sy a kazoo. It was the difference between a symphony and a subway busker.

"We've got her address," Harold declared, a piece of intel he seemed to regard as the key to winning her over. To what end—a workers' paradise, or just the apostles' return to work—wasn't clear. Sy didn't believe she'd sign up to fight for either objective, even if they were achievable. Which he felt pretty sure they were not.

His orders, in any event, were to keep his head down. In a few more months, when he was off probation, Freako could only fire him for cause. Tanager's probation they viewed as a technicality, believing Freako lacked the *cojones* to terminate her for anything short of manslaughter. She was bulletproof, Supergirl in a hardhat.

He would lurk in the shadows, in the cadre's scheme. Tanager, meanwhile, could talk up the return of the cashiered heroes, soon to resume their leadership in the stepped-up struggle to come. At stake were workers' rights, Galvan's legacy, the very dignity of the proletariat.

"We must educate workers to the value of solidarity," Edgar was saying. "This is part of our mission. Anti-Semitism is alive and well in the working class. Racism, alive and well. That's the ugly truth. We can't let our ideals blind us to the facts on the ground.

"But we have to bring them along at their own pace. We're afraid the rank and file's not ready for you, leadership-wise. It's not personal."

"Okay, but Tanager—"

Joyce interrupted his objection.

"—is a woman, yes. So too Mother Jones and Rosa Parks. So too plenty of Freedom Riders and young girls, not even women yet, who forced open the doors to schools in the Jim Crow South. We hope to show Freako workers that Tanager could be their sister, their wife, their daughter. Women are part of their lives. We hope to show them that this one deserves their respect."

Sy ticked off the standard misgivings. The cadre might not fully appreciate the depth of hostility to women at Freako. The company had given Tanager the exclusive use of a Shasta Airflyte camper, a perk which lent her the appearance, from certain angles, of a tool. He and she worked different shifts, limiting opportunities to connect at the smelter.

Also, apart from a puff piece and some random biographical notes, they had barely a clue who she was. They were betting the farm on a blind horse.

"Simon," Joyce said, her tone insinuating he'd missed the point. "We're still, at this stage of our thinking, in the realm of the abstract."

"Which is why we need to speed things along," Edgar put in. "We need to know if she's friend or foe."

And that was that. Sy had his assignment. Harold passed him a sheet of lined paper with Tanager's address. He looked it over, affirmed that he knew the neighborhood, and made a show of folding it into his wallet.

"One more thing," Joyce said. "We're planning that trip to Mineral. We'd like you to join us. We know it's important to you, so we've scheduled it right after your next swing stint. We'll leave after breakfast, not too early, give you a chance to rest up. We'll stay overnight at Naldo's. Have you home in plenty of time for graveyard."

Harold escorted him through the curtain. They said their goodbyes in the doorway. The air was still hot and dry, even as summer drew to a close. But the bells seemed less ludicrous now, more a harbinger of a change of seasons, whatever that meant here in the desert.

"You'll like Naldo," Harold said. "Just don't mention *Emeralds*. José Castillo especially. Bad memories."

Sy promised he wouldn't. He'd have two weeks to scrape the film out of his head. It was a four-hour drive, more or less, to Mineral. Naldo's real-life wife, Teresa, would be cooking them dinner, maybe breakfast in the morning. So likely a long overnight.

He'd have to ask Tanager if Esperanza could fend for herself for a couple of meals. He'd tell her he wanted to check out London Bridge.

If she offered to join him, and the kitten could survive on her own, he could always change his itinerary.

* * *

The Senator Sam show had resumed. Sy watched highlights on public TV while he ate and Esperanza worked on her fetching.

The cat was distressing the rugs in the small hours, while he was on graveyard. And still distressing Mrs. Hardwick, it seemed. She'd been pittering on the bare floor, having moved the rugs out of her way. He hadn't noticed till the landlord called.

Sy suggested it might be mice. Mice were notorious pitterers.

"I'll have to make an inspection," said Willetts.

Sy appreciated his concerns. And now he had some of his own concerns about mice, so the sooner they set a date the better. He also needed a deadbolt. Only now he was working days. Could Willetts get back to him with regard to an evening visit? He was sure the landlord would want him there when he entered the premises, for reasons of liability. He promised to phone the moment he knew his schedule.

Tanager was rotating to nights. This was a stroke of luck. Sy figured he could park the cat at her place for an hour or so, sometime between her pre-shift ablutions and whenever she left for the smelter. Her mother, Rosa García Tanager, and Lainie could help her babysit. Lainie would get a kick at how Esperanza had grown.

He'd hide the litter box—relying on cigarette smoke to mask the lingering fragrance of cat piss—and the kitten's stockpile of toys. Barring allergies, Willetts wouldn't find any evidence of felines when he arrived. Anyway, a rash or a sneezing fit proved nothing.

It occurred to him that the successful execution of this subterfuge might drive Mrs. Hardwick mad. That would be unfortunate.

Gaslighting aside, though, it was a perfect plan. He just had to clear it with Tanager.

* * *

The whitecaps' presence, for once, proved a blessing. Bullock couldn't have his converter constipated and retching lava in front of the brass. So day shift saw the return of the connoisseur of light. Simon was back on Easy Street.

They were five days into the ceasefire when the letter arrived. He recognized his father's handwriting, an oddly elegant cursive, as if penmanship had been the one subject he'd applied himself to. It was addressed to Mr. Simon Bussbaum, which he guessed was how they taught it back in the day.

He'd never received a letter from his parents. He'd never written one to them. They'd had no contact at all since he left Queens. His first thought was divorce.

But they were staying together. They just weren't staying in Queens.

Sy's mother had been mugged.

It was the blacks.

Once he'd extracted this nugget—more like a turd, actually, in a toddler's wading pool—he fed the cat and settled in with a beer. Started again from the top. His father's name and address were written fussily in the upper right corner, per his composition teacher. Just below, to the left, was the date, and beneath that Simon's address.

"Dear Simon," the letter began.

"Hope you're getting along OK in Arizona. It's cooling off here in NYC.

"I'm writing to let you know your mother and I are moving to Florida. Your mother thought you should be informed, in case you should ever decide to write, and because we won't be here if you ever wanted to visit.

"This was a sudden decision.

"Your mother was mugged coming home from the beauty parlor. She was pushed to the sidewalk by a gang of blacks, two or three at least, teenagers she thinks but didn't get a good look on account of them mugging her from behind. They knocked her down and took her purse. The police called me at work. I had to pick her up at the hospital. Her right arm is in a cast so it's TV dinners and takeout.

"This city is a sewer now. Worse by the day. Everybody we know has been mugged. Next week we're finally rid of Lindsay. The papers say Abe Beame. Lindsay we voted for twice but he's no JFK. The blacks like him. But the blacks hate the Jews. They don't know what we went through and for thousands of years. Not hundreds. You and your brother don't want to know. You're a hippie, a Yippie. A flower child. You're against Nixon, against the soldiers, you march for Ho Chi Minh and the blacks to move where they want. I grew up in East Harlem before the Jews moved downtown, out to the boroughs, Long Island, and then the Puerto Ricans took over the tenements where they used to come fix the plumbing.

"My father was a baker. So we always had bread. Bread got me through night school. I earned my diploma and then I could buy my own bread after my father passed. And then for your mother and then for you and your brother. You never went hungry, never wanted for bread or meat either. You had shoes to wear, a roof over your heads. This is the difference from Russia or Poland. My parents left their homelands, journeyed across the ocean, that I might have opportunity. To pull up my bootstraps. Which I did. Despite my sons thinking this makes me some terrible person.

"Land of opportunity. Your mother knocked to the sidewalk and breaks her arm in two places so these punks can steal her purse. Not grand larceny I can tell you. But they should choke on every penny. The police won't even look for them, so many muggings they can't be bothered. Only if it's a murder and even then.

"The doctor says her arm will heal. But she is terrified now to walk by herself two blocks to Waldbaum's for groceries. I put in for a transfer to Miami, we have offices there, and they said yes. The company is paying our moving expenses, on account of I've given them all these years of dedicated service. At first we'll rent an apartment in Hollywood, not the famous one but a nice town, safe, half hour from Miami. Your mother's sister Ruth's daughter married a Cuban, a macher, she lives there now, big house. Ruth spends winters there. So your mother will have somebody to talk to sometimes if she can get a word in edgewise with her sister. Florida is a bargain compared to New York, which sucks you dry for the privilege of getting attacked in your own neighborhood. To get your arm broken by thugs and nobody cares. Maybe we can buy a small house now that it's just the two of us.

"We don't know where your brother is. I believe he's on drugs. I worry he'll land in the street. I don't think your mother suspects. We gave him your address when he left New York, maybe you heard from him by now. I'll send you our new address when we're settled, you can give it to him sometime should you be in touch. Maybe he'll think to send us a postcard.

"Take care of yourself. You don't call or write but we don't expect it. You were always the sensible one. Despite being a Yippee and maybe on drugs too but you had your feet on the ground somewhat. Jake we worried about. Maybe you'll go back to college some day. Get a degree, a career. Some security. You see what's happening. Nixon hates the Jews. Kissinger is a shanda, a disgrace. You may not know we voted for Humphrey, your mother and me. Not for McGovern, who was a peacenik like you and your brother. Picked a mental case for his vice president. But we don't vote for Republicans, not even Rockefeller. Republicans hate the Jews.

"We only wanted what's best for you. It's not so easy. One day you'll see.

"Goodbye Big Apple. Hooray for Hollywood (Florida, haha).

"Sincerely,

"Your mother and father"

This was, for his father, a hundred-year blizzard of language, akin to a manifesto nailed to the door of a synagogue. He was done. The god of the Hebrews dwelled in South Florida.

And so the Bussbaums' plodding, secular exodus was complete. All of them sent from Queens—by muggers, Marxists, or moviemakers—to the promised lands in their minds.

Onward and upward. Sy wouldn't miss the apartment, a cluster of boxy carpeted rooms on the third floor of a sixteen-story slab with percussive radiators and an elevator constantly on the fritz. A psych ward of dreary memories, all that remained of his New York youth. His father made no mention of Sy's collections of comics and baseball cards, which his mother had squirreled away after he left for school. So they were history. He wanted to think they'd donated them, if not to somebody's kid then to Goodwill or the Salvation Army. But he knew they hadn't. He'd bet anything his father had dumped them down the incinerator chute with the rest of the trash.

People paid good money for that stuff nowadays. He'd always meant to remind them.

* * *

Dry air was no match for wet dreams. Sy was bathed in a pleasant fuzziness—all he remembered was Linda Ronstadt—when he noticed the light flooding in through the blinds. He hoisted the cat from the crook of his elbow and found he'd failed to switch on the alarm. It was eight-fifty, nearly an hour into his shift. Too late even to call in sick.

He lingered in bed for a bit, Esperanza resettled atop his chest, kneading and purring and drooling. At a lull in the purring they got up and he spooned some slop onto a plate and refilled her water bowl. Then, drought be damned, he showered until the pressure gave out.

Ninety minutes into his shift he sat down for a leisurely breakfast. He had corn flakes out of a plastic bowl and brewed a pot of coffee in the antique percolator he'd got at the Salvation Army, After breakfast he smoked most of a joint and lay on the mattress listening to top forty tunes on the radio, Esperanza curled in his lap.

And then, three or four hours into his shift—he'd stopped checking the time—the rains came.

He was back in the kitchen now, smoking and staring out at the mountains. The room dimmed and the skies darkened. Cotton ball clouds gave way to slate gray curtains of rain hurtling in from the east. There was a thundercrack, then a flash that cast the mountains and puny skyline into silhouette. After the flash it was dark again. He could just make out modest buildings with dull yellow squares for windows. The clouds grew blacker and closer, stabbed by jagged spears of light incoming from every direction. Drum rolls of gusting rain battered the windows and chased the cat from the room.

The street was an asphalt river, overflowing its banks each time a car sailed by. Soon all traffic had ceased, the only signs of life the misty light in boxy adobe houses and barely visible orange-roofed offices, safe harbors from a storm which no one, at this late date, in a monsoon season marked by a ruinous absence of storms, could have expected.

It was a gift, a glorious surprise. His nerves crackled with inklings of euphoria. He'd had inklings before, but always under the influence, brief spells in controlled environments. He'd assumed substance-free euphoria was reserved for your Joans of Arc, your Bernadettes of Lourdes, your Vincent van Goghs. Not jack Jews from the outer boroughs. He'd had some weed, true. But this wasn't the weed. This was the universe talking.

He threw on his backup coveralls and All-Star high-tops and dug his Salvation Army slicker from a box in the back of a closet. He slipped the oblong hole over his head, reclaimed his watch cap from his groovy Mexican skull, flipped the hood up over the cap. Grabbed a kitchen chair and sailed down the stairs, the poncho floating behind him like Superman's cape.

The rain and wind were relentless. He positioned the chair flush against a windward stucco wall, facing the storm, under the cantilevered terra cotta tiles of the Spanish colonial roof. He noted the location of lampposts and telephone poles and trees, anything tall and rod-like. All those duffers out on the fairways, waving their irons around. Never knowing what hit them.

Each new firebolt made him flinch. The downpour pelted the pavement beyond the eave, dusting his face and tongue with a bracing mist. The thunder coming at shorter and shorter intervals, the nearer the lightning the greater his exhilaration, as if he were witnessing the birth of the world. Or the end of it. But not just witnessing. He was partaking of it, experiencing its power in his blood and bones and soul.

And his loins. He was lusting, he realized, after the universe, horny for all creation. Was this, after all, the secret Wilhelm Reich wanted to share, with his cloudbuster and his orgone box and his cosmic sex energy? Was it portents of boundless, indiscriminate love that had frightened the villagers?

The thunder was now a steady rumble, like a Tommy gun, the lightning rolling and tumbling. A prodigious bolt lit the heavens, then another and another, so fast they blended together and all you saw was a lit-up sky. An illusion of continuity, the way twenty-four frames per second turned into a motion picture. He closed his eyes to take in the sounds of the rain and thunder and rushing water. When he opened them a ten-gallon hat floated by, as if Hoss Cartwright's ghost were riding his trusty steed six feet under the water's surface, taking what shelter it could. And here he was, more alive than he'd ever been, making peace with this beautiful monster storm.

He was nine or so, gazing out on a winter blizzard. A sudden surge crashed through the window into his room. A glass shard ripped a gash in his forearm the shape of a lightning bolt. Paying no mind to

City Hall, which had declared a snow day, his father had gone in to work. His mother had locked herself in the master bedroom.

Jake cleaned the wound with tepid water and paper towels and applied iodine and covered it all in a dozen or so Band-Aids running crosswise along the cut. Then he wrapped his arm in a white cotton pillowcase that absorbed the still-seeping blood in abstract, wine-colored patterns. The grown-up aspirin lived in his parents' room, so he administered four children's aspirin, and when the pain persisted gave him another four. He would have given him more but their father came home and phoned the doctor about him. Then called the super about the window.

Sy was on the couch, starting to doze, when the doorbell rang. Dr. Herschensohn greeted his father, removed his wet hat and overcoat. He set his black bag on the floor and disinfected the wound and sewed it up with eight stitches and replaced the Band-Aids and pillowcase with gauze and a proper bandage. Then he gave Sy something to make him sleep. He praised Jake for his excellent work, addressing him as "young man," and said he'd make a fine doctor.

The gash left a scar in the shape of the Flash's logo, but faint, as if Sy had got a tattoo on a bender and tried to remove it himself. Years later, if anyone asked, that's what he told them it was.

He traced the scar with his finger. The rain had stopped. Azure sky, white clouds, big yellow sun. A child's finger painting. Then a rainbow, a great skybridge over the mountains. Soon the dry desert air returned and the rainbow melted away. He hauled his chair back up the stairs, parked at the kitchen table, and finished the roach. Already the roads were navigable, he could hear the traffic, the city back to its usual rhythms.

He tossed his slicker in the tub and returned to bed. Esperanza came out of hiding. She curled up at his feet, the white of her face and chest obscured, paws over her eyes, a virtuoso of sleep. He reached over and felt her ribs to make sure she was breathing.

It was a meteorological fluke, that splendid storm, the last gasp of the driest monsoon season since Wilhelm got run out of town. Over before you knew it. And too little, too late, experts agreed, to make a dent in the drought.

* * *

One shift to go. Number Three was down. He grabbed a broom and pretended to sweep. Skimmers could furrow their brows and claim to be working, but everyone else had a standing order to look busy on day shift. Most complied by pushing dust around in random patterns, listlessly and pointlessly, the way kids push peas and carrots around their plates. This was the catch to day shift.

Sweeping at least kept him clear of the platform, where Bullock was shmoozing a couple of whitecaps and waiting, apparently, for a ladle of matte. A ceasefire, then, if not détente. Sy was leaning on his broom, contemplating a break, when a claw grasped his shoulder.

He knew it was Sarge. He turned his head, smiled the sad smile of the busted. Sarge half-grinned and crooked his finger. "Come," he said.

Sy followed him to the salt dispenser.

"Goddamn it, Bussbomb." Then words seemed to fail him. He shook his head in despair, or possibly disbelief.

"Overslept. Sorry."

"Sorry don't cut it, son. Sorry and a quarter gets you a cup o' coffee. You need to call if you're not gonna be here, period full stop exclamation point. You don't call, it's a delinquent absence. A delinquent absence puts stress on the unit. That ain't right. Even let's say you don't give a shit about them, think about yourself. A delinquent absence is a blot on your record, a big red ugly blot."

He waited while Simon contemplated the ugliness of the blot.

"You're still on probation, Bussbomb. Shape up. End of lecture."

"Won't happen again. I just overslep—"

"—Stop right there. Don't matter you got hit by a runaway eighteen-wheeler. Your car expires, don't matter. Your *mother* expires, same deal. Find a phone. Whatever it takes. Read me?"

Simon raised an eyebrow, under his metal hat.

"So what have we learned today? Call. That's the magic word. Period full stop. Long as you're breathing, call. You're intubated, laid out in the ICU, you inform your nurse it's a matter of life or death, can she call on your behalf. I'm saying we got to hear from you.

"Number's there on your letter of hire. In the unlikely event you don't have that document framed and hung over the fireplace I can jot it down for you. Keep it in your wallet. Give it to your girlfriend. Work with me here, Bussbomb. Probation's not a damn joke."

"Sorry."

"Screw sorry. You're a good hand, son. Just act like you give a shit. Don't care if you do or not, just work with me here. Now get back to your sweeping. And put your cheeks into it."

He took off and Sy resumed slow-dancing with his broom. Then Bullock rolled the converter in. After a while he motioned Sy to start punching.

They didn't speak. He hadn't spoken with anyone, really, his crewmates worried, perhaps, about guilt by association. Day shift and all. They were seven or so hours in when Bullock poured the last of four ladles of copper and signaled Simon to come and help mud the lip. Sy expected Bullock to ask why he'd missed yesterday's shift. But Bullock kept him waiting until they were done, and he'd whistled to Chief to bring him some fresh matte.

They watched the crane sail down the aisle.

"So," Bullock said.

He stepped to the center of the platform, where he could monitor Chief's progress. "What, like you don't know? That what you're telling me?"

"I'm not telling you anything. Don't know what?"

Bullock's mouth opened wide enough that his chaw was visible. "Christ, Bussbaum, she's *your* lesbian lover. I mean goddamn."

An impulse to violence was tempered by the certainty that Bullock would beat him to a pulp. Plus he wanted to hear about Tanager.

"Say it. Say you don't know."

"What are we doing."

"Humor me. C'mon, say it."

It was a game Sy couldn't win. No point resisting.

"I don't... fucking... know. Happy now?"

Bullock considered this. "I dunno. Not all the way. Happy*ish*. Y'know, not quite there, but in the neighborhood. Like I can smell it, I just can't taste it. There a word for that?"

"What is *smell*." He saw Chief's crane lumbering toward them and contemplated his getaway. "Fuck's sake, Bullock. I'll go ask Chesney." He turned to leave but Bullock grabbed his arm. Sy yanked it away.

"No, hang on. It's just—someone on graveyard left your sweetie a gift."

"A gift."

"Well, kind of, yeah. A rat, the way I heard it."

That tore it. He felt himself starting to shake.

"See what you miss when you're MIA?"

"You *heard* this."

"Everyone's heard it. Everyone that showed up for work. Big news yesterday. Dead rat, Norway probably, decapitated. Doing the backfloat in her *toilette* when she came on graveyard."

He was a psychopath. Or sociopath. Sy wasn't sure of the difference.

"Her *toilette*."

"*Toilette*, right. Her personal crapper. Not a hundred percent sure brown rats can float, tell you the truth, 'specially with their heads lopped off. And the backfloat? I don't think so. Game little dyke, though, Tanager. Back on the job last night, like nothing happened. Then *two* rats last night. Goddamn shame. You hate to see that shit."

Sy was trembling now. His teeth hurt. Bullock was grinning. Arced a mouthful of tobacco juice into the crane aisle.

"I'm told everything's being done that *can* be done to bring the perpetrator—or perpetrators—to justice."

Bullock had done this. He was the mastermind. No telling what came next. Bullock himself had called the smelter a labyrinth, waxed poetic about vanishing into its dark, uncharted spaces. The place was a maze of secret nooks and blind corridors, every shout cloaked in a deafening roar. Perfect setting for mayhem. Dead rats were a warning, a low-rent horse's head under the sheets.

"Fucking psycho," he muttered, not far enough under his breath.

Bullock's expression turned grim. "Fuck you just say?"

Chief clanged a ladle off the rim of the furnace. Bullock was in Sy's face. Sy took a step backward.

"I said you're a psychopath, and to go fuck yourself." He was shouting, but barely heard his own voice over the din. Then he spun and stomped off. Bullock would have his hands full till the end of the shift. Wouldn't need him again. And this last half hour was when the whitecaps melted back into their paperwork. No one would miss him.

He'd hang in the empty locker room, then hightail it to Tanager's.

In the passageway to the showers was a time clock flanked by row upon row of metal slots. Each slot held a card with the name of an hourly worker. An octagonal notice read "Stop! Employees clocking in after the start of their shift or clocking out before the end of their shift will be subject to disciplinary action." Beside it hung a shorter warning, in Spanish, under the word "*¡Alto!*"

The cards were arranged alphabetically. He scanned the Ts. There was a Brian Turley and a Sean Tester, a Trujo, a Thornton, a Thompson. Tanager, most likely, was on the honor system. Only three or four cards separated *Bullock* from *Bussbaum*. Sy plucked Bullock's card and slapped it across his palm. Then he dropped it back in its slot.

It was too early to clock out. He was in the shower when he realized B shift would be passing through in a while on their way to the shop floor. Someone would wonder why he was there, in civvies and ready to go. There would be questions. Dawdling was risky.

But clocking out early was riskier. Better to forget his timecard, plead a brain freeze at the inquisition.

He heard footsteps. He slipped into a toilet stall and tried not to breathe. He heard boot heels on the tile floor. Another stall opened and closed. He gave the intruder a minute to drop his pants and quietly made his escape.

He took the scenic route, the better to dodge inbound pedestrians. The smelter's interior seemed endless, a great dystopic carnival tent with cloistered chambers and secret corridors. But its perimeter made for a longer trek than he'd figured. He'd only been in the belly of the beast. He'd never taken its full measure, just as he'd never taken the time to stand and marvel at the vastness of its surroundings, this drought-parched nowhere in the middle of which, to his wide-eyed amazement, he now found himself.

The complex went on forever. Beyond it, to the east, lay brown rolling hills which might have bordered the mine but might as easily have been New Mexico. The desert played tricks on you, the dazzling austerity, the play of the air and the light. Closer to hand were low buildings and irregular structures he didn't recognize, esoteric varieties of heavy equipment employed in ways beyond his capacity to guess. He did pick out an end loader, a big yellow Caterpillar, and took some solace in this. But it was small comfort.

In three months on the job he'd learned only what he'd wanted to learn. He would have flunked a multiple-choice quiz on how ore was dug out of the earth, how it was then transformed into the substance of pots and pans, electrical wire, statues of liberty and forgotten generals. He had only a primitive understanding, for that matter, of how converter furnaces worked. Punchers had no need to know.

A train snaked out of the emptiness. Tracks ran past the far side of the smelter, maybe forty yards from where he was standing. But he'd never caught sight of the train, which delivered ore from the mine, ten or so miles away, to the crusher. The crusher was either part of the mill or another name for it. Once the ore was crushed it was liquified in flotation cells, where some of the waste sank to the bottom. The tailings got dumped and the company got the copper.

He was sorting this out in his head when the train screeched to a crawl, a dozen or so cars freighted with heaps of rock. It came to a stop near one of the low buildings, the twin stacks looming behind it, peeling the paint off every car and truck in the lot.

He resumed moving his feet. From beyond the parking lot gate he could make out strains of country, resolving, a few paces in, into a vaguely familiar baritone. A lament to an ex-old lady, from what Sy could gather, regarding a new old lady, allowing as to how the new old lady didn't measure up to the ex-old lady, how what he had now wasn't even love, really, but insisting nevertheless—Sy wasn't sure he heard this correctly—that it "wasn't bad."

Marx called religion the opiate of the masses. But he'd never heard country music.

Sy took the source for a car radio, some early bird waiting for carpoolers. Then he saw Bullock, arms crossed, his lower half draped in its orange jumpsuit, leaning against the driver's side door of Sy's truck. Some of Bullock's cronies were there, cranemen Sy knew slightly, mingling with a half-dozen men from different parts of the operation. A few had been at the Wagon Wheel. They lingered around the truck, swigging beer, while drinking songs wafted out of a boom box balanced atop the cab. It was sort of a cut-rate tailgate party. Sy was the guest of honor.

"Gentlemen," Bullock announced, raising his arms in mock homage. "Himself has arrived."

Most of A shift was shuffling into the lot now, headed for home, the Wheel, or their local watering holes. Some, diverted by country tunes and the smell of impending trouble, drifted over to join the gathering herd. There were a few friendly faces. Chesney, looking worried. Gabby too, clutching a small pile of Watchtowers. Witnesses were all right. They didn't salute the flag, didn't believe sinners burned in hell for all eternity.

On the other hand they were pacifists. Pacifists being, at this particular moment, the last thing he needed.

Bullock reached up and killed the music.

"Philly Fucking Bussssbommmm," he said, stretching it into a paragraph. "Wait, 'Fucking' ain't right. I forget, what was your middle name again? Junior? Julius? Sounds like?"

Sy tried to make himself big. It was what you did with a grizzly, he thought. Either that or play dead.

"Get away from my truck."

Bullock put a foot on the running board, ran a hand along the edge of the bed, patted the spare tire attached to the side. Adjusted the mirror and combed his hair.

"Oh, this your truck? Is that an order?"

"It's a request."

"Denied. I asked you a question."

"I heard you."

"Definitely starts with a 'J.' Say it."

"I'm not looking for trouble."

"Were you looking for trouble when you called me a psycho? What about that, Jewboy?" He paused like a man in the throes of a revelation, then turned and raised his arms to the crowd. "Joo-*boy*! Joo-*boy*!"

He heard rumblings of approval. He pretended, without conviction, they were for him, for calling Bullock a psycho. This sniff of fictive heroism puffed him up. As if he'd stood up for Tanager's honor, the way Jimmy Stewart stood up for Shinbone's in *Liberty Valance*.

The man who *really* shot Liberty Valance proved to be John Wayne, the Duke, not Jimmy Stewart. But reality, for the put-upon people of Shinbone, wasn't the point. Shinbone needed a hero, was the point. When the legend becomes fact, as they said at the Shinbone Star, print the legend.

Simon needed the Duke, the Hollywood hero. What he had was Chesney and Gabby.

"I don't care what you do to me," he said at last. This wasn't remotely true. "But why can't you leave her alone?"

Bullock raised his arms in appeal. "Y'all hearing this? Bussbomb here's accusing me of bothering his sweetheart. Who digs girls. Which means—College, are you a man or a girl?"

He'd edged a bit closer. If Sy made the first move Bullock could waste him in self-defense. Yet failing to act meant humiliation.

Check and mate.

"Maybe you just got a thing for hot lesbian love? Maybe she lets you watch. That it? You get off to sweaty babe-on-babe action? You one o' them *lesbros*?"

Sy hated him with a passion. Was *lesbros* even a word?

Bullock spat a loogie of Red Man near his feet, re-crossed his arms. Daring him now to slug him.

Sy took a step backward. "Big he-man, afraid of a girl." He sounded like he was nine. "For fuck's sake, Bullock. I don't want to fight you. I just want to go home."

Bullock spat again. "Go the fuck home then. You don't belong here. Lesbian chicks and Jewboys, Jesus. Go the fuck home. Goddamn fucking pussy. You're not a man, Bussbaum, you're a pussy. Probably what she sees in you."

They were past the diplomacy stage. With his coveralls halfway off, drooping from his extravagant gut, Bullock looked like a low brick wall with a large, angry man standing behind it. No way could Sy end-run him, fetch his keys from his pocket, open the door, clamber into the cab, start the engine—which required mashing a button on the floor, usually more than once—and escape unmolested. As ideas went this ranked as uniquely counterproductive, bordering on self-harm, but at least Sy could blame it on Bullock. He'd just told him to go home. A profoundly stupid idea. But he couldn't think of a better one.

He made for the truck.

Bullock didn't stand in his way. Instead he employed a toreador's move, or a square dancer's, taking one step sideways and launching Sy into a U-turn. Sy landed hard, belly and face first, on the pebbly ground. Palpated his face to assess the damage. He didn't feel any blood, but something akin to a topo map was colonizing his forehead. The terrain of his palms had gone cracked and lumpy.

"Get up," Bullock said.

"What's wrong with you." Not getting up.

"You said you wanted to go home. So go the fuck home. Nobody wants you here. We don't need smartass little college boys. And we don't need your dyke girlfriend. Go the fuck home."

Bullock looked to the dregs of the crowd to confirm his victory. He took a step toward the truck, the boom box perched on the cab. Sy stood up, slowly, to find Bullock had lost interest in him. He was laughing it up with some of his courtiers.

Now or never.

Sy hurled himself at the big man, intending to jump on his back, somehow gain the advantage. Or not *intending*, as cognition had yielded to pure animal rage. Thinking never came into it.

Bullock heard him approaching—the crunch of pebbles under his feet—and wheeled around as he drew close. But he didn't block or tackle him. He reprised his bullfighter's move, dancing sideways and shoving Sy in the back with enough force to boost his momentum into the driver's-side mirror. The round iron frame impressed itself into his face, upper right quadrant, beginning somewhere north of the eyebrow and traversing the bridge of his nose. His eye was throbbing and blurry and basically useless. The collision of nose on frame had kept it from cracking the glass. So maybe his sight would return. His nose felt ruined.

Bullock loomed above him. Reached over and grabbed his boom box.

"Fuck you, Bussbaum," he said. "And your dyke girlfriend, too."

Then he walked away, along with the last of the peanut gallery. Sy heard the crunching of pebbles, was how he knew.

Then voices. Chesney was there, asking if he was all right. Also Ozell, Big O from the Wheel. They grabbed his elbows and helped him to his feet.

"Well," said Chesney, "you're not dead."

He tried to smile. "Reckon I scared him off."

Ozell lit a couple of unfiltered Pall Malls and handed him one. It gave him the world's shortest-lived buzz.

"Gonna scare everyone off, way you look." He took a drag, exhaled, sized him up. "Might want to see a doctor about that face."

Chesney let down the tailgate and they guided him to the truck. They sat on either side of him, like bookends, as if he needed propping up. They sat and smoked, the three of them, watching the cars and trucks clear out of the lot. Gabby conspicuous by his absence.

"You do look like hell," Ozell confirmed.

"He always looks like hell," Chesney said.

Ozell tossed his butt and he and Chesney tossed theirs. Ozell put out his hand. Sy's was tender but he rolled with it.

"We never met. They don't let me out of my crane much. Ozell. Call me Zell."

"Simon. Call me Sy."

Chesney saw they were waiting.

"Ruben. Call me Chesney."

The sun was a great red ball on the horizon, the smokestacks' shadows stretching across the lot. He remembered Tanager, how he'd meant to sneak off and check on her. She was why he'd gone into battle.

"I should hit the road," he said.

Ozell held up a hand." How many fingers?"

"None with my right eye. Three with the left. So I'm gonna say three. Right eye's only good for depth perception. Probably good enough to gauge the curves."

"Probably," Chesney said.

Ozell's expression turned serious, as if figuring the odds. "I'd go straight home now, I was you, put some ice on that. Then get to a doctor."

They stood up and Chesney pulled the tailgate closed.

"Nice wheels," Ozell said. "What is this, 'forty-seven, 'forty-eight?"

"'Nine."

He peered into the cab. "Gun rack's just for show, I guess."

"Bussbaum's new around here," Chesney said.

Sy got in and revved the engine. Ozell came to the open window.

"Hey, man, fuck 'em. Bunch o' damn frat boys, only minus the education. Bullock's the only one looking to mess with the girl. Pretendin' we're some fucking brotherhood, united in all this beautiful blue-collar solidarity. And all the time he's fencing Cuban cigars to the brass. Be gone in five minutes, guaranteed, anyone offered him a nine-to-five gig in an office. Same for the rest of us, just about, me included. You see what it's like. Nobody's here that's got other options."

He thumped the top of the cab by way of a sendoff.

"No lie, man, fuck Bull. Fuck 'em all. Tell you a secret. Everyone but his posse of good ol' boys—the ones come to watch you get horsewhipped—sees right through Bull. Fuckin' Bull, man. That's why they call him that. Most of us just smart enough not to get crosswise with him. No offense. You understand what I'm sayin'. Bunch of motherfucking sheep. Go home and sleep it off."

Sy let out the clutch and pulled away. Through the engine noise and the crunch of the tires he heard Ozell's voice. He could just make out his shape in the mirror.

He was yelling, cupping his mouth with his hands. "Bull ain't shit," he was saying. "Anyone asks, you say Big O told you so."

* * *

First stop was the Circle K bathroom. Above the sink hung a slab of polished metal, less a mirror than a piece of conceptual art. The dull reflection might have been anyone's. He, Simon Bussbaum, was unrecognizable, gone to a murk of form and color.

His face was an ache that began in his head and percolated down to his viscera. His shoulder hurt and his legs wobbled. He wanted to sponge off his surface wounds, but the room lacked a towel dispenser. There was only one of those spring-loaded, continuous roll cabinets with a single, nonremovable length of cloth. The bin was mounted at chest level, where a taller man's solar plexus would be. You had to bend over to dry your face.

The used portion of the towel curled into a loop and got fed back into the bin. A decal warned you not to put your head in the loop. What gruesome decapitation, Simon wondered, had so unsettled Circle K's underwriters and corporate lawyers? The victim's days had been numbered, surely, given the childlike range of his curiosity. But he might have had kids himself, a wife, a mother. You didn't want to think about it.

Anyway, Sy had his own problems.

He opted instead for toilet paper, moistening it in the sink and gently blotting his face. Then he donned his shades and bought a coffee to go. The clerk never blinked. Sy found this encouraging.

The feeling was short-lived. Seeing his face in the truck's glass mirror—the very one that had rearranged it—jogged him back to his senses. The clerk's indifference meant nothing. Indifference was baked into the company culture, as integral to the brand as convenience itself. Nothing to do with him.

Ozell was right. He looked like hell.

His eye was swollen closed. Traffic would be barely a trickle now, which was good. On the other hand, he'd be driving into the psychedelic glow of another enchanted sunset. Rapture, he'd found, was a hazard when driving. He stayed in second gear and rode the brake, his line of sight ranging from the cool of the banded sky to the last flares of the sinking sun. He thought to temper the whiplash by flipping the radio on. But the soundtrack ruined the moment. The moment demanded silence.

He pictured the truck, blurrily, in an aerial tracking shot. A small blue dot inching along a mountainside, bearing him through the desert.

A wandering, one-eyed Jew. He seemed to recall a Brando movie called *One-Eyed Jews*. But there wasn't a soul in Hollywood Jewy enough to back a movie called *One-Eyed Jews*.

One-Eyed Jesuits? Jains? Jehovah's Witnesses? Then it came to him. *One-Eyed Jacks*. He wasn't sure if he'd seen it. He wasn't sure anyone had.

He wasn't sure of anything. Which card was the one-eyed jack, and which the suicide king? And why would a melancholy monarch choose to run himself through with a sword? Why not have some servile courtier pour poison into his ear while he slept in his garden, say, as Claudius did to Hamlet's father? Or maybe an asp, like Cleopatra?

Was Nixon on suicide watch?

The twilight, too, could mess with your mind.

And then, in an instant, he was back on planet Earth. Back in his body, behind the wheel of his old blue truck. It was terror that did the trick. As he reached for his coffee, he failed to detect a curve, regaining the road just in time to thwart his own certain death, a demise more harrowing than a blade to the throat. He was seized by a sudden mindfulness of his sphincter, and he felt his blood beating against his temples. He slowed some more and dialed in a classical station. Because he'd swerved left, the coffee had all spilled on the passenger side. So his lap was mercifully dry.

Still: no coffee.

The pain came in waves. He was exhausted, craving caffeine—or, better yet, a dexie from Dr. Hernández—and only the mix of affliction and fear of death was keeping him awake. Suddenly, here beyond Freako's gravitational pull, the road uncoiled, and he spotted a small overlook he'd never noticed before. He eased off the road and parked by a weather-beaten plaque and a busted telescope. The plaque was a historical marker, one of those greenish rectangles with the telltale curve at the top, all but illegible through the dirt and bird droppings. He recognized Mount Lemmon, its crest poking out of the darkness. The Tucson skyline, such as it was, fluttered in the distance, the city lights winking in the mountains' shadows. He tried to guess, pissing and smoking there in the gathering dark, which came from Tanager's house. He sat on a large rock, his good eye staring vacantly into the valley. Then he drifted off. He snapped to when his chin hit his chest, the cigarette burning at his feet.

Soon he was moving again. There was a pleasant breeze through the windows, Creedence blasting from the radio, and before long the road widened and leveled off and he picked up the pace. A jingle warbled "KTKT, channel 99," and a deejay urged him to keep it right there. Upbeat beyond reason. Overnight temps would be dipping to sixty-eight, but would flirt with a hundred again by mid-morning. "Sixty-eight" was punctuated by the sound of chattering teeth.

Sy switched off the radio. He crossed a dry riverbed and then Wetmore Road and then he was in Tucson. He detoured onto a street of modest adobe homes and pulled to a curb to light a smoke.

Tanager's block was tranquil and well-lit. Colored rocks sparkled in cactus gardens bathed by flood lamps, the only suggestion of motion. He parked across from her next-door neighbor so as not to be visible from her windows. The beige pickup and lemon Bug were both in the driveway.

He checked his face in the rearview. His cheekbone was the color of charcoal, vaguely vampirish, and beneath his disfigured eye hung a hideous purplish saddlebag. His nose looked askew. He took a comb from his pocket and raked his hair, but this only showed off the bruises. It was too dark to wear shades. Nothing to do but ring the bell.

Quasimodo, as played by Mr. Potato Head.

He paused on the doorstep. The TV was on, muffled hysterical voices, canned laughter, random musical flourishes. Ringing the bell seemed intrusive now so he rapped on the door. Stepped back, noticed the knocker. He tapped twice and waited. Finally he pressed the bell but he didn't hear it ring. Tried the knocker again. The voices died down and Tanager materialized in the doorway.

She wore shorts and a faded T-shirt. The shirt said "Armadillo World Headquarters" and featured a drawing of a globe supported by a pair of the weird little creatures, armored mutants halfway between rodents and shellfish. What looked like a two-headed armadillo rested on top, and the two on the bottom appeared to share a tail that was striped like a cat's but shaped like a rat's. Simon guessed the place was a club of some kind.

The logo felt like an opening, a key to the mystery of her recent whereabouts as well as her personal interests, who she was when she wasn't whaling on anodes or doing her laundry. But you could only steal glimpses of women's T-shirts, you couldn't plumb their depths. Her feet were bare and her toenails turquoise. She beamed with a funky magnetism, an irresistible ease she radiated even at Freako, even weighed down by a hardhat and coveralls and metatarsal guards strapped to her steel-toed boots. Yet something was different about her, here at the threshold of this little duplex, her mother, Rosa García Tanager, and Lainie inside, the faint aroma of fresh tortillas wafting out from the kitchen.

She scrunched her eyes and cocked her head for a better angle. Sy couldn't tell if she was more shocked by the state of his face or the presence of his entire person on her doorstep.

She clasped her fingers on top of her head, weaving them into her choppy hair. She'd removed the ring from her thumb. Her earrings were gone. Another garish Sonoran sunset had bit the dust. Her shift would be starting soon.

"Bussbaum, wow. Holy crap."

"I think your bell might be on the fritz."

"Yeah, well. I think *your*s is."

She crossed her arms and crooked her neck. Her neck was long and brown, set off by the yellow of *Armadillo.* "You okay?"

"Been better."

She let out a tortured laugh, a small spasm of disbelief. "Christ, Bussbaum. You look like a bruise." She pushed the door open. "Okay, come inside. Watch your step."

Lainie sat on the living room floor, bathed in television light, talking baby talk to her kitten. This was the way she talked to everyone, he supposed. The set was tuned to The Price Is Right.

Tanager pointed him to the sofa, walked over and whispered in Lainie's ear. Lainie managed a sort of greeting and toted the kitten away. Tanager turned off the set and dragged a beige ottoman from its place opposite an overstuffed chair that faced the TV. The ottoman had a removable top and rattled with what were probably Lainie's toys. Tanager hunched at the lip of the lid, elbows on knees, chin propped on her thumbs, fingers laced over her mouth.

"And... so?"

"Kind of a long story."

"Make it the Reader's Digest version. We're about to eat. Last night of graveyard."

She had a New Yorker's directness, but with none of the bitter aftertaste. A lived-in face, relaxed but alert. She struck him as fetchingly disheveled.

He met her two large eyes with his one open one.

"I heard about the rat," he said. "Rats, I mean."

She laced her hands behind her neck and rolled her eyes. "Fucking hell, Bussbaum. These people are more scared of me than I am of a damn rat. Dead *or* alive. Anyway, it was only one."

"Bullock told me two the second night."

"Bullock," she said. "Fuck's sake, Bussbaum. There *was* no second night. We changed the lock after I found the first one."

She indicated his face. "That what this is about? Were you defending my honor?"

"I wouldn't put it like that."

"Good."

"It's between me and Bullock, really. So... you know Bullock?"

"Everyone knows Bullock. One-stop shopping for hot hams, embargoed cigars and headless rodents."

"He thinks I'm taking your side. Now he's gunning for both of us."

"And *are* you? Taking my side?"

He nodded.

"Well, thanks for that. I mean, I don't really have a side. But thanks for taking it."

A door creaked open. He heard Lainie babbling contentedly. A strange woman, gray T-shirt bearing the legend "Property of Dallas Cowboys," swept in, clutching the flouncing girl by her hand. Tawny and heavier-set than Tanager, a bit younger, long black hair streaked with orange. The kitten scampered ahead and Lainie slipped free and scampered after it.

"Val," Tanager said, waving her over.

Val joined them, grazed the back of Tanager's head in a way that was playful but also, it seemed, not.

"Valerie, Simon Bussbaum. Simon, Valerie."

A wary, half-hearted nod.

"He's been better."

"Hope so. Nice to meet you."

"Emergency meeting," Tanager said. "Won't be long."

Valerie nodded again, knelt down to Lainie's level. "C'mon, Swee'Pea," she said. "Let's play outside for a bit. Kitty's having her coffee break."

The kitten had sought refuge under a weathered sideboard. Lainie was on all fours, trying to follow. Valerie reached down and the girl quit the hunt and took her hand and they stepped out to the front of the house.

He and Tanager sat in silence, listening to the swamp cooler.

"Valerie, she's your sister?"

The question prompted a sad, tolerant smile. "No, Bussbaum. Not my sister."

They did not, in fact, look like siblings. But then Sy didn't much resemble Jake. As a kid he held to the hope they'd been adopted from separate orphanages, and so were genetically distinct both from each other and from the grown-ups claiming to be their parents.

"Unless you mean sisterhood is powerful. Because in that case."

His face fell a little, in the places that weren't damaged.

"But that's not what you meant."

This was true.

"We live together."

"Gotcha," he said.

"We're not roommates, you understand. We *live* together."

"Right," he said, wanting to head off further clarification. "You're saying you don't *live* together, you *live* together."

Tanager leaned forward now, stern but sympathetic, the good cop taking a solo turn in the interview room. The kitten, divining the absence of toddlers, had emerged from its secret location. It was the white and brown one with the Devil Dog swirly coat. It didn't remember him, or Esperanza either, probably. Expressed its will punily but tenaciously till Tanager hoisted it onto her lap.

"That's what they say about me, isn't it?"

Sy construed the question as rhetorical.

"It's okay. You won't hurt my feelings."

"Well, yeah, I guess. Some."

"But not you."

 "Not me."

"Because you didn't believe it? Or you didn't care?"

"Both."

 "No sale. Gotta pick one."

"I didn't believe it. I didn't think it's a sin, like you're not moral enough to work with Bullock. I just didn't think it was true. I really don't care."

Her laugh lines came out. "Not even a little?"

He was busted, then. "Maybe a little."

The kitten sprang from her lap and scampered off.

 "I mean, I don't think they believe it themselves, really. Even Bullock. It's just how they are. Not everyone. But enough. Neanderthals are the real Americans. We've got a skimmer called *Dago,* for god's sake."

The mention of Dago cracked her up. Teeth like a toothpaste commercial. Sy wished he could stop talking.

"And he *likes* it. Crazy. You should hear what they call *me.* All they know is what they know. They're... limited."

"And you?"

"I'm more—surprised."

"Surprised."

"Apparently."

"'Cause I'm raising a kid? 'Cause my ex had a Y chromosome?" She paused, registering what she'd said. "Hey, c'mon. my ex had a Y? That's funny."

He supposed it was. But his face was throbbing again. He studied the nap of the oatmeal carpet, which oozed from under a Mexican rug that anchored the room like a woolly planet. The rest of the room in its orbit.

"My husband. Big brown man, joined the army to save America from small yellow men. Not even drafted. He *enlisted*. To stop the dominos falling. See where that got him. And me. *And Lainie.*" Lost in a brief reverie. "You don't have a girlfriend?"

He shook his head.

"Well, you're at a disadvantage, this part of the world. You're not bad to look at—I don't mean now of course, now you're a freakin' horror show. But last time I looked. And not many guys would do that for a stranger. Getting your brains bashed in like that. That was brave. Stupid, but brave. It's just you're no cowboy. Not even a half-breed Meskin like myself. You're more, I dunno, exotic. And chicks hereabouts, they're not big on exotic. Same as the smelter. 'Round here it's cowboys and bikers, tattooed gun-totin' studs, especially them can hold their whiskey."

"Not you, though."

"Me what?"

"Don't swoon for cowboys?"

"Bussbaum." She scooched forward, close enough that he could smell her shampoo. "I am *so* over cowboys."

She smelled like coconuts.

"I wrote a song about it," she said. "Me and Val started a band."

"Huh. Got a name?"

"'So Over Cowboys.'"

"The band, I meant."

"Ah. Churchy La Femme. Turtle from 'Pogo.' You know 'Pogo'?"

"'We have met the enemy,'" quoting the possum, "'and he is us.'"

"Amen."

"Amen."

"We've got a few gigs lined up. Just bars in town. Passing the hat. You should come check us out."

"I'll do that."

"Great."

"Sure."

He broke off eye contact. Then he raised his hands and let them drop to his thighs, the kind of stupid comical double-palmed slap employed by Pa Kettle when he'd finished his supper.

"Well," he said. "I should go."

"You should go lie down. Have a drink. Have the drink first."

She walked him to the door.

"I'm still worried about what he'll do, y'know. Bullock."

"You think he's gonna mess up my face?"

"No, not that. He didn't even hit me, technically. I'm just an idiot."

"No cure for idiocy," she said. "I'd put some ice on that face, though. I think your nose might be broken."

"Could be."

"See you 'round the smelter, Bussbaum."

"Guess so. Have a good shift." Trying for nonchalance. "Can I ask one question?"

She sighed. "Okay, but just one."

"Paper said you'd left town. Where? And why'd you come back?"

"That's two questions."

"Maybe just answer the second?"

"And that's three."

"Okay, pick any two."

"We were in Austin. They evicted my mom when my father died—company won't let you stay in their shitty little town if you're not on the payroll. I came back for a month, rented this place with money she got from insurance. Also a small widow's pension. Her sister lived nearby, so I went back to Texas. Then her sister, my maiden aunt, got herself married. Family, right? You only have one mother."

"So they say."

They stood in the doorway. Val and Lainie sat in the lemonade Bug, singing along to the radio. Tanager waiting for him to leave.

"Something else?"

"Just that I know some people who'd like to meet you."

"Some people."

"Union organizers. Old school. You'd probably hate them."

"Probably right," she said. "I don't do politics, really. Anyway, I'm a short-timer. This town, this *job*—all of it—it's a temporary condition."

She indicated the logo across her breasts with a flourish like a magician's assistant, conjuring for him the sweet torment of closer inspection.

"Val and me, we're back in Austin soon as we've got the down payment on anything with a roof. Bringing mom with us this time. Not sure about playing the Armadillo. Armadillo's Carnegie Hall. But Austin's rolling in clubs, grab your guitar and go. You can keep Tucson. Definitely keep Freako. Freako killed my father. Who was not a good father, for the record, or a husband either. But they bled him dry. My mom more so. Freako's a death sentence. Give me a firing squad any day."

He passed the Bug on the way to the truck. He waved a tentative goodbye and Val returned it. She didn't make Lainie wave. He sat in the truck and watched as she got out and walked round to the passenger side and lifted the girl over a shoulder and carried her giggling into the house. He kept watching, as if making a picture in his mind, until his mind began to hurt again and he stomped on the starter.

He heard Esperanza mewing as he fished for his key. When she'd had her fill of affection he checked the freezer, bare save for the dregs of a pint of Rocky Road and his empty, second-hand ice cube tray. He fetched the aspirin from the medicine chest and chased a fistful of pills with a Dos Equis. Then he sampled a joint, made short work of the ice cream, and collapsed onto the mattress.

It was good medicine. The fog in his eyes was lifting, and his synapses seemed to be firing again. His last thoughts, as he drifted off to sleep, were of playing cards.

There were two one-eyed jacks and a one-eyed king. "One-eyed jacks, man with the axe"— only the king of diamonds, the one-eyed king, wielded an axe. All the others had swords.

The suicide king, he seemed to recall, was based on some French monarch, a Louis or Henry—no, a Charles—who was driven mad by his son's betrayal. But he didn't kill himself with a sword. He starved to death.

The suicide king was hearts.

* * *

Sunrise. Esperanza in the crook of his elbow. He'd slept in his clothes. Day shift, blessedly, over and done. But he didn't feel blessed. The shocks of the previous day had congealed into a low-grade depression, the same overwhelming gravity he'd felt when he first set foot in the smelter. He couldn't will himself up from the bed.

Aspirin was the motivation he needed. He fed the cat and brewed some coffee, regarding his face in the percolator while he waited. Its convex surface produced a mild funhouse effect, adding warp and puffiness to his eye and nose. But the distortion was incremental. It was his actual face that was frightening, not just its reflection in a kitchen appliance.

He was drinking his second cup when he remembered the landlord. He'd said he'd arrange a visit when he was on day shift again. That was a week ago. Willetts would be growing impatient. But Simon couldn't let him find the cat in the apartment, violating the rental agreement.

This would be tricky now. Plan A had been Tanager. There was no Plan B.

* * *

He was watching a rerun of Sesame Street. It was the episode where the Cookie Monster got amnesia and thought he was a mailbox. Brought to you by the number twelve and the letters Q and X. Bob was about to read a story, "The Queen's Questions," when someone rapped at the door. The kitten hopped off his lap and pranced into the bedroom. Sy was sure it was Willetts.

"Mr. Bussbaum," he confirmed. "I can hear your TV. Please open."

He lowered the volume but left the set on. He'd blame any illegal sounds on Bert or Ernie or the letter Q. The door being flimsy, they spoke in normal voices. "I've been meaning to call you, sorry," Sy told him. "I'm not well."

"Please open the door."

Sy trapped the cat in the bedroom, then cracked the door just enough for Willetts to appreciate his condition. "I'm not supposed to have visitors for a few days. Doctor's orders."

Willetts was dubious. Sy thought he might ask for a doctor's note.

"What happened to—"

"Industrial accident. They think it's a concussion. Also contusions, which you can see for yourself. I don't remember how it happened, exactly. But I'm supposed to stay off my feet."

"You don't remember?"

"Not all the particulars. Blacked out. Memory's fuzzy. That's why I forgot to call you."

"When was this?"

"Two, three days ago? Hard to say. Math gives me a migraine. Can you come back in a few days, when I'm on swing? Before two or so would be good."

"You're returning to work, then?"

"Company doc cleared me. Two more days of rest, three at the most. If you could come back Monday, say around noon, that'd be great."

Willetts peered at his face, then directed his gaze over Sy's shoulder for signs of unwanted occupants. From this vantage point the landlord's mole looked more like a water bug. He stepped back from the door to consult his appointment book.

"Tuesday at noon. Second of the month. Have your rent check for me, please, no need to mail it. You haven't mailed it yet?"

Sy shook his head.

"Fine. And Mr. Bussbaum, this is your final warning. I can't put this off any longer."

"I understand, thank you. I wish we could resolve this today."

"We'll resolve it on Tuesday."

He did, in fact, feel terrible. He let the cat out and they fell asleep to Mr. Rogers' Neighborhood.

Dreamt he was trapped in a mailbox.

* * *

Next morning he threw on some clothes and lumbered downstairs for the mail. A game show was on in Mrs. Hardwick's apartment. Joyless laughter and the voice of The Newlywed Game's unctuous emcee. Mrs. Hardwick had possibly been one, a newlywed, in the long-ago. Perhaps she took solace from arch young couples debasing themselves for kitchenware and Samsonite luggage. Maybe it took her back to her own marriage, however tragic or loveless or humiliating, when her life was bigger than pittering. The TV was the only sound he'd ever heard coming from her apartment.

Amid the junk was a manila envelope bearing three eight-cent stamps. The stamps showed the American flag flying over the White House, and were affixed upside-down. The postmark said Flagstaff. The return address was "Indian Country."

Inside were a dozen or so loose Polaroids. Sy poured them out on the kitchen table. Most were under- or overexposed, instant cameras no doubt challenging Jake's patience and technical skills. Composition seemed not to have crossed his mind. Desert and red rock at odd angles, parts of hogans with rounded roofs, plain one-story houses, some with TV antennas, others with roofs, presumably, out of the frame. A few featured people, mainly Navajos, posed portraits of families spanning three and four generations and snaps of random indeterminate gatherings. Some of the younger men made goofy faces or raised their fists. The girls more sedate, embarrassed by the attention. There was a shot of older men in flannel shirts and cowboy hats, some of them clutching shotguns, and another of ancient women, gray hair pulled back, older than the oldest men, cooking or weaving on looms. One showed Jake shearing a sheep.

And there was one of a bunch of white kids, not including Jake—he could never have managed a self-timer—standing beside a teepee. They had deeply serious faces and held aloft a banner made from a bedsheet. The message was scrawled in red paint: "Free Big Mountain, Peabody Out of Black Mesa."

And, finally, a note, printed in pencil on a three-by-five index card. "Greetings," it said, "from Mother Earth's liver."

* * *

Swing caught him up short. Maybe he did have a concussion.

Crews got only a single day off after A shift now, followed by swing the day after that. Which, suddenly, was today. No way was he going to work. His face was healing, but he felt morose and headachy. The minute Sarge saw him, bruises barely noticeable under his thick glasses and hardhat, he'd want to grill him about not clocking out. Sarge had to know what had happened. Even so, Sy had a brighter future as a liar than as a narc. Especially where Bullock was concerned.

Then there was Bullock. He wouldn't be done with him yet.

The contract gave you two consecutive sick days before you needed a doctor's note. Sy called the number on his hiring letter, as Sarge had suggested, to report his unfitness for duty. The woman who answered the phone—the same woman he spoke to when he called from New York—asked him the reason. He told her "unspecified," adding he hoped he'd be back tomorrow.

He did not hope for this. Likely he wouldn't be ready the shift after that, either, though for reasons more mental than physical. But this was beside the point. The point was he'd need a doctor. The only doctor he knew was Dr. Hernández, his pot dealer, who might be as competent as company docs but lacked an M.D. after his name. Freako's hired guns got paid to keep workers on the job. With sight returned to his eye, though, even the most reputable physician would clear him for active duty.

His best option was to forge a convincing doctor's note. But the one man he knew with the juice to produce a professional forgery, naturally, was Bullock.

He'd think about it tomorrow. He needed a rest. Today was a holiday. He celebrated with aspirin and beer. Parked in front of the TV with his copy of *Ten Days*. One-paragraph introduction by Lenin himself. A preface from the author, John Reed, made clear he'd observed the tumult from ground level, from the outside looking in— and, the uprising being a scattershot affair, he'd only been privy to fragments—and from the perspective of a proud American Bolshevik. He stood against the bourgeoisie, the warmongers, the industrialists, the landlords, the Tsarists, the Mensheviks, the right-wing socialists, most of the left-wing socialists. The Russian masses and their glorious Leninist revolution were the future.

Reed died of typhus not long after publication, the future—what little he'd seen of it—more or less as he'd imagined it. Sy thought this was lucky for him.

"It is still fashionable, after a whole year of the Soviet Government, to speak of the Bolshevik insurrection as an 'adventure,'" Reed wrote. "Adventure it was, and one of the most marvelous mankind has ever embarked on, sweeping into history at the head of the toiling masses, and staking everything on their vast and simple desires."

Sy was keen to learn of the masses' desires. But first he would need to slog through a Siberian wasteland of factions and counter-factions and workers' councils and military and government committees, many referred to by Russian acronyms, plus a thousand or so workers, soldiers, insurrectionists, functionaries, and reactionaries with uncertain affiliations and unpronounceable names. Sy skimmed much of this. He wanted to get to the siege.

He ordered a pepperoni pizza and Coke from some joint whose flyer he'd found on his windshield. Then he fed the cat.

He caught a few minutes of Cronkite. Spiro Agnew, Nixon's junkyard dog—"Pogo" depicted him as a hyena—vowed not to resign if, as seemed likely, he was indicted for bribery. Yankee Stadium—about the only place he and Jake ever went with their father, before they could bike to Shea, the spanking new home of the Mets—had closed for a long remodel. Fans showed up for the final game with carpentry tools to take home pieces as souvenirs.

His pizza arrived, soggy and cold. He ate half and saved the rest. Popped four aspirin with the Coke and plunged back into the revolution.

"Alone among the intellectuals," he read, "Lenin and Trotsky stood for insurrection." Eisenstein had Trotsky *opposing* the insurrection, a change no doubt ordered by Stalin. Reed, free to write what he pleased—or, at least, what would please Lenin and Trotsky—seemed, with the benefit of hindsight, the more reliable source.

The cadre hoped he'd find it inspiring, he supposed, a few ideological quibbles aside. But how could you be inspired, fifty years after the fact, by a revolution which had triggered a nightmare of bodies, purges, gulags, starvation, and misery of every stripe?

Anyway, the book's worshipful, as-it-happened reportage was no match for Eisenstein's delirious, orgiastic mise-en-scène. Reed wrote in breathless, partisan prose, but he considered himself a journalist. Eisenstein was a showman, a genius of spirit and spectacle.

Sy fed the kitten her treats and trudged to the bathroom. Brushed the mozzarella out of his teeth and knocked back another fistful of aspirin. Then he smoked some weed and descended into unconsciousness, the masses' vast and simple desires circling his dreams, taunting him from the just-beyond.

* * *

Willetts arrived at noon, right on schedule. Simon, having passed the night with the ghosts of the landed and dispossessed. was in a defiant mood. Esperanza belonged with him. Private property was theft. This was Indian land. Willetts could go to hell.

Only now he was here. And so, inconveniently, was the cat.

Sy bent down and she leapt into his outstretched hands. He scooped her up and threw her across his shoulder. Then he popped open the door. Esperanza got one glimpse of the stranger and launched herself into the living room, slicing the flesh of Sy's cheek as she lifted off.

"Fuuck," he said. Such was his welcome for Willetts.

The landlord ignored the profanity. Ignored Simon, in fact, for a better view of the apartment.

"That was—"

"Yeah"

"—a cat."

"Uh-huh."

"You swore no pets."

Sy raised a finger to object. "I never swore. But I did say it. I'll give you that."

The landlord shook his head. "We discussed this. It's a violation."

Sy was afraid she'd try to escape through the open door. "Might as well come in."

Willetts swiveled his head, like a periscope, as if to pinpoint the enemy's coordinates. "Having a pet violates the rental agreement. I've warned you. There are no pets."

A watershed moment. He was all but evicted. His imminent displacement, which he'd contemplated all morning, was now assured. The reality of his situation was oddly liberating, as if the rules of engagement no longer applied. Engaging with Willetts at all, in fact, seemed pointless.

"But there *is* a pet," he said. "You saw her yourself."

"Exactly," confirmed the landlord, perplexed. "And this violates the agreement."

"I no longer recognize the agreement."

Willetts looked at him. The cat scratch was morphing into a small mountain range under Sy's left ear, a fresh modification to the changing topography of his battered face. He ran a finger along the bruise to check for blood.

"I don't understand. What are you saying, 'no longer recognize.'"

"I'm saying I don't acknowledge your authority over our choice of residence."

This line of defense surprised them both. That Sy was out of compliance was inarguable. This was a different, more radical position, a doomed appeal for jury nullification. Willetts, unfortunately, being the jury. Also the judge and the executioner.

"'Landlord,' what kind of word is that? You're a *lord*? So I'm, like, your serf? I mean, Gil—it's Gil, right?—you hold the deed to this crappy place. Papier-mâché door, no deadbolt. These useless coolers. That's right, Gil. Total shit. Ever spent more than an hour in one of your own apartments? How do you sleep, charging good money to live in a box that hits a hundred degrees just about every day? Is that even legal?"

Willetts turned his attention to the cooler in the living room, where Sy's hipster proletarian death's head gazed absently into the void. Sy's own thoughts drifted to Palisades Amusement Park, on Jersey's eastern edge—the farthest west he'd ever been before journeying to the desert—where he and some friends would go in the summer. They'd take the A train, like Duke Ellington, then continue past Harlem to Washington Heights. From there they'd hoof it over the George Washington Bridge. They'd sneak into the park through a hole in the fence, and ride the roller coaster using coupons they clipped from comic books. The hole was famous, even the owner knew it was there. This was Sy's favorite memory of America.

"Let me ask you something. Are you familiar with Palisades Park?"

Now it seemed Willetts wished to object.

"Never heard of it."

"Not even the song? Everyone's heard the song. Top of the charts. Freddy Cannon. Don't tell me you never heard the song."

Blank.

"Freddy 'Boom Boom' Cannon? 'Tallahassee Lassie'?"

Nothing.

"Oldie but goodie. But not for everyone. Anyway, here's the thing. Property is theft, Gil. But thieves don't have to be douchebags. We're all on Indian land. This guy who owned Palisades, he could buy and sell a guy like you a million times over. Just like that." He snapped his fingers, generating less a click than a weak flapping sound.

"I mean, God knows what he did to get that rich. We never thought about that. All that mattered to us was he never fixed the hole in his fence. Let kids keep sneaking in. A fat cat, ruling class all the way. But he wasn't a douche. That's the point. Don't be a douche, Gil. Humans have rights. And not just humans. Esperanza—that's my cat— Esperanza has a right to live. As much right as you. More, in fact. Her heart is pure. Her needs are simple. She's only a kitten, Gil. She has a right to a roof over her head."

The landlord's cheeks were turning colors. You could hardly pick out his mole now.

"Mr. Bussbaum," he said.

"Call me Simon."

"Mr. Bussbaum. Are you... a communist?"

It was a fair question. "Am I a communist," turning it over. "I don't think so. Anyway, not a good one."

But good enough, anyway, for Willetts.

"Well, I want you gone. You *and* your cat. This is not up for debate, Mr. Bussbaum. That animal does not have a right to *this* roof. And neither do you. Please be out by the end of the month, or you'll force me to call the sheriff."

He grabbed his briefcase and made to leave.

"I'd like to tell him a few things myself," Sy said. "And one more thing. Tell Mrs. Hardwick I'm sorry."

"You're sorry? Sorry for what?"

"In case she thought she was losing her mind. Hearing things, you know. Pittering."

Willetts declined to answer. Then he was gone. Esperanza appeared as soon as the door shut behind him.

He never asked for his check. Even Willetts wasn't that big a douche.

* * *

He spread his brochures on the mattress and studied the pictures, the cat gnawing happily on the corners.

The pickings were slim. He'd seen Mount Lemmon, if only from his truck. Been to Bisbee, Tombstone, Old Tucson. The Petrified Forest was hours away, nearly to Big Mountain, where Navajos, under federal threat of relocation, were letting his brother squat. This left the Desert Museum, a 98-acre zoo where the animals roamed, uncaged, in semi-natural habitats. The brochure boasted more than a thousand native plant species, and mentioned a demonstration of birds of prey in free flight. But the next demo wasn't for several weeks.

He headed there anyway. Followed his possibly broken nose in a sort of driving trance, unsure where he was till the museum loomed in his windshield, inevitable as dream logic. He paid his entrance fee through a window in a small adobe building and stopped in the gift shop for fortifications. Coppertone, peanuts, a canteen he filled at a water fountain. A baseball cap with the museum's logo, a big cat of some kind. Couldn't go on safari without a hat.

He saw hawks, roadrunners, lizards, rabbits, Gila monsters lurking among the rocks, endless varieties of cactus. There were walled expanses of mammals, foxes and bighorn sheep and a mountain lion. Prairie dogs, bats, coyotes and road runners both. He wandered a couple of hours, pausing now and again to stand and watch. All at once he felt faint and in danger of sunstroke. His head was heavy, drenched in the sweat of his cap. His water was gone. A party of javelinas grunted and snorted nearby. They had huge heads with conical snouts and thick, powerful bodies, like the bastard children of pigs and bears. They seemed to be mocking him.

He wrung out his cap and trudged onward. At the end of the trail he stopped in a coffee shop. He was the only customer. His waitress wore orthopedic shoes and a lanyard with glasses that rose and fell as she breathed. Behind her right ear, a pencil she didn't use to write down his order, a cheeseburger and fries and a large Dr. Pepper with extra ice. She brought him a regular burger, a bag of chips, and a Pepsi, small and iceless. He let it go. Wondering if she ever got to visit the animals.

He watched the clock till four, the official start of his third consecutive absence. He left the waitress a nice tip and went home to feed his domestic, dependent cat. When Sarge didn't call—Sy had thought he might take a moment, on swing, to inform him of his termination—he took a short nap, woke up, had a few tokes, and finished the pizza. Then a beer and straight back to bed.

Birds of prey in free flight. That would have been something.

* * *

His head felt better and his vision was back to normal. The swelling had gone down. His face was beginning to look presentable again, more or less, the less being some discoloration, an off-kilter nose, and now, thanks to the kitten, a new, nasty gash running across his cheek. Sort of a sweet spot of ugly. Not so unsightly that strangers would shift their gaze, but enough to get picked out of a lineup. People lived their entire lives this way, he supposed. He thought he'd go shopping for makeup.

The phone rang at eleven. It was Sarge.

"Philly? How you doin'?"

Sarge never called him Philly, despite having planted the seed in Renfroe's broken brain. Mostly he called him Bussbomb, emphasis on the *bomb*. Being an army man, he didn't believe in given names except, evidently, on special occasions. Had Sarge forgotten that he, not Simon's parents, had christened him Philly? Reptiles lived on a higher plane of consciousness.

"Sarge," he said. "It's still day shift. Swing doesn't start for what, another five hours."

"That's just it. Wanted to catch you."

"You caught me. But you shouldn't have bothered. I know what you're gonna say."

"You don't know diddly, Bussbomb. You're not as smart as you think."

"I know why you're calling."

"*Buss*bomb," he said, leaning hard this time on the first syllable. "Shut up and listen a sec."

He'd heard about Bullock. He'd hashed it out with the brass and convinced them to let Simon stay on. Bullock's behavior—toward Sy and Tanager both—was "inappropriate." Sy could tell he was reading from notes.

"Afraid I also forgot to clock out the other day."

"It happens. Not the end of the world, son."

This was definitely suspect. He was a probationary employee. Any little thing could be the end of the world for a probationary employee.

It was the lawyers.

"Company's worried I'll sue, is that it?"

Sarge chewed on that for a while.

"Look, tell you what. How 'bout I just say what I come to say, then you believe what you want to believe." Reading verbatim now: "The Cobra Copper Company takes its responsibilities to its employees seriously. We do not tolerate... do not and *will not* tolerate violence or abusive behavior toward any employee anywhere on our premises. We are committed... We are *fully committed* to a safe and healthful work environment."

There was a pause, the legal demons vacating his body, and then Sarge was back. "Bottom line, we're ready to work it out. You're a good hand, Bussbomb. C'mon back now."

"Sarge, are you recording this, by any chance?"

"I am not. I'm what you call taking contemporaneous notes."

"Okay then, lemme ask you this. You know what went down with me and Bullock. So how's this supposed to work?"

"Now you're talking. So we've got two more shifts on swing, then a couple days off. What say you take the weekend, with pay, then come back Monday, first night of graveyard. Meanwhile I'll have a heart-to-heart with Bullock."

"A heart-to-heart. With Bullock."

"Givin' him the benefit. But hell, son, I'm Bullock's foreman. He reports to me. I tell him to shape up, it ain't a request."

It was, though. They'd just seen how Bullock could gum up the works. But it was no good whining about it. In the unwritten code of the smelter, whiners ranked lower than Jehovah's Witnesses. Plus Sy was a thousand percent sure he was being recorded. Anything he said would, sooner or later, be used against him.

"Listen, son, I get it. Skimmers are hammers, punchers are nails. Law of the hardware store. Push come to shove, we can make other arrangements. I've got four other skimmers on this crew, nothin' says I can't partner you up with one of them—just be careful what you wish for. Worse come to worst, we'll get you transferred to another shift. Bottom line, though, anyone free, white, and twenty-one got a right to earn a living anywhere in the USA."

Sy drafted a speech in his head. But he left it there. Sarge sported a Stars and Bars tattoo he habitually coaxed into a puny ripple, like it or not, by opening and closing his fist. He did this more or less compulsively on swing and graveyard shifts, when the brass couldn't see that his sleeves were out of compliance. Sy had nearly forgotten what a cracker he was.

"Y'know," he said, "I'm not twenty-one yet myself."

Sarge gave out with a soft chuckle, as if sharing a private joke with himself. "Frankly, son, there's some folks might say you ain't exactly white either, strictly speaking. No offense."

"None taken."

"Anyway, don't mind how I talk. Nothin' personal. You look around, we got all kinds. Even got us a girl now. We're what you call an equal opportunity employer."

"God bless America."

"You said it, son."

Sy told him he'd be there Monday.

Suing Freako had never entered his mind. The notion of sticking his head in a towel dispenser hadn't entered it, either, before lawyers inserted it there. Legal action had its appeal. Soaking the company for his injuries, physical and emotional, beat punching a furnace for hourly wages. Except you needed a lawyer to win a lawsuit. And a lawsuit—on what grounds, exactly, he didn't know, though Freako clearly did—would take way more time than he had.

All things considered, *Bussbaum vs. Circle K* seemed like a better bet. He'd just have to scrape off the warning before sticking his head in the loop.

* * *

He doubted they sold makeup at Circle K. But what if they did? What would one of their pimply clerks recommend for disguising bruises? Foundation? Blush? Beef jerky?

He donned his Desert Museum cap and headed to Steinfeld's. The cosmetics person was serving an older lady with blue-rinsed hair and a pasty, lavishly rouged face. Literally red, white and blue. The woman behind the counter wore a tag on her blouse with her name, Helen, and the words "Beauty Advisor." She held up a finger and beckoned him once she'd finished with Mrs. America.

She spotted the problem instantly. "You should see the other guy, huh?" Motherly wink. Probably in her forties. Her skin in its late thirties, tops.

"Something like that."

She took a moment to size him up, head tilted thoughtfully, cheeks scrunched into an attitude of contemplation. Then it came to her. "L'Oréal BB cream," she said finally. "Some say BB stands for 'beauty balm,' others say 'blemish balm.' We'll go with 'blemish.'"

Helen had taken him, perhaps, for a street person, an urchin devoid of friends or resources. The goop was cheaper than some of the other creams on display. And he could apply it with his fingers, so he wouldn't have to buy a special makeup brush. She warned him the stuff came out of the tube white but would adapt to his skin tone, which she judged warm to neutral. She offered to demonstrate but he said he was in a hurry. She told him how glad she was she could help, and be careful who he tangled with.

"Remember," she chirped, "don't drop your hands."

He tried the goop once he was home. He had to slather it on to cover the bruises, which made him a bit shiny in places. But mostly it blended in. Away from the bathroom light you would hardly notice.

He spent the rest of the day washing and slathering, reading the Times and zoning out to the radio. Around four he phoned in a few days' worth of Chinese takeout, egg rolls, Mongolian beef, chicken chow mein, shrimp fried rice. By six, when his order arrived, he was famished. He set the chow mein aside, dumped the rest into red-lidded Tupperware knockoffs he'd scored at the Goodwill. Scarfed the chow mein straight from the box, sitting cross-legged on the floor in front of the tube with the Times for a tablecloth. Esperanza gave it a sniff but preferred her slop.

PBS was airing a documentary. The film was in black and white and had no discernible story, no hero, no soundtrack, no voiceover. And his local, slimmed-down Times had no TV listings. The setting was an army training camp. Could have been anywhere in the country, for all Simon knew. Kids his age cleaning latrines, getting chewed out by officers, talking about suicide. A soldier who'd served in Vietnam told a group of recruits about men he'd served with, men who'd been killed in combat. He said he'd risk his life to save those in the group, if it came to that, and expected the same from them. None of the recruits said a thing.

The film wasn't pro-army, and it wasn't anti-army. It was just— army. Sy wondered if Kelsey's brother, had he lived long enough to see it, would still have quit Freako for Uncle Sam.

He switched off the set and returned to his book. Dismayed to find he was barely a hundred pages in. And he wouldn't reach the chapter titled "Victory," his personal goal, for another hundred or so.

He grabbed a beer and flipped the TV back on. Carson was in progress. No way was he reading a hundred more pages. Not tonight. Not ever.

Four or five days that shook the world, he decided, should last him a lifetime.

* * *

He felt like a trespasser in his apartment. Did not want to be there when Harold called, as he definitely would, to confirm travel arrangements.

He was slow to escape, though.

"Glad I caught you before you left for work," Harold said when he picked up the phone.

He had no idea, then, that Sy was not expected at work. Or why he was taking a break.

"Ready for Saturday?"

"Saturday. Yes."

"We meet after breakfast. Bookstore at nine. "

"Bookstore. Nine. Check."

"We'll probably drive straight through, so have a good breakfast. Or bring snacks."

"Most important meal of the day. Snacks, I mean."

"Right. So... any news? About Tanager?"

"Ah, Tanager. I was about to call. There's news. But it's bad. She's out. Hates politics. Wants to be a singer-songwriter when she grows up. Rockabilly, I think, feminist cowgirl duets and so forth. That's her thing. She's not disposed toward seizing the means of production."

Harold wasn't amused. "You told her we just want to talk?"

"I told her. Just last night. Turned me down flat. Anyway, she's a short-timer. Moving to Austin first chance she gets."

There was a moment of silence. "Fuck," Harold said. "Well, we tried. At least we know where we stand. We'll figure out next steps in Mineral."

Mineral, aka Emerald. Home of Naldo Galvan, aka José Castillo. A pivotal scene in the movie had Castillo manning the picket line, bantering with a pair of company goons in a big black company car. The suit riding shotgun said what a shame it was, natural leader like him, good English, how far he could go. How he was blowing his opportunity, condemning his wife and kids to lives of poverty, squalor, and second-class citizenship. How the Reds were using him for their godless nefarious ends.

Castillo leans against the door. Turns and spits.

"Why don't you wise up, Joe?" says the driver. "Joe, that's your name, ain't it? Hozay means Joe in American, ain't that right?"

Cut to a tight closeup of Galvan, eyes narrowed, framed in the driver's window. POV from inside the car. "*Me llamo José Castillo,*" he says, voice barely above a whisper. "That's *Mister* Castillo to you. In American."

Sy could see him now on the library's wobbly, tripod-mounted screen, *Mister* Castillo, possessed of a quiet, unshakable confidence that the future belonged to the decent hard-working folk of Emerald City, not these carpetbagging fat-cat scum-sucking *pendejos.*

Their vast and simple desires.

"Next steps, absolutely. On to Mineral."

* * *

He set off on foot. The commercial strip near the campus was bustling with Wildcats. Fall semester had begun.

Chuy's had changed. The name now dominated its storefront window, stretching corner to corner in an elegant gold script. Where were the bunny ears, the rabbit-faced succulent clutching his cup of joe? The little café was twice its previous size, having swallowed up whatever once lived next door. The joint whose main attraction was a ghost-ridden TV had vanished into a vast, gleaming cafeteria.

A sandwich board on the sidewalk read "Breakfast all day." This was just what he wanted.

An undergrad greeted him from behind the long, remodeled counter, perky and well-scrubbed.

"Welcome to Chuy's."

He figured her for a sophomore. Same age as Toodles, give or take.

"Lost your bunny ears."

Her perkiness fled. She regarded his face, or maybe his patches of L'Oréal.

"I think you've got me confused," she said. "I don't even ski."

"No, 'course not. Slopes are terrible here."

She looked spooked, suddenly, like a bank teller about to hit the panic button.

"Sorry. I meant *Spence's* bunny ears. Used to be on the window. Is Spence around?"

"Spence?"

"Spencer, the owner? He around?"

She shook her head, a tinge of regret on her ski-bunny lips.

"There's nobody here named Spencer. New management. I'm new too, so. Maybe he's at another branch. Chuy's has three branches now, two in Phoenix and one in Flagstaff. Besides this one I mean. It's just my second week, sorry." She wanted to help. She reminded Sy of the cosmetics lady, only way less maternal.

"You should see the other guy."

A line had formed behind him.

"So what can I get you?"

He ordered coffee and scrambled eggs and toast, hash browns apparently being compulsory, and she handed him a brass stand holding a card with a number. He found a table inside the window. October now, people still dressed for summer. It might not rain for another year, maybe not even then. Maybe Tucson would turn to dust and scatter like so much tumbleweed.

A different student came and set his food down. Soon another brought him his coffee. The eggs were cold and tasteless, the toast merely cold. The coffee was lukewarm. After a while his waitress asked, "Still working on that?" He wasn't but nodded yes. Enjoying the view. He asked for more coffee and she promised to let someone know.

Two enormous color sets hung from the ceiling, both tuned to Hollywood Squares. The sound was turned off in deference to the Muzak wafting in from a network of ceiling speakers. Each celebrity had a gooseneck microphone, and interacted with civilians seated on either side of the emcee. From time to time a tic-tac-toe pattern of squares blinked crazily to indicate a civilian had won a prize.

Sy glanced up to find Zsa Zsa's visages, one per screen. The horizontal row blinked, and Zsa Zsa gazed upward at Paul Lynde, clapping her bejeweled hands in Hungarian showbiz glee. Then a commercial came on. A school bus driver rubbed his shoulder and grimaced as he reached into a canvas bag. He held up a tube of Ben-Gay, contemplating it as if it were Yorick's skull. The Ben-Gay did the trick and schoolkids piled excitedly onto the bus and then Hollywood Squares was back and an undergrad came and refilled his cup.

Maybe Spence was in Phoenix, or Flagstaff. Maybe he'd sold the original Chuy's for a king's ransom and retired in Cleveland, the in-season home of the Cleveland Indians. Having the cap and all.

He left some bills under his plastic eggs and strode into the midday heat.

That night he walked to a downtown theater, the Cine Azteca, housed in a nifty old Spanish Colonial building. The movie starred Cantinflas, the Charlie Chaplin of Mexico. All Sy knew was it had something to do with Don Quixote. Cantinflas played Sancho Panza. There were no subtitles, but dialogue was superfluous. Cantinflas transcended language. Though Simon was likely the only soul in the theater who didn't know *español*.

Most Anglos, he suspected, had no clue about Cantinflas. He dedicated his viewing to Spence, his fish-out-of-water *amigo*, and his Cleveland Indians cap.

When in Rome. His last words, just about.

* * *

Urgent newsman voice, rat-a-tat of a telegraph. Surprise attack on Israel by Egypt and Syria. On Yom Kippur, holiest day of the Hebrew calendar. They'd invaded in early afternoon—overnight in the U.S.—while the army was off in synagogues, begging God for forgiveness. Kissinger, overseer of Nixon's war on Vietnam and, this just in, Cambodia, called the attack "cowardly." Traders warily eyed world markets. Gas stations from coast to coast, fresh off closures to protest price controls, now braced for OPEC to slash oil supplies.

Mostly sunny skies, high of eighty-nine before tumbling into the sixties overnight.

The next voice Sy heard was Paul McCartney's, warbling the opening notes of "Live and Let Die." He switched off the radio. The '70s broke your heart. Elvis was doing Vegas, Roger Moore was trying to do Bond, McCartney—who even knew what he was doing? One more bead of sorrow in a rising tide of despair. Already America had been through Kent State, Wounded Knee, Watergate, Vietnam, Cambodia, Chile. America did not need Wings.

Yom Kippur fell ten days after Rosh Hashanah, the Jewish New Year. Flew in under the radar. Sy's calendar from the bank showed Jewish holidays in gray, nearly imperceptible mouse type. The new year—five thousand and something—had happened while he was working days. It was the shift he played hooky, the day before his showdown with Bullock. So not something he'd notice. He wasn't observant. And he was definitely distracted.

It was ten in the morning back east. Assuming he'd made it to Florida, his father would be getting updates from some rabbi. He'd have traipsed first thing to some Conservative shul for his ritual of atonement. God forbade Jews from consuming news during the high holy days. But there were loopholes. His father would know. This year's bid for forgiveness would involve a personal check to the shul—memo line "Israel"—and a special curse for the Arabs. It would gladden God's heart that his chosen ones kept up with current events. He'd excuse this minor infraction.

It was October, the tenth month of the year. After Rosh Hashanah came the Ten Days of Awe, which overlapped, Sy realized—consulting his bank calendar and his autographed book—with those that shook the world. The profound meaninglessness of this insight caught in his throat. Apart from the cyclical nature of things, the observable fact of recurring phenomena—war, famine, birth, death—Sy had never been clear on the notion of history repeating itself. Not even, per Marx's revision of Hegel (as recounted by Jake), as farce. And what if it didn't rhyme, either, as Twain supposedly said? What if it was merely redundant? What if the moral arc of the universe, instead of bending toward justice as foretold by the Reverend King, just randomly bent?

He was too much in his head. He turned the radio on again. Pop tunes, high-speed chatter, Spike Jones sound effects, ads for local merchants, cigarettes, long distance phone calls, California prunes. He fed the cat and fortified himself with a heaping bowl of Rice Krispies, three slices of buttered toast, and a gallon of coffee. When he'd emptied his cereal bowl he ran it under the faucet and wiped it dry and filled it with kibble. Then he filled another one. He set down two bowls of water, cleaned and topped off the litter box. Threw a change of clothes in a shopping bag and rubbed the cat's head till she reached her limit and ran away. Cats slept sixteen hours a day. She would only know she was on her own during brief, intermittent spells of consciousness. And wouldn't much care.

He got to the bookstore early. Parked a ways off and sat in the truck, smoking and keeping watch. Harold and Pete appeared from around the corner. Then Lencho walked up from farther on down the block. Joyce and Edgar lived above the store and would already be inside. No sign of Dwight. But six was a carload. It was three hours to Mineral. The prospect filled him with dread.

The high sun glinted off the legend, "Vanguard Books/Libros," stenciled in gold on the awning and window. A bookstore sans books, a Potemkin bookstore, Eisenstein again. HQ for political adversaries so dangerous, Harold believed, they'd made Nixon's enemies list. Dick and Henry watching their every move.

The trip played out in his mind. Strategy wasn't the point. Recruitment. That was the point. He, Simon, was all they had, now, with Tanager out of the mix. Their last, best hope. They'd soften him up in the car, treat him like blue-collar royalty. And then the clincher, a one-time-only command performance by Naldo Galvan, the man behind the myth.

The pitch was predictable. You can help these boys. Or you can turn the page.

But there was no helping these boys. John Reed, backed by half the Red Army, couldn't turn these boys into heroes.

With Galvan or without him, the smart money said Freako's men wouldn't join the cadre on an all-expenses-paid Super Bowl junket. Why would they? Pete might have been the only one over thirty who'd ever worked for a living. The young ones in costume, masquerading as working stiffs, awaiting their closeups. And then there were Joyce and Ed, the troop's den mom and dad, decked out in their goggles and engineer's cap, the last, Simon suspected, in converging lines of professional agitators. He could see them at a factory gate, strumming ukes and banjos and singing union songs to picketing workers. Probably clapped on the downbeat.

They had to be phoning him. Weighing whether to send an emissary to his apartment, lest he'd slept in. Under the impression he'd worked a late shift. He felt an onset of *shpilkes*, the same dull nausea he'd come to expect, in his first weeks at Freako, each time he glimpsed the stacks beyond the curve of the mountain. Spectral figures behind the scrim like a dumb show.

"You didn't come all this way to punch a converter," Harold had told him. Yet here he was. It was Harold's harebrained walkout that had punctured the dream, busted him down to a puncher, one more shmuck with enough hand-eye coordination to service Bullock's converter. Best case, Sarge would partner him with a different skimmer, both less loathsome and less competent than Bullock.

This too filled him with dread.

The door swung open, a big "closed" sign framed by the glass. Too far to hear Zuzu's bells. One by one the travelers emerged and placed their bags in the trunk of the Campbells' '64 Fairlane, avocado and white, the only vehicle on the block. They lingered awhile, Edgar visibly antsy. His jitters looked to be biological. But then he tapped his watch and cocked his head toward the store and Harold went back inside.

The Keystone Kommies. All this commotion, and to what end? It was 1973. *Emeralds* no longer forbidden, just mostly forgotten. The red menace had gone out with hula hoops. Avowed Marxists polluted impressionable young minds every day on a thousand American campuses. Who cared anymore, really, but Birchers and Barry Goldwater? What were the stakes? Were they in mortal peril from U.S. intelligence, as Allende had been? Were they afraid McCarthy's ghost would rise from the grave—whether as tragedy, farce, or rhyming couplet—as his father feared Hitler's?

Probably not. But that was their story. And they were sticking to it.

They needed a purpose. A workers' paradise. A walkout. A pat on the head from Naldo Galvan. Didn't matter. A MacGuffin, Hitchcock called it. Something that set the story in motion but made no difference, really, to anyone. Something that drove the plot.

The plot. That was the point.

* * *

He could hit I-10 in minutes. Just that easy to get out of Dodge.

He watched the car pull away. They'd be passing near his apartment. He envisioned Harold pounding his door, the cat cowering within, to see if Sy wasn't dead. He'd have no way of knowing if Sy was dead, short of breaking and entering. But he'd have no use for him in such a condition. Getting no answer would be answer enough.

Sy lit a smoke. When he snuffed it out they'd be gone.

He drove to the bank. Absent a social life he'd amassed a small fortune in union wages, north of a thousand dollars, enough to tide him over till he found more plausible work. He took two hundred in cash and had the banker cut him a check for the rest. He stopped at a pet store and picked out a kitten-sized harness, a six-foot leash, a deep litter box with a metal scoop, and a twenty-pound bucket of litter.

He'd keep the cat in her carrier—hoping Tanager wouldn't miss it—till she, Esperanza, got her sea legs. He'd leave the new box in the bed of the truck, weighed down by the bucket, and wrap it in a Hefty bag after he'd filled it up. In this way Esperanza, her leash hitched to the bed, could do her business. When the time came he'd see how she did in the cab, minus the carrier.

First, though, the harness. Kicking and screaming. When she was finally suited up she wriggled manically and attempted a long, comically awkward jump to the nearest chair, falling back on her haunches like a blackout drunk. Once she regained her bearings she went into a gallop, but couldn't quite work her legs and plunked on her side. Tried again. Plunked again.

At last she surrendered, collapsing in sort of a silent protest. When she hadn't budged in a while he took pity and set her loose. She spent a few minutes licking the fur where the harness had been, but bolted the instant she realized her motor skills had returned.

No one had mentioned this at the pet store.

He'd settled on Berkeley. College town. Not too hot, not too cold. He'd heard about Telegraph Ave., the Free Speech Movement, People's Park. He'd read the usual Kerouac, smatterings of Ginsberg. Ginsberg wrote *Howl* at the Berkeley library. A place where white belts and shoes—much less Haggard's "manly footwear"—were definitely not in fashion.

A roll of the dice. He mostly knew Berkeley from movies. And so most of his knowledge, inevitably, was unreliable. But San Francisco was just over the bridge—the Bay Bridge, whose westbound upper deck Dustin Hoffman, emboldened by cinematic license, drove east to Berkeley in *The Graduate*— and Oakland was right next door. This much he was sure of. And he could always head farther north, to Oregon, or Seattle, even to Canada, where he'd half-expected, a lifetime ago, to seek refuge from Nixon's draft. The idea was to travel light. He'd figure it out once he got there.

He packed his bags and hauled them down to the truck. One fit behind his seat, the other he scrunched on the floor on the passenger side. He hid the TV as best he could under a beach towel he'd found at the Salvation Army. The towel featured a brown bear and the legend *California Republic*. The litter was in the truck bed, holding the box in place.

He contemplated his death's head. With his hardhat trapped in his locker—and never having thought to smuggle out a sample of blister copper—the skull was his only keepsake. Just the same it seemed to belong there, strapped to the swamp cooler, a torso-less bust on its vibrating plinth. He admired it from across the room, a failed museum piece, the installation's shadow cast by the mid-morning sun over the length of the wooden floor. In the pattern of light and dark he could make out the weave of the knit cap's tip, as if Paul Bunyan—said, in certain mythologies, to have dug the Grand Canyon with his axe—had tipped over dead, stiff and straight as a redwood, at his feet.

He took the cap. Left the skull.

He abandoned the useless rugs, the useless electric fans, assorted items from Goodwill and the Salvation Army—his toaster, his percolator, his inch-thick mattress—along with the kibble he'd put out when his next stop was Mineral.

He wrote off his cleaning deposit. The place was a wreck, the fridge was alive, and the smell of cat piss, now that he was leaving it behind, had somehow assumed a new, acrid prominence. The deposit equaled a month's rent. Willetts could keep it. And Simon would skip that final payment. It all worked out. Even Steven.

He whistled and Esperanza trotted out from the bedroom. He knelt and she sniffed his hand and he threw her over his shoulder. She nestled in the crook of his neck all the way down the stairs and into the cab of the truck. Purring like mad. This was a relief. He didn't want her making the trip in a carrier or especially, now that she'd tried it on, in her cute little straitjacket.

Tuxedos weren't the brightest bulbs on the tree, Tanager had warned him. He'd seen no reason to doubt it. But she was a sweetheart, Esperanza, a goddamn sweet little soul.

* * *

He wouldn't reach Berkeley overnight. It was after two. With a couple of rest stops he expected an eight-hour drive, give or take. He'd shoot for L.A., find a motel with rooms far enough from the registration desk to sneak in the cat under cover of darkness.

The fastest route had him hanging a left in Phoenix. So he'd have to skip London Bridge. Decided to have a look at the school where Reich sent his son, Wetmore Elementary, near Tucson's northern limit. It was a single-story building, like everything else in town. Cactus plants here and there, like everywhere else. A sprinkling of American flags. He eased into a parking area. Kids were visible in the classrooms, hunched over their desks. There were low brown hills in the background. These, he knew now, were the Catalina foothills. He thought of the girls on their spiritual journey, the house of the super-caring people. Beyond the hills, farther off to the east, was Mount Lemmon. So many life zones.

He got gas and supplies at a Circle K and drove north till he had to turn left in Phoenix, where the Interstate veered west. This leg of the freeway cut through as desolate a stretch of emptiness as he'd ever seen, more forbidding in its way than the darkest streets in the most bombed-out parts of the Bronx—he'd seen pictures—a valley of dirt and rock ringed by low mountains. There were highway signs with the names of towns, but no signs of life other than several trailer parks and a couple of gas stations.

But his gauge was redlining. Gas was just what he needed. Plus he needed to stretch his legs, and the cat had been cooped up going on five hours. She was a good traveler, barely a peep. Mostly curled up on the seat where he could rub her head. But five hours was a lot, for a cat. She deserved a break.

An Arco loomed on his right, backed by a cloudless sky of orange and powder blue. A sign said "Quartzsite," which he took for a typo. Then he pulled into the station. It was the Quartzsite Arco. So maybe a pun. A site for quartz. Sort of a shibboleth, the way Houston Street, in New York, sounded like "house." You knew or you didn't.

The lights were on. But he didn't see anyone working. The sun floated above the horizon, which was low and flat, nothing but stunted mountains off in the distance. He got out and touched his toes a few times, as much to confirm his existence as to stretch his back. He poured some litter into the box, put out some kibble in the opposite corner of the bed. Saddled up the cat and closed the gate on the leash to keep her corralled. It was hotter than Tucson at this hour, with a breeze that just made it worse. He was pretty sure this was the Mojave.

At last an attendant came out to the truck. Sy asked him to fill it up.

The attendant wore jeans and the top half of an Arco uniform with his name, Todd, embroidered over the pocket. He was thirty or so and hadn't shaved in a while. "Don't get many customers out of season," he said, explaining his absence. "Big gem show in February. That's our Christmas."

Sy said he was headed to California. Todd laughed.

"You and everyone else comes through here traveling west who's not in the market for gemstones. You're already there, just about. Wind's right, you can spit to California from here." He held a finger up but didn't bother to spit. Happy for company.

He used the fuel tank cap to hold the nozzle in place. He'd just grabbed a squeegee when he saw Esperanza.

"I'll be damned. Got you a little travel companion."

Sy introduced him, which Todd got a kick out of. Esperanza was trying to eat and hissed at him.

"Ferocious little guy."

"She's a girl. But definitely." He'd never once heard her hiss before. Not even at Willetts. "Got a men's room I could use?"

Todd pointed him to the office. "Just inside. It's open."

He was behind the register when Sy came out. "Seventeen gallons. Six-eighty, cash American. Cost you a lot more in a week or so."

Sy nodded. Not wanting to get sucked into the Middle East. He slapped a crisp new ten on the counter and studied a map of Quartzsite through the plexiglass shield. He'd more or less memorized it by the time Todd gave him his change.

"And ten," slapping the last dollar down. "Good luck in California."

He saw it the instant he opened the door. Esperanza had slipped her harness. He felt his chest seizing up. He raced to the truck and examined the leash. But she wasn't attached. He ran around the truck, checked underneath. Then he circled the station. Calling but not shouting her name, sing-song voice, not wanting to spook her.

Todd came out to see what the trouble was.

Sy indicated the truck bed.

"Aw, hell," Todd said. "She couldn't have got far."

They looked inside the station, then walked a ways up the road. The moonscape went on forever. She'd be the only thing moving if she was out there. Easy to spot. So she probably hadn't gone far.

"She's around here somewhere," Todd said. Trying to be reassuring. "Believe it or not there's a couple thousand people live around here, I'd say. RV parks mainly. Church back that way. There's a shop, a few diners. A laundromat. Someone'll see her, take her in. Mark my words."

Sy couldn't breathe. It felt like a heart attack, or a collapsed lung, and he held up a hand to stop Todd from talking. In a minute or so his breathing returned.

"I'm gonna drive around a bit." Still doubled over, speaking into the blacktop. "Fuck. Fuck fuck fuck."

Todd studied the horizon, reading the light the way Bullock read the flame of his furnace. "Gonna be dark soon, But I'll pray for you. I'd try this side of the Interstate, I was you. More people here. There's a wildlife refuge across the freeway, let's hope she's scared of traffic. Most cats are. Got one myself, Pumpkin, orange and round. Yours is a bitty thing. Cute though. Someone'll take her in. Strays get lots of folks to look out for 'em in an RV park."

Esperanza wasn't a stray, or a pumpkin either. She was family.

"I need to find her. There a motel or something?"

"Super 8 just ahead," gesturing toward California. "Can't miss it. I'll keep an eye out, meanwhile. I see her, I'll call the manager. No phones in the rooms yet."

Sy hopped in the truck. Cruised Route 95, the narrow highway that crosscut the Interstate, first north and then south, where the refuge was. All he could see in the dimness was emptiness, no place for housecats and hostile habitat for creatures of any kind, natives included. Now it was twilight. He booked a room at the Super 8 and scarfed pretzels and Chips Ahoy he washed down with lukewarm tap water and lay in bed fully dressed, staring at the bulb in the ceiling, cursing himself and wishing for Esperanza's safe return. Even knowing this was the dark side of the moon, hundreds of miles from his former apartment, the only home she might think to return to.

It was dark outside and utterly silent, save when a car zipped by on the freeway. Esperanza didn't deserve this. But he did. Yom Kippur had ended at sundown. So he couldn't atone if he wanted to. All he could do was pray she'd be terrified of the Interstate, that she'd wander into an RV park searching for kibble and a good Samaritan would show her some Christian charity, here at the crossroads of I-10 and Route 95. He'd resume the search in the morning.

He slept in his clothes, fitfully. Sometime during the night he woke to the sputter of an electrical short, a sound like a Whoopee cushion—

a sound, that is, like extended farting—and the overhead bulb flickered and popped and the room went black. He stared into the darkness till the sun came up.

* * *

Sunday morning. He searched for a couple of hours, driving up and down the few paved streets, wandering on foot into trailer parks to look for Esperanza or someone who might have spotted her. But the parks looked mostly abandoned. Not a soul at the laundromat. After a while he saw one of the cafés had opened and he stopped but nobody had seen her. The cashier promised to keep an eye peeled. Sy bought a coffee to go and drove to the Arco to check in with Todd. Todd hadn't seen her either.

"Tell you what," he said. "You go on your way, on to California. I can tack some notices up, the church, the laundromat, places like that. I'd hate for Pumpkin to go missing. I'm happy to help if you want me to, just say the word. I'll call the second I hear anything."

Simon, with no better options, thought he could live with this. Todd seemed sincere. The plan gave him hope. Carrying on beat spinning his wheels in the purgatory of a Super 8, a condemned man waiting to hear from the governor. Only he didn't know where he'd be. He had no address and no phone number. He had no way of getting in touch with Jake or even his parents, not that they'd be any help. The only living soul who might help was Tanager. But he couldn't let Todd call Tanager. Tanager could never know he'd left Esperanza to fend for herself in this endless valley of rock and dirt.

Todd took a business card from the counter and scribbled his number on the back. Said to call anytime. Sy wanted to cry. Told him it was a mitzvah.

Todd looked puzzled.

"It means thanks a ton," Sy explained. "In the sincerest fucking way possible."

Twenty minutes later he was in California.

* * *

In summers, on their way out of Palisades Park—after a day of gut-churning rides on the Cyclone and Tilt-a-Whirl, dips in the saltwater pool, the obligatory tour of the animal freak show—he and his friends would stop at the goldfish booth on the midway. A dime got you three ping-pong balls, which you lobbed toward a bowl holding a goldfish. The bowl was the size of one of those fortune-telling Magic 8 balls, the prophet of choice for seekers too lazy for Ouija boards, and the fish circled in tight neurotic laps. The bowl's mouth was no bigger than a baby's fist, so even a near-perfect toss bounced off the rim. You won by landing a ball on the water's surface.

Sy always won. That is, he lost, but kept playing until he won. The prize was the goldfish.

The real winner, though, was the goldfish, however short-lived the victory. It made Simon proud, always, seeing the tiny creature scooped from its bowl. Because what was its crime, really, besides being a goldfish? If he could rescue one from its puny, watery cage, wasn't this a step in the right direction? It wasn't Atticus Finch, standing against Jim Crow on behalf of an innocent black man. But it was something. His friends would whoop it up like he'd hit the jackpot—sarcasm being their native language—as if the goldfish were made of gold. As opposed to a living, breathing thing, not so different from a two-headed turtle, say, or a two-faced cow. You couldn't laugh off a two-faced cow.

The freak show was a grim, what-if funhouse mirror—there but for fortune, or grace, or whatever—a rebuke to the numbing normalcy of life in the outer boroughs. The midway brought them back to themselves. The geezer who ran the booth—though what Sy had judged to be geezerhood, looking back, was probably middle age—would dump the grungy water from the bowl into a sandwich bag, then scoop the fish into the bag. Then they'd all traipse east over the Hudson, where mobsters slept with the fishes till their bloated corpses bobbed to the surface. The goldfish belly up, usually, by Jackson Heights, the final stretch on the E back to Queens. Every one of them, a dozen or so at least, given a burial at sea, sent off with a gentle flush of sparkling blue water. They were his only pets.

Until Esperanza.

People's Park was disappointing, a beacon of '60s resistance—the site of the "Bloody Thursday" battle between protesters and cops—

reduced now to a barren patch of dirt and trees, lacking either the solemnity befitting the dead and wounded or the celebratory spirit of Yippies levitating the Pentagon. Telegraph was as groovy as advertised, a long stretch of head shops, book and record stores, and street merchants brimming with people who looked like Sy, people who called themselves freaks and the newsmagazines insisted on calling youths. At its northern terminus Telegraph gave way to Sproul Plaza, where, a decade ago, Mario Savio had exhorted students to put their bodies on the gears and the wheels and the levers, to grind the machine to a halt. Sy wasn't sure, thinking about it now, which machine he meant.

The campus was bustling and green. But the housing market was grim. Berkeley was all motor inns and apartments and student housing and, nearer the freeway, hourly-rate fleabags where hookers could take their clients. Rental agencies had nothing. Index cards on the Co-op's bulletin board advertised rooms with kitchen privileges. But Sy didn't want any roommates. After three nights in a grungy motel he gave up the search.

He ended up in the Mission, across the bay, holed up in a cell-like chamber in an SRO next door to an XXX movie house. The place was even grungier than his motel but affordable for the longer haul, if it came to that. His room was on the fifth floor and featured a bed with a stained mattress and a basin sink he was sure had served as a urinal. The bathroom was down the hall. A lot of the tenants had problems with drugs or alcohol, and some couldn't reliably hit the toilet—they settled for close, as in horseshoes—which explained why people pissed in their sinks. Most, like Sy, were just passing through, between jobs or marriages or otherwise down on their luck.

He called Todd from a payphone to check in. But there was no news.

One of the older tenants had a nephew who managed a moving crew. For a while Sy paid for his pot and cigarettes by maneuvering bureaus and sectionals down the narrow stairs of eccentrically painted Victorians. But the work was hard, the wages low, and his co-workers sketchy, especially the driver, who smelled like gin and yelled at the customers. One day the nephew sent the crew to the wrong address. And then, apparently, called it a day. Sy never got paid. Called it a career.

His nest egg was still intact, mostly, and Freako had sent him his final paycheck care of the SRO. He found a studio whose landlord, as far as he could make out, wasn't a douche. It was clean and quiet, tucked away in an alley behind a lesbian bar. It had a Murphy bed and an ironing board that folded down from a wall. Todd was his first call from his new, private phone. Still nothing.

He made his second call the following day, inquiring about a cryptic help-wanted ad for someone with a "valid driver's license" who was "honest, responsible, and organized." A cryptic woman invited him in for an interview on what turned out to be an enormous floating ship, a transfigured commuter ferry, docked at the Embarcadero. He arrived to find people zooming around on roller skates, arms out for balance on the choppy water. The job was delivering federally controlled pharmaceuticals to drug stores and hospitals, the manager explained, and didn't involve roller skating. But Sy would have to be bonded, which involved a background check. And he'd need a California license.

When he'd passed his driver's test he took his temporary license to the manager. When the background check failed to turn up his hitchhiking bust he was hired.

He'd finally shed his New York license, then. He was a bona fide resident. California was the Golden State. Its motto was "Eureka."

The weather was glorious. Indian summer. The company owned a fleet of small trucks, light and zippy, and he passed his days consulting Thomas guides, smoking weed and cigarettes, and listening to AM radio. Evenings and weekends he had to himself. The Mission thrummed. The subway was barely a block away, a spanking new system with clean trains that ran under the bay to Berkeley. But it was meant for commuting and shopping, not for exploring. The trains went hardly anywhere Sy wanted to go.

Where he wanted to go was the movies. And movies, suddenly, were everywhere. The locals could keep BART. He had his sky blue '49 Chevy, minus the gun rack—he'd tossed it into a dumpster somewhere in SoCal—and accessorized now with flattering blue-and-gold tags. And the granny-geared transmission, with its odd, lower-than-low first gear, proved a blessing in San Francisco. Save for its squishy brakes and miserable gas mileage, the truck was the perfect vehicle for climbing the city's endless, endlessly scenic hills in slow-moving traffic.

He used to ditch high school sometimes to spend the day at the movies, sort of a mini-film festival. He'd stash his books under his bed and take the F into the city, and if he could find a seat he'd pore over the auteur-leaning ads in the Village Voice—checking them against all the listings fit to print in the Times—and map out a plan of action. If the train was crowded he'd get off at a central location, Lex and 63rd, say, and wing it.

When the planets aligned he could manage four films in a single day. Three, worst case. On 3rd Avenue alone was the one-two combo, the Baronet and Coronet, with Cinemas I and II right next door. Across town, on West 95th, was the Thalia, and below that, Broadway at 88th, the New Yorker. You had the Elgin in Chelsea and the Waverly and Bleecker in the Village. None of these places showed popcorn movies except for the Elgin, which ran all-night triple features on weekends for stoners and meth heads and high-school kids with nowhere else to make out.

San Francisco, too, was crawling with arthouses. They didn't show the underground artistes his old prof claimed to go drinking with, cultural Jacobins whose abstract, scratch-and-sniff experiments in camera-free moviemaking Sy found impenetrable and suspected his prof, in his heart of hearts, did too. Mainly they featured foreign films, indies, revivals, and new releases that never got to the desert.

There was, in the fog of the Outer Sunset, a cozy loft theater started, supposedly, by that sharp-tongued *critique de cinéma,* a local girl turned belle of Manhattan cultural circles, who'd taken such perverse delight in subjecting a dirt-poor miner to public ridicule. The place was a hole in the wall at the top of a rickety flight of stairs, and showed obscure films he'd always needed to see, whether he knew it or not.

He forgave her.

He forgave everyone, nearly. Everyone but Bullock. Bullock could choke on a mouthful of Red Man and drown in his black, nicotine-clogged vomit. Wished him the worst. The rest he forgave. His parents, Jake, Tanager, the Keystone Kommies. Even Willetts. Supporting characters in search of a plot, some story in which they could find themselves, by which they could get their bearings. One confident, commanding voice, God or Trotsky or some unseen planetarium guide—or José Castillo, aka Naldo Galvan—to show them the way.

Mankind's marvelous adventure.

City of Emeralds. What if, instead of playing out on the library screen, the film stock *had* melted, the story replaced by a lava lamp? Might the folly of his wanderings in the desert—and the emptiness, in the pit of his stomach, knowing they'd come to nothing—have been avoided? Had this trip, in short, been necessary?

He dreamed about Esperanza.

A recurring dream had some trailer park denizen taking her in, declining to notify Todd. Not wanting to give her up. Usually some old couple, retired, living on Social Security. Maybe a son killed in Korea. Maybe a grandson in Nam. a kid in prison, a daughter too busy to stay in touch. Scrawny kitten sniffing around their motor home. They feed her, let her sleep on the couch, call her Kitty or Tux, something dopey and obvious, misspelled perhaps, in keeping with her adopted town. Run of the trailer park.

Once he dreamed she'd melted into the wildlife refuge, gone feral and learned to survive by her wits. No landlord to authorize her existence, no self-appointed guardian feeding her slop and referring to her by four lilting syllables *en español*, poorly pronounced, meaning "hope" to him and *nada* to her.

This dream never recurred. But it never left him. What did he hope, in the end, for Esperanza? Was she better off as a pet or a predator, hunting rodents for food and amusement till she ran afoul, at last, of the law of the jungle? Was it instinct that drove her to escape, some animal need to take her place in the natural world? Or was it simply, as Tanager said, that she wasn't the brightest bulb on the tree?

Sometimes he dreamed he was back in the smelter, waves of lava lapping from the upturned mouth of the furnace, crashing down to the tracks. Sometimes he dreamed he was somebody else.

He forgave the makers of *Emeralds*, whose rendering of history had proved unreliable, calamitous even, but whose struggle to forge a mythology of working-class heroes—to mold copper dust into legend— was a labor of true believers. Sincerity being, after all, the main thing.

And he forgave that flannelly freshman from Plattsburgh, or Watertown, who, in his crazy pot-addled wisdom, had conferred on Simon his secret identity, the Buzzard, a misguided slander from which Sy continued, despite everything, to draw sustenance.

The kid, thankfully, had vanished into the north woods, just as Jake had vanished into Indian Country, his parents into their Sun Belt shtetl, Tanager, by now, into the honky-tonk heart of Texas. Esperanza into the unknown.

The Buzzard, though, would shine on forever, or nearly, a fixed star outside history, above it, unaffected by the machinations of humankind. History, for the Buzzard, didn't repeat. It didn't rhyme. History was a mirage. A trick of the light.

Simon Bussbaum, meanwhile, focused on laying low, staying high, minding his head. Not too high. More of a middling high. He'd taken to haunting the Camera Obscura, an odd little Lego building at Lands End shaped like a pair of binoculars, or arguably a camera, topped by a chimney-style pyramid. Inside was total darkness save for a luminous, concave surface in the center of the room. By some miracle of ancient science this horizontal screen reflected, from the light of a pinhole in the pyramid, a constantly moving image—Sy thought of it as a soothing, painterly sun you could stare at for hours on end—of the breakers beating against the cliffs, seals rollicking in the surf, whatever made itself known to the primitive lens in its slow, 360-degree revolutions. A movie, basically, of real life, each enhancing the other. It was mesmerizing.

Everything—as the dormouse said, or was it the white rabbit?—was everything. The living universe framed, no ideas but in things, not just the crashing waves but deserts and mountains and forests, animals human and elsewise, forever, without meaning or purpose. Images as ethereal as a dream, all time spread out like a liquid map.

It wasn't a burning bush, or any man's marvelous adventure.

It wasn't love.

But it wasn't bad.

The Buzzard, then. Definite article.

Like the Flash. Or the Man of Steel.

Riding a thermal, blissful and otherworldly, spiraling up and up.

* * *

THE AUTHOR

Barry Bergman is a New York City refugee, long ago replanted in the SF Bay Area. He's been a newspaper reporter, a magazine writer/editor—with scores of bylined stories in *Sierra*, *California*, and *Mother Jones* magazines—and a communications pro at UC Berkeley and assorted nonprofits. Before earning his journalism degree at San Francisco State University, he worked in a variety of industrial settings, including two years in an Arizona copper smelter, an experience he would eventually reimagine as the fictional background for *Proles*, his first completed novel. He's currently working on a new novel in a house he shares with his journalist wife and two cats, Cosmo and Mookie, in Berkeley, California.